TRADING INTO DARKNESS

TRADING INTO DARKNESS

THE MAGIC BELOW PARIS™ BOOK TWO

C. M. SIMPSON
MICHAEL ANDERLE

LMBPN Publishing
PMB 196, 2540 South Maryland Pkwy
Las Vegas, NV 89109

First US edition, March 2019
ISBN 978-1-64202-148-6

TRADING INTO DARKNESS TEAM

Thanks to our Beta Readers

Mary Morris, Nicole Emens, Larry Omans, Charles
Tillman, and John Ashmore

Thanks to our JIT Readers

Dorothy Lloyd
Diane L. Smith
Misty Roa
Angel LaVey

Editor

SkyHunter Editing Team

DEDICATION

This is for all those who believed in me enough that, eventually, I had the courage to believe in myself.

Thank you.
—C.M. Simpson

To Family, Friends and
Those Who Love
to Read.
May We All Enjoy Grace
to Live the Life We Are
Called.

— Michael

SHADOW-RAID AMBUSH

The trail ahead passed through a tall stand of calla shrooms, but Marchant had no time to admire their graceful white trunks or the soft glow coming from the undersides of their caps. Nor did she have time to collect any of the smaller shrooms and toadstools growing at their feet. Stretching her magic into the cavern around her, she knew Mordan had sensed the ambush, too.

The big kat stalked silently a half-dozen yards to her right, moving through the cavern dark as Marsh adjusted her eyes to see better. The problem with calla shrooms was that they were hard to see over...unless you weren't from the world below and were built a little taller and wider than its inhabitants.

But Marsh wasn't that lucky. She was slender and slight of build like all cavern folk, her skin pale and shaded like the cream-colored stones among which she made her home. Her eyes were a touch darker than her skin, with green flecks, and a golden tinge, and her hair a disciplined cascade of copper drawn back into a braid to keep it out of her eyes. She didn't need it blocking her vision, even when she was using her magic to see.

She walked down the path, drawing on the shadows as she went and asking them to show her who else shared the spaces they connected. Carefully, she gathered the shadow threads that answered her so she could see what they revealed.

Not that the shadows spoke, but they connected the spaces in the cavern, and what they touched, Marsh touched too—which meant she could use the shadows to transmit an image of what was in the dark or use them to hear what was spoken out of range of her ears—if she could find the right connecting thread.

She kept going forward, knowing she was moving farther into the trap that had been set. She had the kat, though, and the big beast was confident they could take the small force that awaited them. Marsh just had to draw their attention until she was ready...

Before she could do that, though, the threads slid out of Marsh's grasp, and she frowned. Someone else was using the shadows, pulling the threads she was calling on to search the dark right out of her fingers. Someone was using the shadows to shelter those waiting in ambush around her.

Marsh pulled on the threads, trying to take them back, but the other mage had a stronger grip and she couldn't. Maybe she and the kat had made a mistake. If they were facing a more powerful mage among their attackers, they might *not* be able to take them down.

The attack began before she could act on that thought, the first strike coming from behind. Marsh felt the twist of the shadows and bounced two quick steps forward, pivoting even as the darkness came alive around her. Shadows thinned and dropped away, revealing the body heat of those hiding beneath them.

The damn shadow mage had cloaked the waiting force so well she hadn't seen through it using either her shadow magic or the nature magic that allowed her to sense the life forces around her.

"*Merde!*"

One of the ambushers laughed.

"Got you this time, girl!"

"Yuh think?" Marsh stepped forward, pushing her hands in front of her and then taking them wide.

He gave a startled shout as a wall of shadow slammed into his chest and threw him back. More shouts came from either side of him as the attackers emerging from the shrooms were also flung back. As they fell, Marsh brought her arms back down and drew her sword.

Magic was good for some battles, but the blade was always there when she needed it, and she could always call a shield to her arm. Behind her, the kat roared, and a man screamed.

"Yield! I yield!"

There was a growl, and he yelled again. Shortly afterward, there was another scream. The shield could wait. Marsh gave the fighters in front of her a feral grin, lifting her shield arm and opening her hand. Shadow drew together above it, forming an ebony dart. Marsh flicked her fingers, pointing at a man on the ground, and the dart flew toward him, slamming through the fabric of his cloak to pin him in place.

"Hey!" he shouted, and Marsh laughed.

Truth be told, that *had* been a little close for training purposes. When she called and directed the next two darts, she made sure they dissipated into harmless smoke just before they hit the tunics of her other targets. Both men stopped their advance and dropped to the ground as though they'd been hit, waiting for the battle to end.

Behind her, the screams had stopped. By her count, Marsh figured the kat had taken down the other three members of the raiding party, which was strange because she was sure there was supposed to be one more. She reached out with her mind, touching the threads of shadow that connected her with whoever else might be hiding in the dark.

Once again, they slid out of her control, refusing to show what or who shared their touch.

"Roeglin!" Marsh growled as he slid onto the path beside her.

She caught the movement from the corner of her eye, but only barely. Turning, she raised her sword, calling shadows to form a shield on her free arm. His blade slammed against it seconds later.

"Getting careless," he said as they broke apart, circling each other warily.

Marsh knew she was in trouble when the air at her back moved. She turned side-on, keeping her shield between her and the mage even as she parried the blade coming at her from behind.

Mordan, she called, using her connection to the kat to show her where her opponents stood.

The silence that met her was far from reassuring.

Marsh backed up so both opponents were in easy view. Roeglin she knew, but the shadow guard who'd stepped into the fight was new. Faced with two experienced swordsmen and no kat to help her, Marsh knew surprise was her only hope for a win. Tossing the sword into the air, she made a quick sweeping gesture with her hand.

Black tendrils lashed out, snaking around the shadow guard's feet...or they would have if he hadn't quick-stepped to one side and brought his shadow-coated blade down to sever them. Marsh realized that she and Roeglin weren't the only ones who could work shadow magic. The guard retaliated with a dart that Marsh caught on her shield as Roeglin's eyes flashed white.

Merde, Marsh thought, wondering what the mage was trying to conjure in her mind.

The calla shrooms around her began to shake, furtive whispers of movement, becoming less subtle with every passing second. Marsh drew on her nature magic to sense the life forces in the cavern, but whatever was coming toward her was either dead or not really there.

Nice! That was one way around Roeglin's mind magic. Ignoring the shivering shrooms, Marsh focused on the shadow guard, lunging toward him so that he had to step back and parry. As Marsh pressed her attack, Mordan slipped out of the shrooms behind Roeglin, snaking a paw around the shadow mage's ankles and pulling him over.

His startled shout distracted the guard, and Marsh pressed forward. Unfortunately for the raiders, Mordan wasn't finished. Even as Roeglin fell, the big kat leapt, crashing into the side of Marsh's opponent and bringing him down.

Roeglin got off the ground, sputtering.

"One of these days, you're going to be somewhere the kat can't reach—and then you're actually going to have to work out how to get yourself free."

As he spoke, the others picked themselves up off the ground, some dusting off their tunics and armor and others resettling their weapons. The kat moved between them, nudging each with her nose until they caressed her head, letting her know she was forgiven and they were all right. As much as Marsh had tried to convince Mordan that this type of "play" was necessary so they could learn to stand against other hunters, the kat didn't like it.

"So," Marsh asked, looking at Roeglin. "Did I pass?"

He curled his lip.

"You got lucky, but yes, you passed. You can have a cookie. I'll let Brigitte know."

Well, *that* was more sarcasm than she needed, but speaking of cookies...

"How's Aisha doing?"

"She doesn't want you to leave, but we've convinced her we need her to help keep Lennie busy, so she'll let it go."

"Oh, she will, will she?" Marsh didn't know whether to be annoyed or relieved that the five-year-old had been convinced to stay at the fortress while she and Roeglin joined the teams restoring the trade routes between the Four Settlements.

She was going to miss having the little brat along—and at the same time, she wasn't. Five really was too young to be in the middle of a battle, no matter how well the kid had coped with it in the past. Everyone was still waiting for her and Tamlin to fall apart over the disappearance of their parents, but neither of them had.

That was good, too, but it was also bad since it put the pressure right on Marsh to find them. She only hoped she could do that before anything worse happened to them, assuming they *were* still alive.

"You ready to recharge some glows?" Roeglin's voice cut through her thoughts, and Marsh groaned.

While she'd reached the point where drawing on the shadows and staying connected to the hoshkat no longer completely drained her of energy, she still struggled when it came to charging the glows.

"Everyone can do it," both Roeglin and Tamlin assured her, but Marsh found using her magic to charge the pale purple gemstones more draining than asking the shadows what lay on the other side of a cavern or searching for the life forces of other creatures. Maybe everyone *could* do magic, but it was like sword-fighting, or cooking, or studying in that it required practice, and not everyone was good at all the different varieties.

It would explain why most people lived their whole lives without knowing what they were capable of. Some abilities didn't naturally bubble to the surface, and some weren't as strong. Maybe that was why she could work with shadows and not with light. Strengths and weaknesses, and all that.

Or it could just be because you like hiding in the dark.

Roeglin's voice in her head was something she would never get used to. Speaking of different kinds of magic... Well, he could walk through people's minds, and the person whose head he thought was the most fun to walk through right now was hers. Marsh let her body do the talking, punching him in the shoulder before the thought crossed her mind.

"Betcha never saw *that* coming," she muttered, a smile tugging at the corners of her mouth.

"I should have," he grumbled, rubbing his arm. "You hit hard…every…single…time."

"So, no glows?"

"Ha! Nice try. Just for that, you can do extra."

Nice way to remind her he was the one in charge. Marsh sighed and fell in beside him as they headed back to the shadow-mage fortress. If she was lucky, this would be her last training session before they headed out to begin restoring the trade routes. The Master of Shadows had decided the road to Ruins Hall would be the first one worked on, and he was sending ten of his best shadow guards to join the force the Ruins Hall founder was building.

Together, they would re-forge the path to Kerrenin's Ledge and the other two settlements that made up the Four Settlements community. Together, they would force the raiders out of their lands and make them give back the people they had taken—*if* they could re-connect the caverns.

"Together," Roeglin agreed, and Marsh knew she was never going to get the damn man out of her head.

He was there to stay, and not in a good way.

"Hey!" But whatever Roeglin was going to add was lost. They'd reached the entry to the fortress, and Aisha was waiting.

2

THE MASTERS DECIDE

An hour later, Marchant closed her eyes and bowed her head. At this rate, she was going to see purple gemstones in her sleep...and not a single damn one of them was going to be glowing.

"Aagh!"

She drew a deep breath and straightened, settling her fingers against the top of the stone and gently stroking down. The movement was supposed to draw the light out of the air and coax it into the glow stone, but either there was no light in the air around her, or it was hiding too deeply in the shadows to be found. Marsh had been trying so hard to discover it that she was finding it difficult to believe *anything* could make the stone brighten.

Okay, maybe she could set it alight. That would *always* work.

Right now, all she wanted to do was tear the stone from its stand and hurl it across the room. Knowing her luck, though, if she did that, it would hit the wall and shatter, and then there would be no way to charge it. She sighed and wondered what would happen if she tried charging it with heated shadow.

Sure, it wouldn't glow with visible light, but most of the people walked the caverns using heat patterns to enhance their vision anyway—and it would be easy, so easy. Marsh traced a line down the gem and into the stone. Heated shadow could burn as brightly as any light if folks were looking at it right.

Repeating the gesture, Marsh let her mind wander, playing with the idea of shadow-heated glows. Would it make them harder for the raiders to find and put out? Would being hidden from normal sight be protection or hindrance? Would...

"That's not a bad idea, Marsh, but I don't think it'll have the same effect on the shadow monsters as filling it with light."

Marsh started, her concentration crumbling into a thousand pieces as Brigitte's voice broke into her thoughts. The journeyman had a point. Marsh stared down at the stone.

At first glance, it didn't look much different from an uncharged glow, except maybe a little darker, as if a shadow had been cast across it. But if you looked at it closely, the shadow flickered and wavered like a candle burning dark—and if you looked at it as heat instead of light, it burnt like the sun above the surface world.

Aisha stood up from behind several rows of brightly shining glows, her blue eyes dark with concentration. Shaking her head so her dark curls bounced, the little girl crossed to the workbench and studied what Marsh had done.

"Monsters won't like the hot *and* the bright," she commented, and with a twist of her hands, turned the dark flame to a living beacon of white and yellow.

Marsh yelped and skittered back as her eyes began to water and heat licked at her face. Aisha laughed but looked expectantly at Brigitte.

"What do you think?"

To give her credit, Brigitte managed to keep a straight face, even if laughter bubbled in her azure gaze and she avoided looking Marsh directly in the eye.

"I think I'll have to ask the Master of Shadows what he thinks," her instructor said. "That's an interesting idea the two of you have come up with."

It was kind of Brigitte to give her credit, Marsh thought, but most of it should go to the child. *She*, at least, knew what she was doing.

Marsh might have been cross with Aisha, except the little girl hadn't meant anything by it. The kid loved playing with new ideas, and Marsh had just handed her one on a plate. Marsh stared at the flaming glow, letting its light draw her in like a campfire would, and then she blinked.

"I'm sorry?"

"I asked if you thought you could try another one," Brigitte said in a voice that told Marsh she'd said it more than once.

Marsh nodded.

"Sure. I can't get any worse, right?"

This time Aisha caught herself before she commented. Marsh saw the child open her mouth to agree and then hastily bite her lower lip. It made her smile. Maybe five-year-olds *could* be taught diplomacy, or maybe Aisha had a better sense of self-preservation than anyone gave her credit for. Whatever the case, Marsh was glad the girl had decided not to say anything. She wasn't sure she could handle sympathy right now.

With a sigh, she stood up and stretched, then walked over to the box of uncharged glows, taking one from the top and returning to her workstation. Setting it down carefully, Marsh lowered herself to her knees, running her hand over the glow from gem-tip to metal setting.

Right. Let's do this.

An hour later, when she was trembling with fatigue, Brigitte laid a hand on her shoulder.

"Time to stop," she said. "You've done enough for the day."

She had?

Marsh surveyed the gem, relieved to see a soft glow coming from within the stone. At least she'd done *something*. Roeglin's voice shattered the illusion.

"You could *almost* use it as a night light."

Brigitte groaned, and Marsh closed her eyes as Aisha sprang to her defense.

"It's a good light," the child declared, seeing their reactions and coming to stand beside Marsh.

She put her hand gently on Marsh's shoulder, patting her like she was a puppy.

"It's a night light," Roeglin argued as he stepped into the room.

Marsh waited for Aisha to argue that it wasn't, but the girl shifted uncomfortably beside her. After a moment's silence, she patted Marsh's shoulder again, this time reassuringly.

"It's a very *good* night light," she said, and Marsh sagged.

Brigitte stepped in.

"It's more than enough for today," she repeated. "Class dismissed."

She hesitated, and Marsh hoped she wouldn't try to be supportive. The Deeps knew she'd had about all the support she could handle. As if sensing this, Brigitte turned her attention to the newly-arrived mage.

"What can I do for you, Ro? I take it you had a reason to come to see me, other than upsetting my students?"

Relaxing as Roeglin's attention shifted, Marsh pushed herself slowly to her feet. She was about to gather her newly created night light when Brigitte spoke.

"Leave that there, Trainee. I'll pack up today. You and Aisha need to get ready for dinner."

Well, at least she hadn't told her she needed a break. Marsh turned for the door and looked at Aisha.

"Bath time," she said, and the child pouted.

"Not dirty."

"Yeah? I can smell you from here."

"Can. Not."

Marsh started walking. In truth, all she wanted to do was curl up in a corner and cry. After proving her mastery of shadow this morning, the afternoon had served as a reminder of just how much magic she *couldn't* tap into.

And she needed to do this. Every mage on the trade route had to be able to charge the glows or they wouldn't get the road opened anytime soon, and they had to. The

Deeps knew what the raiders were doing while they had Ruins Hall isolated. Marsh hurried down the corridor.

She had to work out what she was doing wrong and fix it. What good was she going to be otherwise? A heavy sadness settled over her, and her eyes prickled with tears of frustration. Why *couldn't* she call the light?

Before she could start chewing over the problem again, Aisha interrupted. The little girl ran to catch up and slipped her hand into Marsh's.

"It's okay," the child told her. "The shadows won't talk to me. Only the rocks."

Marsh wasn't sure how that was meant to be comforting, but at least the girl was trying. They walked in silence for a few more moments and then Aisha asked, "Do I really smell?"

As Marsh opened her mouth to reassure the child, another voice cut in.

"Of course you do. You stink. You smell worse than a mule when Mordan's been chasing it."

Roeglin's taunt might have worked, but Aisha had had four older siblings, and her brother Tamlin was merciless. The little girl knew exactly how to deal with the shadow mage's teasing.

"Worse than you?" she retorted, and Marsh sputtered, turning in time to catch the look on Roeglin's face.

Aisha giggled, and Roeglin's surprise turned to chagrin.

"Ha. Ha," he said. "Very funny."

He turned to Marsh.

"I need to see you," he told her, and again Aisha leapt to her defense.

"Nuh-uh. Brigitte said we had to have a bath for dinner."

"That's not going to taste very nice."

Marsh rolled her eyes, but Roeglin hadn't finished. He fixed the pair of them with a stern gaze before focusing on Marsh.

"*After* your bath, and *after* you've delivered Aisha to her brother," he said. "My office."

His office. Well.

Marsh wondered what she'd done wrong but decided not to ask. It was probably something to do with her utter hopelessness at recharging the glows, and she probably wasn't going to like it. Her heart sank. What if he told her she was grounded until she got her head around it? What if…

Not all shadow mages can recharge glows, Roeglin told her, pulling her fears from her head and interrupting her thoughts to reassure her, *and you're not grounded.*

"Half a turn," he said out loud as he turned away. "Don't be late."

"Yes, Master Roeglin."

Marsh couldn't bring herself to use just his title. It wasn't that she didn't want to acknowledge his rank; it was just that she didn't feel comfortable calling him "master." She could handle calling the heads of the school or the others by the title alone, but not Roeglin. She needed to use his name as well. Maybe it had something to do with the way she'd met him.

He hadn't been a master then.

Okay, he *had* been a master, but he hadn't been *her*

master. She could get her head around the title, but not around calling him by it. Stupid, really.

To her surprise, Roeglin didn't have anything to say to that. He merely quirked an eyebrow at her, smirking as he headed up the next flight of stairs. Marsh escorted Aisha to the communal baths and got her clean, then led her back to the quarters they now shared and dressed her in a fresh robe before delivering her to her brother.

"I have to see Master Roeglin, so you've got dinner duty," she said when Tamlin answered her knock.

His dark eyes flicked from Marsh to Aisha, and he nodded. Any other time, he might have argued about having to mind his sister when it was Marsh's turn, but not when Marchant called Roeglin by his title and rank. It was their code for official business, and Tamlin knew not to argue when he heard it. The boy was settling into the role of shadow-mage apprentice as if he'd been born to it.

"I'll see you after dinner," she told him, and again he nodded.

She'd rescued the two children from the shadow monster ambush that had deprived them of the rest of their family, and she took her duties as a surrogate parent seriously. If she couldn't find any other family members willing to take them, or if she failed to rescue their parents —something she didn't want to think about—she'd be all the family they had. And until she got things sorted, she needed to be that family for them, regardless.

That meant making sure she checked in with them every day, like their parents would, making sure they were okay and listening to their hopes and fears. She made it part of their daily routine, no matter how busy her day had been, how fraught, or how exhausting. At first, she'd been worried, but they seemed happy enough. The fact that Aisha shared her room helped.

Marsh wondered how they would do when she had to travel, but pushed that thought aside. It was hard not to look back as she left Tamlin's quarters, but she managed. She didn't want to be a *clingy* parent. Knowing the boy would look after his sister, Marsh hurried to Roeglin's office.

The shadow master's greeting was straight to the point and not exactly a welcome.

"I noticed you're having trouble charging the glows."

As an opening line, it stopped Marsh cold. She froze two steps into his office.

"Close the door behind you."

When she had, Roeglin gestured toward a chair. Marsh was still searching for the right words as he continued.

"You're not in trouble," he assured her, and she tensed, knowing there was a "but" coming.

He did not disappoint her.

"But we are going to have to think of alternatives if you can't call the light into the glows."

Marsh swallowed, clenching her jaw to stop herself from forbidding him from saying what came next. After a quick glance to make sure she was waiting, Roeglin went on.

"If you can't manage it, we'll have to add Aisha to the team."

Now she *did* have something to say.

"No!"

Roeglin tilted his head toward her, raising both eyebrows.

"I beg your pardon."

It wasn't a question, but Marsh answered it anyway.

"You are *not* putting her out where she might be attacked."

"I'm not asking. The *Master of Shadows* is not asking. That decision has already been made. Time is running out, and we do not have the luxury of waiting for you to develop the skill. As your master, I know you won't be able to do it in time, and maybe not at all, and as the liaison between the shadow mages and Monsieur Gravine, I cannot continue to wait."

"But—"

Roeglin raised a hand, and Marsh stopped. His face softened.

"I'm sorry, Marsh, but we are out of time. We have a week at most, and we need to reorganize things to allow for Aisha to come with us."

"Does that mean you'll allow Tamlin to go, too?"

He shrugged, and a wry smile curved his lips.

"We won't have much choice," he admitted. "I can't see the boy letting his sister go into the caverns without him."

"And she'll be taking the kit and Scruffknuckle," Marsh added, trying to comfort herself more than anything else.

Roeglin sighed.

"She will." He paused. "Has the other kit shown signs of making an attachment?"

Marsh shook her head.

"No, although it's not short on choices. There are at

least four beast-speakers who would love to have its company."

"Including the Master of Beasts…"

"He's not forcing the issue. He says the choice is for the kat to make."

That decision had won the Master of Beasts Marsh's respect. She had a feeling he could have coerced the kit's will to his own but had chosen not to, despite the prestige such a companion would bring. As for her own attachment to the kit's mother, she knew that was temporary. As soon as she had helped the great beast retrieve her missing kits, Mordanlenoowar would be gone.

She sighed and returned to the subject at hand.

"I don't suppose I can change your mind?"

This time Roeglin's lips quirked briefly upward, and he opened the top drawer of his desk.

"Here," he told her, placing a glow stone on the table and picking up a short-timer. "You charge that by the time the glass runs out, and we won't need to take her with us."

Marsh wanted to give up then and there. She knew she couldn't charge the stone, knew she didn't have a hope in all the Deeps, but she wasn't going to give in so easily. Maybe the idea of Aisha's impending danger was just the incentive she needed.

3

AN UNWELCOME ASSIGNMENT

M arsh's fears for Aisha's safety were not enough. By the time the dinner bell had rung, Marsh had not managed more than the faint 'night light' effect she'd achieved earlier. When she ignored the bell, Roeglin stood and came around the desk.

"It's enough," he said, laying a hand on her shoulder.

Marsh shrugged it away, stroking her fingers down the crystal's side once more and trying again to call the light from the room around them. Roeglin grabbed her wrist, pulling her hand away from the crystal, his voice sharp with rebuke.

"You've done enough."

Marsh stifled the urge to jerk her wrist out of his hand and smack him upside the head. He was right, and she hated it, but she also couldn't argue with him. She really had done enough—if only to prove that she *couldn't* do it.

Aisha was going to have to go with them. Tamlin, too.

She let her shoulders slump and bowed her head, and Roeglin let go of her wrist to return to his desk. Opening a drawer, he pulled out a small bag and placed it between them.

"Have a cookie."

His words made Marchant lift her head. She was going to refuse, but he'd opened the bag, and the smell of Brigitte's baking hit her. Marsh grabbed two. All she wanted to do was sleep, but she wasn't about to fall asleep in Roeglin's office. She wanted to make it to her own room, at least.

The trouble was, she'd pushed the magic just a little too far, and she'd been tired to begin with. Fatigue crawled along her limbs, making her eyes heavy even as she bit into the first cookie in an attempt to restore her fast-fading energy.

"Who's looking after Aisha?" Roeglin asked as Marsh lifted the cookie a second time.

The damn thing was heavier than it looked, but it tasted amazing.

"Tamlin," she replied around a spray of crumbs.

Roeglin ignored the mess, and Marsh focused on taking another bite. The master's next words made her frown.

"Good, because you need to sleep."

Marsh wanted to argue that she didn't, but that would have been a blatant lie. She *did* need to get some rest. Worse, she didn't think she could stop herself from doing so. Her body was going to do what it wanted, and what *she* wanted didn't matter.

"Brigitte's going to kill me," Roeglin muttered, and Marsh managed to lift her head.

Roeglin caught her look and went on to explain.

"Because I let you push yourself too far, so you'll be out of action tomorrow."

Roeglin had been doing magic a whole lot longer then she had, but Marsh still didn't want to hear it.

"I've got—"

"Nothing," Roeglin snapped. "Your day's clear of anything but sleeping and eating—and that includes looking after your kids."

Marsh wanted to know exactly how he was going to enforce that but realized it was more a question of where she was going to find the energy to defy him. The cookies helped a little bit, but she was going to have to head to her room soon, or she'd disgrace herself by curling up under Roeglin's desk and falling asleep on the floor.

Roeglin snorted.

"Well, we can't have that, can we?"

He waited, then pushed his chair back.

"Come on," he said, standing as Marsh struggled to her feet. "I'll walk you to your room."

Oh, he would, would he?

"I can tuck myself in," she snarled, frustration at her failure leaking into her voice.

Roeglin raised his hands in mock surrender.

"Not saying you can't, but you've got to get there first, and I don't want you falling down on the way. Lennie would take several large chunks out of my hide. Brigitte, too, I imagine."

As badly as she wanted to smile at the idea of Lennie and Brigitte taking bits out of Roeglin's hide, Marsh glared at him. She hated to admit it, but the man had a point.

Right now, her room seemed several caverns too far away, and she honestly didn't know if she was going to make it.

"Fine."

She pushed herself to her feet, and Roeglin came around the desk and tucked her arm through his.

By the time they got to her room, he'd wound his arm around her waist and Marchant was thinking curling up under his desk would have been a lot less embarrassing. She was convinced of it when Tamlin and Aisha came out of the room. The boy raised his brows and turned to his sister.

"You can sleep in my room tonight."

Marsh's face went bright red.

"It's not what you think."

Tamlin gave her a pointed look.

"Uh huh. We're going to be late for dinner."

Tamlin would have turned down the hall if Roeglin hadn't explained.

"I'm putting her to bed."

The kid arched his eyebrows again.

"I can see *that*."

Roeglin groaned and hurried to explain.

"No. I asked her to do work in my office—"

There was a snort from the hallway behind them as someone tried to not to laugh. Roeglin looked toward it and Marsh slipped her hand free of his arm, pushing the door open and stumbling through it to escape the embarrassment in the hall. As she crashed onto her bed and closed her eyes, she heard Brigitte.

"Honestly, Ro. I'm going to take away your license to talk. Tamlin, Aisha can sleep in her own bed. Marchant's been working on her light magic and is exhausted. She won't wake her."

"Well, why didn't they just say that?"

Marchant didn't hear the answer to that one, and she fell asleep without hearing them close the door. When she woke, Brigitte was shaking her, and she'd brought a meal. The woman didn't waste any words.

"You're needed in a meeting." She watched as Marsh got up and then pointed to the food. "Make sure you eat. Aisha's with Tamlin, and they'll join us later."

Marsh did as she was told, stretching away the fatigue that lingered in her tired muscles and then reaching for her clothes. She was glad she didn't have to wear the robes given to most apprentices. The trousers and shirt she pulled on were more comfortable. Their soft, dark cloth was better than any she'd worn as a messenger for Kearick, and her sword belt fit the pants perfectly. Robes would have gotten in the way. Even the boots were an improvement, better than she could have afforded on Kearick's stingy wages.

Thinking about her former employer made Marsh remember the artifact she still had stowed in her backpack. While the supply master knew of it, she'd let Marsh take it back and hadn't told anyone else she still had it. Marsh frowned, nudging her old pack farther under her desk as she sat to eat. She still had to deliver the darn thing whether or not she got paid for it.

She'd thought of locking the pack in the chest she used for her clothes, but had reasoned that was the first place anyone would look for it. Instead, she'd tucked her old travel pack in the farthest, darkest corner beneath her desk and called on the shadows to conceal it. So far, not even Aisha's curious eyes had noticed it.

Thinking of the child made Marsh glance toward Aisha's bed. It was empty, but it was made, and Marsh breathed a sigh of relief. That was one less thing to deal with when she saw the child next. After finishing what was on her plate and draining the mug of lukewarm chocolate, she headed for the door.

Brigitte was waiting in the corridor.

"This meeting," Marsh said. "What's it about?"

"Restoring the trade routes," Brigitte told her, and Marsh felt a shiver of excitement.

When they reached the Shadow Master's office, however, she realized Brigitte hadn't told her everything. The room was crowded, even though it was one of the largest offices she'd ever been in. As well as her and Brigitte, Roeglin, Gustav, Aisha, Tamlin, a man whose uniform identified him as head of the shadow guard, three hoshkats and an unusually quiet krypthund puppy were present.

Marsh was two steps through the door when she registered the presence of the children and came to an abrupt halt. She turned to Brigitte, about to demand an explanation, but the woman took her by the arm and guided her into the group. She addressed the Master of Shadows before Marsh could speak.

"Sorry we are late, Master."

He'd looked up as they entered, and now he shook his head.

"I'm sure you came as soon as you were able." He turned

his attention to Marsh. "It's good to see you recovering, Trainee Leclerc."

As a warning of her position in the hierarchy, his use of her training title was effective—and Marsh wondered why he'd felt the need.

"Thank you, Master of Shadows," she said, and let Brigitte guide her to a place beside the children.

She still wasn't very happy with them being here, but she knew she'd have to wait to see why they were in attendance.

"If you'll all sit," the Master directed, and waited until they'd done as he bid. "As you know, the trade routes must be restored sooner rather than later. To this end, we have been testing all of our mages so we know how quickly the glows might be repaired."

A hollow feeling settled in Marsh's stomach, but the Master of Shadows wasn't finished.

"We cannot afford to ignore the abilities of one of the most skilled at calling the light that I have seen in all my years."

Aisha wriggled happily in her seat, and the Master smiled.

"Apprentice Aisha Danet will be added to the team containing her guardian Marchant Leclerc." He caught Marsh's half-gasp of protest and silenced her with a stern gaze as he continued, "And Apprentice Tamlin Danet will be joining her."

Again, Marsh drew breath to argue, but the Master of Shadows still hadn't finished. His gaze moved over the group of mages and guards gathered before him.

"I understand that many of you will have concerns

about including one so young on this journey, but the task is urgent. I believe we are more than capable of keeping one small child and her brother safe. After all, it has proven possible in the past."

Marsh wanted to argue that the caverns were much more dangerous now than they had ever been, but the Master of Shadows was well ahead of her.

"With the danger growing, I am still confident that we can keep them safe, given that they will be with a force of experienced shadow mages and guards, as well as one of the most dangerous beasts known to the caverns."

The tone of his voice said his mind was made up, but Marsh decided she had to try.

"Master of Shadows," she began, and he turned his face toward her. Marsh noted that it was wiped carefully clear of any expression, but she didn't let that deter her. "With respect, but it is still not safe for a child to be outside the monastery, and there may be an alternative."

He raised his hand, and she stopped.

"You are right about it not being safe, but without reopening the trade routes utilizing the forces being built by the Ruins Hall founder, not even the monastery will be safe. Letting Aisha use her skills will allow us to restore that safety sooner. As for the alternative, it is a good idea, but I'm afraid it will not suffice for safeguarding the trade routes since the ability to see the heat from the flames is not possessed by all."

That was something Marsh had not known. She'd thought everyone could see the heat stored in the objects and creatures around them. The Master of Shadows caught her look, and it was as though he'd read her mind.

"Not everyone," he confirmed, "and enough can't that we need the light."

Marsh wanted to keep arguing but decided not to. The Master of Shadows had a point. Besides, he'd clearly made his decision, and she didn't want him angry with her.

"Yes, Master," she said and looked down at her lap.

As she did, Mordan nudged her with her head, and Marsh felt the big kat's presence hovering at the edge of her mind. She quietly laid her hand on the kat's head and opened the link between them. Mordan crept into her mind, her presence brushing against her doubts and fears and reassuring her as it passed.

Mordanlenoowar was traveling with Marsh and her cubs. Mordan's kits were traveling with Marsh's cubs. There was no danger in the cavern that could stand against her pride and the pride from the Protected Cavern when they hunted together.

Marsh stared at the kat.

The Protected Cavern?

And the kat replied by sending her a picture of the monastery with its fortified walls and gated barbican.

The Protected Cavern.

The idea that the kat saw the shadow mages as a separate pride and their fortress as a cavern amused Marsh, and she smiled. She wanted to know what the big kat thought of the shadow mages, but Brigitte's elbow in her ribs jolted Marsh out of her head and she looked up. She found herself staring straight into the Shadow Master's eyes.

"Care to share?" he asked.

Marsh gestured toward the kat.

"She says the children will be safe with her and the kits along."

The Master arched one eyebrow and settled back in his chair.

"Indeed. Well, since the children will be accompanied by such an impressive menagerie, as well as one shadow master, a journeyman, a trainee, and an entourage of guards, I'm sure you have no objections to them joining the team you will be a part of, do you?"

"No, Master."

"Very good. Now, Brigitte, in the absence of your original master, and in the face of her poor judgment in leaving you behind, I'm assigning you a new master." He indicated Roeglin. "Master Leger will take over your training. In addition, the last journey showed that you have the skills of a journeyman, and I am promoting you to that rank. As of now, you are no longer an apprentice. Welcome, Journeyman Petitfeu."

A soft congratulatory murmur rose around them, but it took Brigitte a moment before she could stutter her thanks. The Master of Shadows smiled and nodded, but he was already continuing to the next topic.

"Master Envermet," he said, addressing the head of his shadow guards, and the man straightened, turning his attention solely to the Master.

Following the Shadow Master's gaze, Marsh recognized the man from the morning's training. No wonder he'd been hard to beat! She listened as the discussion turned to the distribution of the shadow guards between the team and the monastery.

It was followed by talk of rotations, supply lines, and

timelines, and her mind began to wander. On the other side of Brigitte, Aisha twisted restlessly in her seat, and Scruffknuckle sat up to put his head on the little girl's lap. The movement drew the Master's attention, and the discussion paused.

"Journeyman, Trainee, you are dismissed. Take the apprentices and their menagerie with you. You have an afternoon left to train in."

"Thank you, Master," Brigitte answered for all of them and rose from her seat.

Marsh was quick to follow, making sure Aisha and Tamlin rose also.

Truth be told, she was happy to leave the office, although she didn't know how she was going to be able to concentrate on any kind of training knowing Aisha would be heading out with the repair teams.

4

SHADOWS OF THE PAST

In the end, Marsh didn't have to worry about training. As soon as the door to the Master of Shadows office had closed behind them, Brigitte gave her a stern look.

"Your orders were to rest for the day," the newly-made journeyman said. "I'll take the children."

Well, Marsh thought, *that tells me!*

But she didn't argue, and was secretly relieved. Without the meeting to distract her, she'd realized just how tired she still was from her activities the day before...and hungry! She wondered if Brigitte would notice if she went down to the dining hall first.

It turned out that Brigitte had a limited ability to read minds...or maybe she'd just been around mages long enough to know what they needed. Either way, she detoured past the dining hall on the way to delivering Marsh to her room. Aisha was delighted.

"Cookies!"

"You're going to get fat," Tamlin teased, but Aisha didn't let him deter her.

"*My* cookies!"

"Two," Brigitte ordered, and Aisha pouted.

But she didn't argue, and Marsh relaxed. It looked like a lot had gone on while she'd been out training with Roeglin and the guard, and the children were in good hands. That made it a lot easier for her to leave the kids in the journeyman's care and sleep.

Watching them as they ate only confirmed that the children were fine. The three of them laughed and joked, letting Marsh eat in peace, and she couldn't help thinking how different Aisha's reaction was compared to the first time she'd seen Brigitte.

Back then, the little girl had taken one look at the woman's shadow-monster-dark skin, screamed, and locked herself in the closest room, asking the stone to protect her. Now Brigitte's ebony skin and midnight hair no longer bothered the little brat. It was good to see.

Once they'd eaten, Brigitte, Aisha, and Tamlin walked Marsh back to her room before leaving to go to class. Marsh barely heard the door close after them, drifting into oblivion seconds after her head hit the pillow.

She woke much later to darkness, but it was a darkness in which she was not alone. Quiet steps reached her ears, furtive rustlings from her desk and the soft clink of the lock on her clothes chest as it was opened...even though the key still hung around her neck.

Adrenaline surged through her and Marsh woke properly, but she forced herself to lie still; perfectly still, lest the intruder realize she was awake. Keeping her eyes closed, she stretched her mind into the darkness, blending the magic she used to sense nearby life forces with the magic that let her see what lay in the shadows. It was strange to see her room clearly lit, and stranger still to see a face from the past staring intently at her belongings.

"Mikel?"

His head snapped around as she sat up and he bounced to his feet, spinning toward her as he pulled a short, sharp blade from his belt.

"Hey!"

Marsh pushed her blanket down and rolled off the bed, just as Mikel leapt to plunge his blade into the place she'd lain, but Marsh didn't stop. Kicking clear of the bedding that had followed her to the floor, she rolled to her feet, calling a shadow shield to her arm even as she drew a sword out of the surrounding dark.

Mikel turned, his face following her movement, gazing unerringly at her despite the lack of light.

"Where is it?" he demanded, his voice hard with frustration.

"What?"

"Your delivery."

"Why?"

Marsh resisted the urge to glance toward the desk, forcing her eyes to stay fixed on Mikel's face.

"Kearick wants it back."

"I haven't delivered it yet."

Marsh retreated as Mikel stepped away from the bed.

"That's why he wants it back."

"So he sent you to take it? Nice to know he trusts me."

"That changed when you didn't make the delivery when you hit town."

"I was kinda busy at the time."

"The delivery comes first."

"Not when I'm not getting paid, it doesn't."

"Nice to know where your loyalties lie." He glanced around the room. "So, how much are the mages paying you?"

"I'm a trainee."

"Hence why Kearick wants his delivery back."

Marsh was about to say Kearick only had to ask when Mikel's face hardened.

"Where is it?"

"I'll make the delivery when I get back to Ruins Hall."

"I can make it now."

Which begged the question…

"How did you get here, anyway?"

His mouth tightened.

"Some of us can travel without roads."

"And the raiders?"

"What raiders?"

His words gave Marsh a sense of unease.

"You didn't see any?"

"Saw some troops camped out at the junction. They didn't see me."

Mikel stepped forward, the dagger held before him. "Where is it?"

"Not yours to take," Marsh said, and tilted her chin toward the door. "I'll deliver it when I get back to the Hall."

"That's not what Kearick wants."

"Then Kearick can send me a change of instructions."

"Not happening. Last chance!"

"Get out of my room."

Mikel's attack came with his reply. "Have it your way."

Marsh brought her shield up, blocking his lunge even as she struck out with her blade. It bit into Mikel's unprotected arm and he swore, backing up so he could shift the dagger to his off–hand while he drew his sword.

"Wasn't going to kill you..." he said, but Marsh didn't let him finish.

"Guess that's changed now," she told him, forcing him back with another strike, which she reversed and turned into a thrust. He ducked the first and stumbled back with a curse, but Marsh's relentless push forward caught him in the gut, and he cried out in pain.

"Time I returned the favor," Marsh told him and ripped the blade free.

He screamed, dropping to his knees as she pulled her sword back for another strike. She had started to bring it forward when his blades clattered to the floor and he rolled onto his side, groaning as he grabbed at his stomach.

"My death won't stop them," he said. "Ruins Hall will fall, and then they'll..."

He stopped speaking and moaned as another wave of pain rolled over him.

Marsh didn't know what to say. She kicked his sword away from him and was about to do the same for the dagger when the door to her room burst open and light flared around them.

"Back it up, Marsh."

"Stand down!"

"Back it up!"

Marsh raised her shield to block the light, but she

recognized Master Envermet and Roeglin's voices. When her thighs hit her desk, she stopped, listening as the two mages grabbed Mikel and dragged him out of the room. The light did not diminish, and she realized it was coming from a small round rock that had been pitched in through the doorway. She stayed by the desk until Brigitte appeared and dispelled the light.

"Are you hurt?"

Was she?

Marsh looked down at herself and realized she wasn't.

"You want to dispel the shield and blade?"

In truth, she didn't, but this was Brigitte, and the journeyman's eyes were dark with concern. Marsh closed her eyes and willed sword and shield return to the shadows. They unwound, freeing her hand and arm, and Marsh opened her eyes, again and looked at the mess. Now, in addition to her scattered bedding, blood pooled on the floor in the middle of the room. Brigitte followed her gaze.

"You got him good," she said.

"Will he…" Marsh couldn't bring herself to finish the sentence.

Brigitte shrugged.

"I don't know. It will depend on what the rock wizards can do between them."

"What about Lennie?"

"I hadn't thought of her. I'll see…" Brigitte turned her head toward the two anxious faces peering through the door. "Tamlin, see if Lennie can help with the intruder."

He went, the sound of his running footsteps fading as it echoed down the corridor. Brigitte tried to fix Marsh with a stern gaze, but the smile that flitted across her lips ruined the effect.

"You were supposed to be sleeping."

Marsh swallowed, feeling the first onset of nerves. A shiver ran through her, and she raised her hand so Brigitte could see it shaking.

"Believe me, I'd have preferred not to have had someone try to kill me."

"Was that what he was here for?" Brigitte turned toward the door. "Come on. We'll head down to the dining hall so Roeglin can send someone to deal with this."

Marsh pushed herself off the desk, but instead of following Brigitte out of the room, she crouched beside the desk and reached into the shadows cloaking her pack.

"We need to find a safe place for this," she said, holding it up. "It's what he was sent for."

"Sent?"

Marsh walked to the door, shouldering the pack as she went. Aisha grabbed her hand as soon as she stepped into the corridor.

"You 'kay?"

Marsh wanted to tell her that she wasn't okay, but that wasn't what the little girl needed to hear.

"I'm fine now that you're here," she said, and was rewarded by an approving nod from Brigitte. She tapped the pack. "You gonna help me find a safe place for this?"

Aisha regarded her with wide eyes and shook her head.

"Master of Shadows will help," she said.

Marsh sighed and looked at Brigitte. The journeyman shrugged.

"The child has a point," she said, "but I think we should

hand it over to the Supply Master for the time being. The Master of Shadows is busy."

Busy with what? Marsh wanted to ask, but she had a fair idea. When she'd last seen him, the Master had been mapping out how they were going to restore the trade routes, starting with the one to Ruins Hall. She couldn't have slept that long...

As she followed Brigitte down eerily silent halls and corridors, Marsh revised that. There was none of the day-to-day hustle and bustle that she was used to. As they descended the stairs to where the Supply Master laired, Marsh had to ask.

"Where is everybody?"

"Dinner. We were coming to get you when we heard the ruckus."

Ruckus. Well, that was one way to describe it, Marsh thought. On the other hand, it also explained why no one had come earlier. The sleeping levels were quiet during training and meals. She'd been lucky to wake up at all.

"Wondered when you'd be down," the Supply Master said when they reached her. "Roeglin said to expect you."

That had shown a lot of faith, Marsh thought, given that she hadn't decided what to do when he'd left.

"How's Mikel?" she asked, and the Supply Master looked at her in surprise.

"Mikel?" she asked, lifting Marsh's pack and carefully taking the artifact out of it.

"The seeker. The one who attacked me."

The Supply Master's reply was delivered with a non-committal shrug.

"Roeglin said they'd be questioning him, so I guess he's

still alive. Lennie went past a little while ago. She must have been able to make a difference."

"Is she okay?"

"She looked a bit tired on the way back, but that big guy was with her, so I'm guessing she'll be okay."

"Henri?"

"I think so. The missing husband's brother." The Supply Master reached under her counter and pulled out a heavy stone box. "This should do the trick."

Eyeing it, Marsh had to agree. She watched as the Supply Master laid the artifact inside the box and closed the lid. What surprised her was that the woman did not lock it right away. Instead, she ran her finger around the seam where lid met body, and the stone melded together until the seam was gone. After that, the Supply Master slid a lock through each of the corners of the box and closed them.

Marsh thought that might be overkill, and her thoughts must have shown on her face because the Supply Master caught her gaze and gave her a tight-lipped smile.

"The Master of Shadows said he wanted it as secure as I could make it. I'm nearly done."

Nearly? Marsh stared at her, but the woman didn't explain any more. Instead, she turned to the wall behind her counter and laid an open palm on the stone. Now that she was paying attention, Marsh noticed the padlocks set in orderly rows along the bottom of the wall. More padlocks were scattered over the wall like random decorations, and she couldn't work out why.

As she watched what the Supply Master did next, Marsh realized what the explanation might be. The stone crept away from the Master's hand and left a hollow in the rear wall that would easily fit the box. The Supply Master picked the box up from the bench and lifted it to the shelf, sliding it easily into the gap. When she was done, she rested her hand at the top of the hollow she'd created and the stone flowed back, working its way around the box and smoothing itself over until the hollow had disappeared.

When it was done, the Supply Master moved her hand down until it was at the midpoint of where the shelf would be. Closing her eyes for a moment, she let her hand rest there, and then she lifted it away. Staring at the spot, Marsh saw that a simple loop now protruded from the wall. Catching her look and smiling silently, the Supply Master took another padlock out from beneath her counter and slipped it through the loop.

"There," she said. "All done, and if the fortress is attacked, I will simply erase the locks from the wall. There will be no clue as to where the artifact has been hidden. It is all we can do to make sure it does not fall into the wrong hands."

Staring at the wall, Marsh felt a part of herself relax. If the Supply Master removed the locking point, there would be no way for anyone to tell that this wall was any different from the others, and in any case, most treasure hunters would assume that what they looked for would be found on the shelves in the storerooms beyond.

They would be mistaken.

"Is there anything else?" the Supply Master wanted to know.

She looked at Brigitte, but the journeyman shook her head.

"Did Master Leger leave any instructions?" Brigitte asked, and it was the Supply Master's turn to shake her head.

"No." She cast a glance at Aisha, drawing Marchant's attention to the child's look of wide-eyed fascination, "although I think the little one might be better off in the company of her brother."

"Point taken." Brigitte turned to the door. "Come on. Let's go find Tamlin."

Marsh turned to follow and tripped over Scruffknuckle. The krypthund pup gave a startled yip, flipped her a filthy look, and bounded out from under her feet. Aisha laid her hand on him as he went past and he skidded to a halt beside her.

The child shot Marsh a look dirty enough to match the pup's as she walked Scruffknuckle out the door. Marsh rolled her eyes.

"He should know better than to get underfoot," she grumbled, and Aisha glared.

"You should watch where you're stepping." Before Marsh could find a reply to that, the child stalked down the hall, leaving Marsh frozen and staring before following in Brigitte's wake.

They had just reached the stairwell when Roeglin came out of it. His eyes were shadowed and his mouth was set in a straight line, but his face lightened when he saw Marsh.

"Trainee Leclerc," he said, "if you would come with me."

"Coming." Marsh turned to Brigitte. "Journeyman Petitfeu."

Brigitte made a gesture of dismissal and took Aisha's hand.

"Looks like it's just you and me, kiddo. Let's go find your brother."

Roeglin didn't say anything as he hurried ahead of Marsh down the stairs, and Marsh didn't bother asking where they were going. She had an idea she already knew, and she wasn't looking forward to the meeting ahead.

5

A CHANGE OF PLANS

Mikel was tied to a chair in the middle of a stone-lined cell when Marchant arrived. Gustav and Master Envermet stood against the far wall behind him. The seeker ignored them, lifting his head when he heard the door open. His lip curled in contempt when he saw who Roeglin had brought.

"Well, if it isn't the little girl who wants to be a seeker!"

Marsh made a show of looking over her shoulder.

"No little girls here," she said, turning back and looking Mikel up and down, "but there *is* a heaping great turd that needs to be moved to a latrine."

Mikel gave a short, sharp laugh in reply, sobering as Roeglin stepped closer. Marsh stayed where she was, waiting to see what Roeglin might do next. Mikel flicked the shadow mage a quick glance and turned his attention to Marsh.

"Tell me, why haven't you joined the winning side?"

Marsh made a point of looking at the other mages in the room before returning her gaze to Mikel. She hesitated as her gaze passed over Roeglin, but he gave her the smallest nod and she replied.

"I thought I already had."

Again, that snort, this time of derision.

"These guys?" He rolled his shoulders, turning his head to take in the shadow guard, the bodyguard, and the shadow mage. "They're outclassed and *way* outnumbered. They don't stand a chance against what's coming."

"What's coming?" Marsh put her hand on her hip and cocked her head. "I thought you worked for Kearick."

"Kearick's just the next boss up. There are others far more powerful…" His eyes darted around the cell as though expecting one of those "others" to step out of the shadows. When none did, he continued. "And they are closer than you think. Ruins Hall will fall, and this fortress will be next. We're looking forward to making it our home."

Marsh raised an eyebrow and waited. With any luck, she'd be able to get him to talk some more. Mikel stared back, and the silence between them grew. Marsh sighed and looked at Roeglin, but, before she could say anything, Mikel spoke.

"You need to make your delivery," he said, "or I'll just be the first. That artifact is not a toy for inexperienced girls to play with."

Marsh turned back to him, real anger stirring for the first time.

"I wouldn't be so inexperienced if Kearick had helped me find an apprenticeship. I bet he didn't even approach you."

Mikel laughed.

"He didn't, but even if he had, I'd never have taken you on. You don't have what it takes to be a real seeker." He gestured around the cell. "The fact that you ended up here is proof of that."

Tamping down her outrage, Marsh forced herself to smile.

"And yet, I *did* end up here. I survived the ambush and made it on my own with two children in tow through caverns I'd never seen, and I rescued others on the way. If that doesn't show promise, I don't know what does."

She stopped.

Mikel was staring at her.

"What?"

He licked his lips and then replied.

"You survived the ambush outside Ruins Hall *and* made it back?"

"Your point?"

"We were told there were no survivors."

"Well, they were hardly going to admit to failing, were they?"

Mikel drew a breath, the look on his face moving from straight calculation to concentration as he looked her over. Marsh had the impression he was studying her, or maybe looking for something he might have missed the first time.

Whatever it was, he didn't tell her whether he'd found it when he continued. "The artifact belongs to us. It needs to be wielded by someone who knows how to use it."

"I don't suppose you'll tell us how?"

His lip curled. "Not a chance."

Marsh laughed. "You don't *know* how!"

From the look on his face and the flush rising over his skin, she'd hit the mark. She laughed again.

"*You* don't know how it works, and *they* wouldn't teach you. It's like they don't trust you." She paused, ignoring the scowl he directed her way. "Maybe *I'm* not the one who's on the wrong side. Maybe you'd do better working with us."

He shook his head.

"No."

"Why not? It's not like you're important to them."

Again, that look of scorn and defiance.

"How would you know? You couldn't even make it through the front door. All *you* were considered good for was being an unwitting courier."

The words stung, but Marsh tried not to show it. Instead, she shrugged as though they didn't bother her.

"Just goes to show that everyone makes mistakes."

This time she turned to Roeglin.

"Is there anything else, Master?"

The shadow mage shook his head.

"I think that's all. You are dismissed."

Marsh turned toward the door, but she had barely moved two steps before Mikel spoke again. "It really *is* too bad you have to die."

She paused, then forced herself to start moving again. His words bothered her, but there was nothing to be gained by answering them. Even so, she was shaking when the door clunked shut behind her. Since Roeglin had dismissed her but not told her where to go, Marsh decided to see if she could catch up with Aisha and Tamlin in the dining hall. A little bit of time in their company would go a long way toward making her feel better.

For now, she felt...ruffled. There were no real emotions, just a strong feeling of unease, as if her whole world had shifted but she didn't know how. It was as though her reality was somehow less real, an unnamed thread stalking closer with every step she took. Emerging into the corridor outside the dining hall was a relief, and Marsh hurried to find the children. They waved as she came through the door, their faces lighting up as she crossed the floor toward them. Marsh wondered what she'd done to make them so happy.

You survived.

Roeglin's voice in her head made her pivot toward the door, but not before she saw some of the joy fade from the children's faces. She wondered what had them looking so concerned?

We need to eat, and then we need to see the Master of Shadows.

Roeglin didn't wait for her response but hurried over to get his meal. Marsh followed, her unease growing as she loaded her plate and returned to where the children were waiting.

"Are you okay?" Tamlin asked and Marsh nodded.

Mindful of Roeglin's message, she dug into her food.

Marsh nodded. "You?" she asked through a mouthful of crispy shrooms.

Tamlin nodded in return, following her example and digging into his dinner. Beside him, Aisha did the same. It was as though both children could sense the urgency in the air.

"Lennie?" Marsh added, and Tamlin chewed quickly and swallowed to clear his mouth.

"Tired, but okay. She couldn't fix it all, but she stopped him from dying."

Marsh wondered what good that would do Mikel, given that he seemed intent on staying on the wrong side and they couldn't really spare the men to guard him.

None. Roeglin's response had a final note, and Marsh shied away from asking him when Mikel was going to die.

She could have done without the shadow mage's response.

It's done. We'll bury him in the morning.

Marsh coughed as her food formed a lump in her throat. Roeglin didn't say a word, just silently passed her a glass of water. The two children watched them, concern shadowing their eyes. Brigitte took in the scene but didn't say anything. Roeglin added nothing more but cleared his plate in record time, nudging Marsh to do the same before getting up to leave.

Marsh followed, eating as she went, and stuffed the last forkful of food into her mouth just as she reached the stack of dirty dishes and added her plate to the pile. She was glad when Roeglin detoured back to the table to address the children.

"We have a meeting now, so you need to train with Brigitte. Practice your glows; you'll need to be as good as you can if you're coming with us."

Aisha's face lit up, and Tamlin looked happy, then worried.

"She's too little," he whispered, and Roeglin shook his head.

"Not anymore," he told the boy. "She has the skills of a grown-up and a brother to protect her, and we need her."

The look Tamlin gave the shadow mage was a cross between pride and consternation. Marsh knew exactly how the boy felt. On the one hand, it was good to see Aisha's skill recognized, but on the other, it was terrible to see her going into danger to use it. Marsh wished there was another way but she acknowledged that there wasn't.

The children were coming with them; there wasn't any other option if there was going to be a world for them to grow up in. All any of them could hope for was that they could create a world where the siblings could grow up safely once they'd secured the caverns and driven off the raiders.

Yeah... Once all that had happened, *and* she'd found their parents.

"I'll catch you both at bedtime," Marsh said, and shared a glance with Roeglin. "Sooner if I can."

Tamlin gave her a dark and dubious look and Aisha waved with one hand, while patting Scruffknuckle with the other. The hoshkat kit had reappeared from its wanderings to lean against the little girl's leg and wrinkled its lips in a silent hiss of disapproval.

They were sure signs the child was worried, but Marsh couldn't fix that. All she could do was try to keep her promise and catch them at bedtime, even if it meant taking a break from the meeting to do so.

I'll see what I can do, Roeglin assured her as he led the way to the door. Out loud he added, "Trainee, we need to go. Journeyman, you're in charge. Apprentices, do as Journeyman Petitfeu says."

There was nothing Marsh could add to that, so she followed Roeglin out to the corridors leading to the Shadow Master's office. Neither of them said a word, Marsh because she was trying to work out what she had to do next, and Roeglin, because... Well, Marsh didn't know, and she didn't have time to ask, even if she'd thought he *would* tell her.

I wouldn't.

Of course, he wouldn't. Marsh rolled her eyes and came to a halt when they arrived outside the door to the Master of Shadows' office. Roeglin raised his hand to knock, and both of them jumped back in surprise as the door was wrenched open. Master Envermet looked around it and gestured them both inside.

"It's about time," he said. "What did you do? Stop to eat?"

Marsh shot a startled glance at Roeglin, but the shadow mage took the question in stride.

"Trainee had to eat, and I needed to make sure the apprentices were set to practice their lessons."

The *trainee* had needed to eat? Marsh struggled to keep her disbelief from her face as she followed Roeglin into the room. Gustav was also there. The Master of Shadows waited for Roeglin and Marsh to sit before he began.

"What we learned from the seeker who attempted to take the artifact means we cannot wait any longer," he began. "If what he says is true and Ruins Hall is expected to fall, we have to do everything we can to reach them in time to save it. It also means I have to alter the plans to repair the trade routes. We will need an advance force to scout the way and report what they find."

He looked at Roeglin.

"You will be in that force. Who can you reliably reach, apart from Marsh and me?"

"I can reach Brigitte and the children," Roeglin told him. He swallowed as though afraid to disappoint the man but unwilling to lie. "I…I haven't tried with anyone else."

"How long would it take?"

"To establish a connection?"

The Master of Shadows nodded.

"A week, possibly two. It depends on what the connection is based on."

The Master frowned.

"We do not have the time." He drew a breath, drumming his fingers on the desk for a moment before clearly coming to a decision. "I'll send Tamlin with the second, and Brigitte and Aisha with the third."

He raised his hand as Gustav started forward, his mouth open in protest.

"I promised protection for the child, and Tamlin is able to conceal himself in the shadows where his sister cannot."

Marsh refrained from pointing out that Aisha could hide inside the rocks. The Master had a point. If danger struck, Tamlin could escape. Aisha would be stuck inside her rock with no way of knowing what was waiting outside. Without Brigitte's help, she might step straight out into a raider. Roeglin shot Marsh a sharp look, but the Master of Shadows hadn't finished.

"As you can see, there will now be three teams."

He pointed at Marsh and Roeglin, then Gustav.

"You two, and you, will be accompanied by three of the shadow guard to form the first team. Master Leger will lead it." The Master of Shadows turned to Master Envermet. "You will lead the second."

He looked at Roeglin.

"And Brigitte will lead the third. Your team," he continued, "will act as forward scouts. You will go ahead, trying to reach Monsieur Gravine in time to warn him of the coming attack. You will also warn Master Envermet's team of any forces between here and Ruins Hall—which you will *avoid*. The second team will be a larger force designed to take out such threats."

He raised a hand as both Roeglin and Marsh opened their mouths to protest Tamlin's presence in the team.

"The boy is needed, and he will be protected. There will be two guards with him whose sole task will be to keep him safe. It is the best I can do. Further, they will act as a message unit to the repair team following behind. Without more mind mages, the best I can do is have runners between the second and third teams." He looked at Roeglin and Marsh. "Tamlin is the first runner for the second team, and he will only leave if it is unsafe for the repair team to continue."

Silence followed his words as the truth of what he was saying sank in. If the runners had to go, Master Envermet's team would have fallen. The Master of Shadows gave them a moment to digest this information, then went on.

"Master Roeglin, your team is to go around everything in your path. You are not to engage. You are not to let them know you are present or that you have passed. Your sole priority is to reach Ruins Hall and give Master Envermet the information he needs for the repair team to work safely. Do you understand?"

"Yes, Master of Shadows."

"And do you accept the mission?"

"Yes, Master of Shadows."

"Good. Master Envermet will take you to collect your guards. You will leave tonight and travel as far as you can before you rest. Go and prepare for your journey. Master Envermet, I expect you to return with Journeyman Petitfeu so we can discuss your missions in more detail."

"Yes, Shadow Master."

As Marsh rose from her seat, intent on following Roeglin from the room, the Master of Shadows added one more thing.

"The artifact will stay in our keeping," he said, and could only be addressing one person.

"Yes, Master," Marsh acknowledged.

She did not stop as she replied. Roeglin had reached the door, and she hurried to keep up, Gustav on her heels. As they arrived at the door, Gustav turned back to the Master.

"I'd like to take Henri and Jakob if I may, Master."

There was a heartbeat of a pause before the Master of Shadows replied. "Yes."

"Thank you, Master." Gustav left the office, hurrying to catch up with Roeglin.

"We'll meet you in Stores."

Roeglin nodded but continued his quick pace down the hall. Master Envermet jogged after them to join him. He glanced at Roeglin and Marsh.

"I know you have to prepare, but if you would accompany us, I could introduce you to my guards?"

Marsh nodded and Roeglin made a sharp movement with his hand, indicating that Envermet should lead them.

"After you, Shadow Captain."

Master Envermet obliged, taking them up two stair-wells to reach the shadow guards' quarters. He marched into three rooms in quick succession, not bothering to knock at any of them. The first guard to come stumbling into the hall had a shock of red hair and dark blue eyes. He was buckling his belt and his leather tunic needed fasten-ing, but he was fully dressed with his weapons already at his hip.

The second guard was dark-haired with dark eyes, and his skin was the color of coffee. His belt was already buck-led, his weapons settled over his hips, as he pulled the tunic's fastenings tight. The third guard was dark-haired and blue-eyed, and stood a head shorter than the second. She scanned the hallway as she emerged, her eyes traveling swiftly over Marsh and Roeglin.

When she was done with them, she inspected her two brothers in arms and then went over their armor and harnesses, making sure they were sitting correctly and were secure. When she finished, she stood in front of the redhead.

"Your turn," she snapped, and poked him with a stiff-ened forefinger.

He flinched away from it but inspected her in return, adjusting a strap that hung a little looser than the rest. Marsh frowned. She hadn't seen anything wrong with the strap, but it had clearly needed adjusting. As the guards finished inspecting each other, Master Envermet returned. To Marsh's surprise, he had one more guard in tow. She was grateful when Roeglin asked the question that ran through her mind.

"I thought the Master of Shadows said three guards...."

"You need a guide," Master Envermet replied. "This is Clarinay. He knows the caverns better than most and can take you by the fastest route."

Clarinay had skin the color of stone, tousled mouse-brown hair, and dark gray eyes. He looked at Roeglin and held out his hand.

"Wanderer. It is an honor to meet you."

Wanderer?

But no one had time to answer Marsh's questions, and Roeglin did not reply. He took Clarinay's hand and shook it, not taking his eyes from the man's face. Marsh did not miss when Clarinay looked over the group before returning his attention to Roeglin, nor did she miss the way his eyes swept over her, taking in her dress, her weapons, and her face.

It crossed her mind that Clarinay might be something more than a guide, but Master Envermet gave her no time to think about it.

"I need to return to the Master of Shadows, but these are the guards for your team. I trust you will care for them as if they were your own."

Roeglin turned to face Envermet.

"Master of the Guard, while they are under my command, these guards *are* mine."

They held each other's gazes for a long moment, then Envermet nodded and turned away. Marsh wanted to know what Roeglin had really promised the shadow guards' leader in those few short words, but she wasn't game enough to ask, and Roeglin was already leading them back to the lower levels.

"This way."

Their first stop, with the guards in tow, was Tamlin's room. At Roeglin's knock, the boy came to the door.

"She's in your room," he said, catching sight of Marsh.

"We'll go there next," Roeglin told him. "In the meantime, Marsh needs to say goodbye."

He stepped out of the way so that Marsh could crouch in front of the boy.

"The Master of Shadows is sending me in an advance party," she said, "and he wants us to leave now."

Tamlin's face became troubled.

"When will you be back?"

Marsh cast Roeglin a querying glance.

Can I tell him?

The shadow mage nodded.

"I don't know, but," she said, holding up a hand to still the boy's protest, "you and Aisha will be following in two separate groups."

Again he started to protest, and again Marsh held up her hand.

"You're needed in the second group with Master Envermet so Master Leger can pass messages back, and Brigitte will be protecting Aisha in the third as they repair the glows. Okay?"

It *wasn't* okay. It was never going to be okay to send a child into danger to do an adult's job. Never. Not even if she could do it better than most adults they knew. Tamlin laid his hand on Marsh's arm.

"Hey, it's all right," he said, then, as though reading her mind, he added, "She'll be fine. Probably better than most grown-ups."

Marsh bowed her head and cleared her throat, then mimicked his gesture, laying a hand on his shoulder.

"Right. Anyway, Tams, I just wanted to say goodbye before I left, and to wish you the best of luck in your task. Master Envermet is going to be making sure the path is safe, so I want you to look after yourself, okay?"

"Yeah, okay, *Mom*," he said, giving her as broad a grin as he could manage before pulling out from under her hand and turning away from the door. "You better go and say goodnight to Aysh, or she's gonna be really mad at you. I'll see myself to bed."

Before Marsh could respond, he'd closed the door in her face. She crouched there a moment longer and then sighed. Resting her head against the door for another heartbeat, Marsh drew a deep breath and pushed to her feet.

"I've got to go see Aisha," she told Roeglin. "See if I can't get another door slammed in my face."

The shadow master gave her an odd look and shrugged.

"Sure, if that's what you *want*."

Marsh glared at him and stalked past, leading the way to her room.

"No parent wants that," she said, "but..."

She arrived before she could finish her sentence and pushed open the door. What she saw made her come to a sudden halt.

Curled along the wall of Aisha's bed, Mordan raised her head, her lips curling upward in a feline snarl. Snuggled in the curve of the big kat's belly, Aisha was sound asleep, one arm thrown over Scruffknuckle's neck, her head cushioned by one of the kits, and the other kit lying around her legs and feet. The mother kat hissed quietly, but it was too late; Aisha stirred, opening her eyes and lifting her head enough to see Marsh.

"Marsh? Look! I *sleeped*."

Marsh gave a short laugh and crossed the room to wrap her arms around the child.

"Yes, you did."

"You sleep now?"

Marsh shook her head, the smile fading from her lips.

"I'm sorry, Aysh, but I have to go."

"Where?"

"To Ruins Hall."

Aisha struggled free of the animals curled in her bed and swung her legs over the side.

"I come too."

"Not with me."

The girl's mouth set in a firm line.

"Yes!"

"No."

"*With you!*"

Marsh forced herself not to shout back. It required effort, but she managed to keep her voice even as she placed her hands on the child's shoulders and looked into her large blue eyes.

"With Brigitte. Tomorrow. To fix the glows because I can't."

Marsh delivered the order as firmly as she could manage and Aisha stilled. When the little girl replied, it was in a very small voice. "Promise?"

Marsh nodded. "Promise. Tonight, you need to sleep,

and I have to go ahead and make sure it's safe for you to go out, okay?"

Aisha studied Marchant's face with serious eyes and then nodded. "Kay," she said, and wriggled back onto the bed, worming her way between the sleeping animals and wrapping one arm around Scruffknuckle's neck before draping the other one over the kit she was using as a pillow. "Take Dan."

The animals rearranged themselves around her, all except for Mordan. The big kat stretched and yawned before hopping carefully from the bed to stand in front of Marsh.

"Bye, Marsh," Aisha mumbled sleepily, turning onto her side. "Love you."

"Love you, too, kiddo. Sleep well," Marsh murmured, then hurried from the room, the hoshkat padding at her heels with one of her kits following in her wake.

Roeglin, the three shadow guards, and their guide were waiting in the hall, carefully out of sight of the child in the room. They turned and led the way down the hall as Marsh emerged, not a single one of them commenting on the presence of the kat as she quietly closed the door behind her.

Marsh hurried after them, trying to ignore the way her eyes were blurring. She hoped Roeglin and the others wouldn't notice as she dashed a hasty hand across her face, but if they did, they said nothing as they returned to the stairs and made their way to the Supply Master's office.

6

ONE WITH THE SHADOWS

Gustav met them in Stores as he had promised, and he had both Henri and Jakob in tow. Neither man looked impressed, but they didn't complain as the Supply Master sent her apprentices hurrying away to gather the supplies they needed. Roeglin introduced them to the shadow guards.

"Clarinay, Zeb, Gerry, and Izmay—Henri, Gustav, and Jakob." Roeglin fixed them with a stern look. "You are all mine and will look after each other."

"We will look out for each other," they answered, but the way they eyed each other looked more like they were sizing each other up as opponents rather than comrades.

Marchant glanced at Roeglin and raised an eyebrow when he met her eyes. He followed the flicker of her gaze and shrugged.

They'll be fine, he said, accepting the pack handed to him by one of the Supply Master's apprentices. Out loud he added, "And we need to be going."

Marsh didn't have anything to say to that, and none of

the guards had anything to add either. Mordan studied each of them carefully. Marsh wished she had time to link with the kat and gain her perspective, but she knew she didn't. Roeglin led them swiftly through the halls and out of the gates, breaking into a steady jog as soon as they hit the trail beyond.

Marsh adjusted her eyes so that she was seeing mostly through the faint traces of heat blooming from the fungi and rocks in the cavern. Every now and again, something burned bright across her vision; small bats hunted through the air around her. It made her wonder what else might be abroad.

As soon as she'd thought of it, she let her consciousness slide a little, tapping into the energy that let her sense what other life might be nearby. It was harder to do on the move, but Marsh made herself remember that all living things were connected. According to the Master of Beasts, they all were part of a web of life stretching around the planet, even the most insignificant.

Focusing on that thought, Marsh sought those connections. In her mind, the fungi grew and stretched into a single massive forest, the tallest callas linked to the tiniest blue button in a tangle of gleaming threads—and crawling or flying between them were a multitude of brighter points of light: beetles, centipedes, frogs, spiders, and moths. Marsh let their forces flow over her and then moved her focus to the trail ahead and the expanse of fungi on either side.

Her mind assessed her eight companions, absorbing their presence in a flawless display of light as she moved among them. Outside their tightly packed lanterns of life,

Marsh sensed Mordan, the hoshkat pacing them through the dense growth to their right, smaller lifeforms fleeing her tread. Occasionally, she'd catch a glimpse of the kat's brilliant life force moving between the rest.

As soon as Marsh was sure she had the hang of seeing through her mind, she let herself surface enough to register more than the sound of her feet hitting the ground. Hanging onto the sense of life around them was difficult once she began relying on her eyes, but Marsh managed it. It didn't take long before they reached the place where the glows by the side of the trail were dark.

Marchant's first instinct was to stop, but she squelched it down as Roeglin kept up the pace. The cavern around them seemed to grow darker and more ominous and Marsh turned her head, using the direction of her eyes to guide where her life-sense focused. They'd been running for an hour before Roeglin slowed the pace to a walk.

By then the lit glows were well behind them and the cavern silent around them. They'd reached one of the small roadside stops the shadow mages provided for caravans, and Marsh regretted not having any rock wizards along to secure the space. She said nothing as Roeglin called a halt, though.

"We will reach the junction in another three hours," he told them when he'd caught his breath, "but we'll be walking the rest of the way. Take a breather. We'll move on shortly."

As the guards settled onto rocks around the rest stop, Roeglin came over to Marsh.

"What are you doing?" he asked, and Marsh blinked.

Up until that moment, she'd been sending feelers out

into the dark, sweeping the area around them in a search for what lifeforms might be nearby.

"Sorry?"

"Your eyes: they're green," he said. "Bright green. What are you doing?"

"I'm trying to sense the life around us."

"Why?"

"If there are raiders, I'd like to know they're there before they know we're coming."

He looked thoughtful for a long minute and then nodded.

"How do you feel?"

His question puzzled Marsh until she thought about it, and she realized what he was really asking. She *was* a little weaker than she should have been.

"Oh."

"Hm."

Marsh blushed, feeling like she'd been caught in a rookie mistake, but then Roeglin spoke.

"I like the idea, but I need you on your feet, too. Save it until we're an hour off the junction. I think we'll be safe until then. After that, I want you scanning. Something tells me they're waiting."

Marsh wanted to know how he could be so sure, and he explained.

"It makes sense for them to be watching the fortress to make sure we don't send reinforcements, and to make sure nothing gets through if we do. If I thought you could sustain it longer, I'd get you to keep scanning, but moving and scanning? That's a new one for you, right?"

Marsh nodded. She'd only just thought of it, and it had been a little more taxing than she'd anticipated.

"Good. Eat something. Drink something. Take a breath. Tell me when you're ready to get moving."

It didn't take long, and soon they were back on the trail. Roeglin had used the stop to partner each shadow guard with a caravan guard, and he'd paired Marsh with Clarinay.

"You're my scouts," he said, and Clarinay had given Marsh a doubtful look.

Roeglin caught it.

"She used to be a courier, and now she can sense a little of what lies ahead of us before we can see it. Take her with you. Teach her what she lacks." He glanced at Marsh. "Treat it as an extension of your training."

Marsh wasn't going to argue. As skills went, learning how to scout sounded like a good thing. She decided she'd couple those skills with the ability to blend with the shadows, and then wondered if she'd be able to master it.

You can only try.

Marsh frowned. It was disconcerting the way Roeglin kept popping into her head like that. She wondered if there was any way she could stop him.

You want to learn?

"You're the only mind mage I know."

The amusement left his mind-voice.

But I'm not the only mind mage there is.

"Will the raiders have them?"

Do you want to find out the hard way?

"No."

Then we'll see if you can learn.

67

Marsh was reminded that not everyone could learn every kind of magic.

"When?"

After we reach Ruins Hall.

"I can't stay in Ruins Hall," Marsh told him. "I have to try to reach Kearick."

"Why?"

"He's working for the raiders, and he has to be stopped." Marsh paused. When she continued, her voice was slightly softer. "And he's already sent one assassin to retrieve the artifact. I doubt he'll stop there."

"You've signed on as a trainee at the monastery," Roeglin told her. "You can't just leave."

"He needs to be dealt with."

"Agreed, but not by you, or at least, not on your own."

"Agreed," Gustav said, joining the conversation with a single decisive word. "Not on your own. Monsieur Gravine will have something to say on this matter as well."

Marsh sighed. She was about to reply when Clarinay tapped her and Roeglin on the shoulders.

"Time we went ahead," he said. "We're getting close."

Roeglin nodded and slowed his pace. Clarinay signaled for Marsh to follow him into the shadows alongside the path. When they were a few steps away from the trail and out of sight around a large boulder, Clarinay turned to her, his gray eyes gleaming.

"You're noisier than I'd like," he said. "You need to move more quietly, like the shadows."

His eyes turned a dark storm-gray and then went completely black. Marsh watched as his body darkened and faded, blending with the shadows, even to the way he looked when she sought heat instead of visible shapes and outlines. She started when he solidified in front of her, his heat signature growing brighter the more solid he became.

"Can you do that?" he asked, and Marsh shrugged.

"I can try."

"Do so."

"Care to give a girl a hint?"

"Think of yourself as part of the shadows, no more solid than the air that makes them. A beast that prowls their depths yet remains alone."

Marsh drew a deep breath and let it out slowly. She pushed aside the thought that they did not have a lot of time. Roeglin would not have stopped. He might already have led the others well beyond the point where they stood. Taking another breath, Marsh sought the shadows.

By keeping her eyes open and on Clarinay's face, she was able to see when she'd made it—and then she looked down at herself and saw only shadows. Clarinay did not give her time to celebrate.

"Let's go. We can move faster this way as well."

He did not wait for her reply but moved away, and Marsh was hard-pressed to keep up with him. She discovered that seeing as part of the shadows was different than seeing when she was solid. To her surprise, the path to the junction was clear of anything that might harm them—and nothing lay in wait on either side. Together, she and Clarinay leapt through the shadows.

They flew through the dark, sweeping around the stems of calla shrooms and leaving no mark on the patches of blue buttons and brown noses as they passed through them. The mushrooms and toadstools shivered but did not bruise, even though Marsh's shadowy feet touched their caps. As soon as they were sure the junction was clear in both directions, Marsh and Clarinay returned to the path.

When they saw Roeglin and Gustav ahead of them, Clarinay tapped Marsh on the shoulder and steered her off the path.

"It won't do any of us any good if we get killed by our own," he explained as he left the shadows to become flesh and blood once more.

Taking the hint, Marsh followed his example. She hadn't known she'd been so light as a shadow. The sudden return of the weight of what she was carrying came as a surprise, and her knees buckled. Marsh caught herself before she could fall and straightened up.

"Well," she said, "*that* was new."

She watched as Clarinay ferreted around in one of his belt pouches and was surprised when he pulled out two of Brigitte's cookies.

"You need to eat," he told her, passing her one, "and we have to get back to the others."

Marsh accepted the treat, biting into it as she followed Clarinay back to the rest of the team. She was comforted that he demolished his own cookie faster than she did.

"Didn't see a thing out there," Clarinay reported and Marsh nodded, too busy chewing to do more.

"We'll hit the junction then, and head toward Ruins." Roeglin looked from Clarinay to the gathered guards. "And we'll look for somewhere to camp along the way."

The junction was as clear as it had been when they'd checked it before. Nothing moved in the shadows. Nothing moved amid the rocks and crevices of the tunnel walls.

Nothing, that is, except Mordanlenoowar, and the hoshkat showed no sign she'd found an intruder. It was unnerving, but Roeglin wasn't looking any gift horses in the mouth. He signaled Marsh and Clarinay to go ahead.

"Find me a campsite," he ordered, and Marsh followed Clarinay into the shadows again.

This time she remembered to check ahead of them for what other life might lie on the trail ahead, and just like the last time, she found nothing out of place. There were the usual insects, centipedes, a scorpion, some bats, and a rat or mouse or something equally small, but nothing big. Nothing like the hoshkat, or even remotely human-sized, waited on the road before them, and it remained that way until they reached a point where the trail widened into another small cavern.

This one held more shadows and more life than any they'd yet passed, but still, nothing that might threaten them. It was also the most likely point they'd seen for a campsite in over an hour.

That's our camp. Wait there, Roeglin said, speaking clearly in her mind. Marsh stopped.

She was standing at the edge of a large pool of water, and she looked up and across to where Clarinay had knelt at the edge to dip his fingers into the water before raising a cautious handful to his mouth.

"Roeglin says we'll camp here," she told him, and he raised his eyebrows, glancing around them and nodding.

"It's a water source, but there's nothing else here," he answered, then added, "Not yet, anyway."

It was poor comfort, and a good reminder that other things moved along the glowless trails—and that creatures congregated near water. Marsh shrugged. Clarinay could be as gloomy as he liked; it didn't alter the fact they needed a break. Even so, she said nothing when the scout melted into the shadows. Instead, she followed his example. One more check around the cave wouldn't hurt.

It wasn't as though they'd missed anything, but it was always possible something had moved in while they'd been stopped at the pool. Moving in the opposite direction to the one Clarinay had taken, Marsh wove through knee-high brown-nose toadstools and some kind of ferny shrub growing in the glow of a cluster of golden gleams. Emerald highlights winked and moved across its leaves, and Marsh paused to take a closer look.

The fern was covered in green-carapaced beetles, all milling and jostling for space on its long, delicate leaves, their shells glinting in the golden gleams' glow and the dark blue outlines of their jaws shining. Marsh stepped back and made sure not to brush the leaves as she went past. Shadow form or not, she didn't want to risk a bite.

Her circuit of the cavern meant she met Clarinay in the middle. She wasn't sure, but she thought the scout tried to stealth his way past her, and it made her think. If she encountered another shadow mage in this form, how exactly was she going to stop him?

Intrigued by the problem and darn sure the situation would occur, Marsh tried the age-old tactic of sticking out her foot and attempting to sweep his out from under him. To her surprise, she connected with his ankles, but before she could do anything else, he hopped over her foot and took two swift steps before pivoting and coming back at her. This time, though, he pulled a blade out of the shadows and swung at her head.

Marsh responded by drawing a shield to her forearm and raising it in self-defense. Clarinay's sword slammed against it with more power than finesse and Marsh staggered back, pulling a sword of her own from the air around them. Clarinay gave her a brief but fierce grin, looking for all the Dark like a ghost in the shadows.

Marsh grinned back.

This might not be how Roeglin would have had them spend their time waiting, but it *was* fun. She enjoyed sparring. Looking at the serious cast to Clarinay's face, though, gave her second thoughts. It *was* sparring, wasn't it?

You'd better hope so, Roeglin said, *because Clarinay knows his way around a blade.*

Hot damn! Marsh felt her grin grow wider and pretended to take a wide stroke toward Clarinay's head. He didn't buy it, swatting it away with a short blade he called to his other hand and reaching for her with a swift thrust.

Marsh twisted to one side, turning to bring her shield between them, and Clarinay laughed. Warily, they circled each other, then Clarinay made a lightning-fast lunge toward her, forcing her to skip back and breaking her concentration. She wasn't paying attention to where she put her feet or the fact that she had shifted out of the shadows and tripped on a thick clump of rosebud toadies. Stumbling, Marsh recovered her balance, only to go down when her other foot caught on a stone.

What the... Her mind spun as she tried to make sense of what was happening, falling heavily and having to scramble out of the path of a swift follow-up stroke. Her shield hand landed in a patch of brown-noses, shattering their delicate caps and rewarding her with a spray of gray slime and a dusky cloud of spores. Clarinay's sword vanished and he became solid in the blink of an eye, reaching out to grab her by the arm and pull her clear before she could breathe too many in.

"Not bad," he said when he'd set her on a boulder covered in nothing more than crusty lichen. "Tell me, what did you learn?"

"That brown noses have gray snot?" Marsh asked, surveying her hand with regret.

Clarinay rolled his eyes.

"Be serious. What did you really learn?"

So there had been more to the sparring than letting off steam? Marsh frowned, thinking back over the battle and settling on the one point she thought he might be looking for.

"That we come out of shadow form when we fight?"

"Close," he said. "That we have to concentrate on staying in shadow form or we return to our natural selves."

"I was close."

"But not right. Now, what else did you learn?"

"That we can hit each other with shadow weapons when we're both in shadow form."

"Exactly." Clarinay said, looking a little bit pleased.

Given it was the happiest Marsh had seen him, she'd take that as a compliment.

"Is there anything else I need to know?" she asked, and Clarinay shook his head.

"Those were the two things I wanted you to work out," he said. "Now you can help me dig the latrines."

Marsh stared at him, and he gave her a brief smile.

"We're here first. Least we can do is get that set up."

He made a fair point, even if Marsh didn't like the idea that it meant she'd be doing a lot of digging when she was on point. Roeglin was unsympathetic.

Quit your bitching.

Marsh rolled her eyes even though she figured he wouldn't be able to see her.

And thank you very much.

"We'll put them in that alcove we passed just before the pool."

It made sense. The alcove was well away from the water, so there wouldn't be any contamination. It was the ideal place for a latrine, and it shouldn't have come as a surprise when they discovered they weren't the first people to have thought so. Marsh and Clarinay stopped digging at the same time, their noses catching the unmistakable cue that this place had been used before.

Without saying a word, they filled in the shallow trench they'd just dug and studied the ground around them. Whoever had been here had passed by a couple of days ago. Now that they knew there *had* been someone going through, they both surveyed the area more closely. It took them several minutes of casting about to realize that their previous visitors had camped on almost the exact site they'd chosen for their own camp.

"Do we move?" Marsh asked, and Clarinay hesitated.

After a moment's thought, he nodded, surveying the cavern.

"Over there," he said, choosing a spot closer to the cavern's edge and separated from the water source by several thick clusters of shrooms, as well as a few short stalagmites and clumps of boulders. "If we're lucky, they stuck to the trail and the campsite and won't be as familiar with that part of the cavern.

"You're thinking they might come back?"

"Not going to risk it."

His answer was short, and Marsh gave herself a mental kick. She should have thought of the possibility, but it hadn't crossed her mind. Clearly, she had a lot to learn.

Clearly, Roeglin said, agreeing. *Make sure you do.*

Marsh wanted to come back with something sarcastic, but she couldn't think of anything. Roeglin had teamed her up with Clarinay for a reason, and it wasn't his good looks.

His what?

The thought had not amused Roeglin at all, and Marsh snickered.

"When you've quite finished."

Clarinay had noticed she wasn't paying attention, and he wasn't pleased. When Marsh looked toward him, he pointed to another niche in the cavern wall.

"Put the latrines over there," he instructed. "I'll clear a space for sleeping here."

"Oui," Marsh returned, and set to work.

By the time Roeglin led the others into the cavern and along the trail, the latrines had been dug, and Mordan-lenoowar was warming herself by a small fire built from dried shroom husks. Clarinay was instructing Marsh on the local flora and fauna and discussing the traces of whoever had come before.

"They left nothing in the water," he was saying, "so

there is a fair chance they'll be returning. The way they dug in their latrine points to that, too."

"How?"

In response, Clarinay had her remember the depth and angle at which they'd discovered the previous trenches and how it set them up for future use. Marsh had to admit he had a point. If she'd been planning on returning and re-opening the toilet pits, that would be the way to do it.

"We need to build a waystation here," he said as the soft tramp of feet reached their ears.

Marsh couldn't agree more, but it reminded her of something else. "Where is the next waystation?" she asked.

Clarinay gave her a shadowed look. "There isn't one. Most caravans make the journey from Ruins Hall to the monastery without stopping."

Even the slow ones? Marsh wanted to ask, but she didn't, because Roeglin and the six guards chose that moment to arrive. The rest of the evening was taken up by the routine of setting up camp and eating before watches were posted and sleep was ordered.

7

SHADOW MONSTERS

Roeglin listened to Clarinay's report of the suspected raider campsite and nodded. The guards around the campfire exchanged glances and then stared warily into the darkness beyond the campfire's subdued glow.

"Be alert tonight," Roeglin ordered when he spoke to Gustav and the guards.

To give them credit, none of the guards rolled their eyes at his instruction. They all just nodded solemnly and turned toward Gustav to set the watches. When Roeglin realized none of the mages or scouts had been included, he tried to protest, but Gustav wasn't having it.

"With all due respect, Master Leger, keeping you safe is *our* responsibility. We'll see you through the night."

It was as close to a dismissal as Marsh had ever heard the bodyguard give, but Roeglin didn't take offense. He just nodded and turned away, pausing before he left.

"If your people need relief, please let me know."

"Very good, Shadow Mage."

And that had been the end of that. Roeglin had returned

to the fire and insisted Marsh debrief him on what she had learned that day, and then he had ordered her to rest. He'd turned to Clarinay next, and the two of them had huddled together in hushed conversation long after she closed her eyes. They were still talking when she finally drifted off to sleep.

The shadow monsters struck during the night. They needed no latrines or paths, and they did not use either of the trails leading into the cavern. Marsh woke to a firm hand covering her mouth and nose. It released its grip as soon as she opened her eyes, and she saw Gustav crouching above her. He raised one finger to his lips. She nodded, and he pulled his hand away.

He moved his hand from his mouth to his ear, indicating she should listen. The gibbering chatter of shadow monsters was unmistakable and Marsh rolled swiftly and silently out of bed, reaching for where she'd draped her armor over her pack.

Gustav helped her check that it was clear of creepy-crawlies and then stayed to make sure she put it on right, checking her straps and weapons before he stooped to lift her blanket from the ground. He shook it out and shoved it into her hands.

Across the campfire, Henri was doing the same for Roeglin, and Gerry's hands were being swatted away from Clarinay's buckles. Mordanlenoowar stood at the edge of the camp. When the big kat saw Marsh stuffing her blanket into her pack, their eyes met, and then Mordan slipped quietly into the surrounding dark.

Happy hunting, Marsh thought and felt a snarl curl through her mind.

Mordanlenoowar was hunting but was not happy. The prey was not what she preferred. The shadow monsters tasted...wrong, even though they needed to die. Marsh sent the kat her sympathy, along with a curt order to kill them all—and overlaid those thoughts with the hope that the kat returned safely.

The kat was more pragmatic, touching Marsh's mind with the urgent need to protect her kits should Mordan fall.

It will be done, Marsh assured her, pulling her pack on as the link between them went quiet.

Marsh didn't wait for orders but hurried to follow the hoshkat into the night, determined to protect her partner no matter how firmly Roeglin demanded she remain behind.

When this is over, you and I are going to discuss the matter of pets, he growled, and Marsh flipped him a mental finger.

Mordan was more than a pet.

I ought to freeze your mind and stuff you into a box, he muttered, and Marsh wondered if he could.

As tempting as it would be to prove the point, now is not the time, he told her, then left her head.

The shadow monsters had not waited. They came sliding through the darkness, homing in on the campfire and the human movement around it. Marsh was tempted to stand in their path, interposing herself between them and her traveling companions, but Mordanlenoowar had other plans. She'd caught a different scent—human, belonging to the one thing that could open a gateway in the shadows to let the monsters through.

Without the raider's mage, the shadow monsters would

not have had a way into the cavern. If he were gone, there would be a limit to how many reinforcements they could call. The mage was going to pay for his intrusion into the cavern. He was going to pay for letting the monsters loose.

Mordanlenoowar would ensure he opened no more gates.

Marsh caught herself smiling as the hoshkat crept closer to the gate. The mage had stepped clear, moving from the other side of the portal into the cavern through which the shadow monsters leapt. Marsh heard shouts from the direction of the campsite but did not let herself be distracted. The mages did not work alone, so there would be another one close by. She circled in the opposite direction from the one the hoshkat had taken.

That way, even if the mage saw her, it would not foil the big kat's attack; Marsh would not risk that. She took a moment to become one with the shadows so she could move through them without fear of making a sound. She'd counted half a dozen shadow monsters slipping through the shrooms. She could not tell how many were in battle but knew the guards would make a good accounting.

All she and Mordanlenoowar had to do was stop the flow. Even as she thought it, another half-dozen or so shadow monsters howled out of the gate. Marsh noticed something else slipping through the gate as well, and fixed her attention on it.

As she watched, the figure of a second shadow mage became clear. This one was more interested in what lay through the gate behind him than anything that might be waiting for him in the cavern. He kept looking over his shoulder as though that would save him from whatever was coming.

At one point, he angled his head around the edge of the gate, catching the eye of his fellow mage. As soon as he did, he waved his flattened fingertips across the front of his throat, signaling for an end to something.

The gate?

Marsh glided closer, catching the darker bulk of Mordanlenoowar creeping across the cavern floor. The big kat was positioning herself for an attack. She didn't even look toward Marsh, who was getting ready to take out the second mage. The way the guy kept looking back at the gate, this was going to be easy.

Let them close it first! Roeglin's voice was desperate in her mind, and Marsh passed it along her link to the kat. Mordanlenoowar's growl filled the air, and the mage nearest the kat looked desperately around. As his gaze swept the cavern, it fell across the gate and turned from concern to near-panic.

Now he could see what had his partner so worried. Now he looked as frightened as the second mage. For a whole second, Marsh wanted to know what could terrify two mages hardened to working with the shadow monsters and all the risk *that* entailed, and then she didn't care. She just wanted them to close the portal before whatever was beyond it got through.

The shrieks of the shadow monsters paled in comparison to the sounds following them. These screeched through the air and the shadows between, sending shudders along Marsh's fingernails before grating up and down her spine. They made her want to curl up in a ball on the floor of the cavern and rock herself in the comfort of the dark. They made her want to flee.

Marsh took a deep breath and divided her attention between the portal and the shadow mages. If they didn't get the gate closed before whatever was coming made it into the cavern, she was going to have a fight on her hands —and if they did, she was going to gut them both to make sure they never opened another gate. *Ever.*

It was the least she could do if there were things like *that* in the lands beyond. She didn't realize her attention had closed almost solely on the gate until the high-pitched keening coming from beyond it stopped, and she saw that the portal no longer hung at the edge of the trail. It took her another two heartbeats to comprehend that the two mages were moving, and not in the direction of the shadow monsters and the camp.

No, the misbegotten sons were making for the junction her team had passed earlier that day, and they were moving just as fast as they could get their legs to take them. Time she put an end to it.

But the hoshkat was faster. Even as Marsh started to move, Mordan leapt into the air, slamming her forepaws between the shoulder blades of the closest mage. He hit the ground with a bone-jarring thud, and the kat launched herself from his back, digging deep with her hind claws and leaving furrows as she sprang toward the second mage.

The first man momentarily lay silent as she leapt away, then let out a deep groan. Marchant changed course, reaching him as he pulled himself up onto all fours. Marsh did not hesitate, putting everything she had into the downward stroke that drove her blade into his back. Bone grated against her sword, and he screamed before going limp and forever silent.

Marsh paused for a moment to catch her breath and registered the unearthly sound of the shadow monsters' screams coming from the camp. How many had she seen go that way?

"*Merde!*"

All she wanted to do was flee, but she couldn't. Roeglin was her trainer, and—

Master! wheezed through her skull and Marsh snorted, but she ran toward the fight all the same.

Roeglin sounded like he actually needed her help, and that meant he was still alive and still holding his ground with the others.

Move your ass!

Ingrate! Then Marsh thought about how much faster she'd moved when she was one with the shadows, so she tried to do it again, surprised when her body blended effortlessly with the cavern dark and the shadows instantly took her where she needed to go.

Well, that was new—but it was a new she was going to have to investigate later. Maybe Clarinay could explain it. She arrived at the battle between one thought and the next, focusing on remaining in shadow form even as she dropped her metal blade and pulled one from the shadows.

She wondered whether it would work any better than her usual sword, and decided it was worth trying, in any case. None of the guards seemed to be having much luck. A shadow monster screamed as she swung her new sword across its side, and ink flowed out of it, floating like shadow but as sticky and damp as blood.

"Shadow blades!" she cried, swinging again and summoning a shield to the arm she'd raised against the creature's retaliation.

For a moment, she thought her voice hadn't carried. Then she heard Roeglin in her head.

Shadow blades! he repeated, and the tempo of the battle changed.

Marsh heard weapons hit the ground, and then the sounds of injured shadow monsters as the monastery's guards used the darkness against them. In spite of this, they were still struggling when Mordanlenoowar joined the fray.

She pounced into the center of the battle and swiped at the closest shadow monster, her eyes glowing as brightly blue as the monsters' eyes glowed red. The creature she'd attacked howled a challenge, and the kat leapt away, drawing it after her. To Marsh's surprise, the shadow monster turned to go after Mordan, leaving its chest exposed to Clarinay's blade. The scout didn't waste the opportunity.

He drove his dagger into the side of its neck and whipped his sword around to thrust up and through its chest, kicking it off his blades as it fell. As soon as it was clear, he turned on the next nearest monster. There were four, all vying for strikes at Gerry and Henri, who were fighting back to back.

"Not much good to you," Henri panted, parrying a deadly set of claws with his sword even as he blocked a bite with his shield.

"Just. Keep. It busy," Gerry managed, mirroring Henri's moves without being aware of them.

The shadow guard had managed to conjure a shield and sword, but the monster he was facing looked like it had taken on guards before. Marsh cursed, trying to finish the horror she'd injured. Her second strike drew it away from Roeglin's side and directly onto her, and she managed to get under the guard of its claws to punch her dagger up into its heart.

It died with an agonized squeal and flailing claws, but Marsh was already turning away, blocking its death throes with her shield as she stepped around to take out the nightmare keeping Roeglin's shield arm busy. As she reached it, Mordan appeared again, slamming into the shadow monster occupying Roeglin's sword and driving the beast to the ground.

Marsh wondered how the kat was even connecting with the monsters, then noticed that Mordan's claws had taken on a smoky hue and her teeth gleamed less brightly than she remembered. It was a view that vanished quickly, however, as the kat sank her fangs into the shadow monster, her jaws met by a hastily upflung arm.

That wasn't the end of it, however, and the two of them tumbled into the nearby shrooms in a frenzy of flailing claws and teeth. Marsh was worried for the kat, but she had problems of her own. Her target had turned away from Roeglin's shield and was trying to stretch its reach beyond her guard.

This one seemed more flexible than most, and Marsh countered multiple strikes that reminded her more of an attacking snake than a clawed arm. The strikes stopped when Roeglin brought his blade into play, spilling the monster's intestines on the cavern floor.

"I'm not sleeping here when we're done," Marsh managed as the sight and smell hit her, but she didn't have time to dwell on it.

Jakob was shouting as he tried to draw the attention of one of the beasts away from Zeb's fallen body. Marsh looked up in time to see him lash out with a boot, trying to push it off the man, but the shadow monster would not be deterred. Marsh raced toward them as the creature stretched its jaws impossibly wide and bent to bite off the shadow guard's head.

There was no time for finesse or calculation. Marsh hit it side-on, slamming her shield into its ribs and her sword into its side as she arrived and then tumbling over it as her momentum pushed her forward. As she fell, she realized she'd lost her shadow form and was relying on her very human bulk and speed—and she didn't have much of either.

This time, it didn't matter. As the shadow monster twisted and screamed beneath her, Jakob brought his sword down and severed its head from its body, then turned back to take on the next beast that thought Zeb might make a good meal. Marsh struggled to her feet, dragging her sword from the shadow monster's body as she looked for her next target.

To her relief, the odds had evened out, and as she watched, they turned in the group's favor as Roeglin, Clarinay, and Gerry finished a monster each. Marsh looked for bodies and discovered that the monsters dissipated into the darker corners of the cavern. It crossed her mind that they might reform, but she shoved the thought away. So far, there had been no reports of *that* happening.

As she looked for an opening to join the battle, another two shadow monsters went down, and she realized she wasn't needed. All she could really do was to make sure nothing broke away and attacked Zeb.

Good idea, Roeglin managed, deflecting a clawed strike with his shield and jamming his sword into another shadow beast's gut before ripping up and back.

The beast roared as he pulled the blade free, and it roared again as he followed the move with a sword stroke that sliced across its biceps and chest. If humans had come from shadow, she might almost believe the shadow monsters were once men.

Roeglin was silent on that one, but that was because he'd garnered the attention of the next shadow monster, saving Clarinay from what might have been a nasty fight. Marsh turned away, scanning the perimeter of the campsite and sending her senses out into the cavern. She wondered what a shadow monster might look like as just a life force moving through the dark and took a moment to find out.

The ones closest to her looked like boiling masses of purple and black flame, in contrast to the red and yellow of the humans they fought. With that image in her mind, Marsh let her senses float through the cavern, seeking any more human or shadow monster lives. She didn't find any, although she came across Mordanlenoowar drinking at the edge of the pool.

The kat's life force glowed strongly, so Marsh moved on. When her scan revealed nothing, she thought she'd ask the shadows and see if there was anything concealed in their depths that she had missed. She sent her query through the cavern, teasing the shadow threads closest to her with the question.

She came up with nothing save the faint sense of something having passed from the cavern into the tunnel leading to the junction where the trail to Ariella's Grotto met the turnoff to the shadow mage monastery. It was just a tremor, nothing more—and, no matter how much she worried at the threads, a tremble was all she got.

8

SHELTER FROM THE SHADOWS

With a sigh, Marsh let the shadow threads go and opened her eyes.

"So much for looking out for Zeb," Roeglin said, his face so close to hers that she could feel the warmth of his skin.

Marsh gave a yelp of surprise and stumbled back, tripping over Zeb's prone form and falling. She'd have landed on him, compounding whatever injury had laid him out, if Henri, Gustav, and Clarinay hadn't grabbed her and pulled her upright.

"Thanks," she said, her face blazing scarlet. She looked Roeglin straight in the eye. "I scanned the cavern looking for life forces as well as what the shadows could tell me, and it's empty, save for some tremors along the trail leading back to the junction. You'll need to warn Master Envermet he's going to have company. Zeb was perfectly safe."

Clarinay gave a low whistle, Gustav's eyebrows hit his hairline, and sudden tiredness swept over Marsh, making her sway. Jakob was staring at the dark-touched blade in his hand, seemingly unaware of anyone around him. Marsh was about to comment on that when the sudden flare of white as Roeglin contacted Tamlin caught her eye. She focused on it, using it as an anchor to keep herself upright.

"And we need to find another campsite, because I'm not sleeping here…Master."

Marsh didn't let herself stop, but turned back to the trail and headed in the opposite direction from where she'd felt the trembling sensation of someone's passage. As much as she wanted to pursue it, she had to take a message to Monsieur Gravine, and she had to do it fast. The incursion they'd just faced proved that.

They really didn't have time to sleep…or to stop. They had to… She heard a flurry of movement behind her, and Roeglin's voice in her head.

Trainee Leclerc!

Marsh kept walking. She was sure the trail wasn't empty; she was sure there had to be someone living along it—a prospector, a farm, a… Surely the damn mage knew of *somewhere*! He was supposed to be the Wanderer.

Whatever that was.

"I'll tell you about it one day," Roeglin answered, coming alongside her and laying an arm over her shoulders.

At least he didn't try to stop her.

"To answer your question, a prospector lives about five miles down the next side trail. He'll just be waking when we arrive. If we wait for him to come out, he might lend us his hut for the day."

"And if we don't?"

"One of us might get shot with a crossbow bolt."

Marsh almost stopped but forced herself to keep going. A cabin, right? It was better than spending a night in a gut-soaked cavern that raiders were using as a thoroughfare. If Roeglin caught the hitch in her stride he didn't comment, just matched her step for step and pointed out the turnoff when she would have missed it.

Clarinay surprised her by materializing out of the shadows ahead of them.

"The road ahead is clear," he said, and then, catching Marsh's look, he continued, "You're in no condition to scout tonight."

The surety in his words was almost enough to have Marsh protesting that she was more than able to scout, but she knew she wasn't. She was exhausted, and the new use of her shadow magic, the battle, and the search for danger as the others had ended the fight had taken more out of her than she'd realized.

Rather than respond, she kept her silence and watched as Clarinay faded into a background of stone.

"Keep going," Roeglin said. "We all need the rest, and stopping's not a good idea."

"I don't know, boy," Gustav teased. "Henri, Jakob, and me? We're fine."

"That's why *you're* carrying Zeb," Roeglin retorted.

They were? The shadow mage moved down the trail, taking Marsh with him. Five miles had never seemed so long in all her life, and what they found when they arrived was not what they'd hoped for.

For one thing, it was quiet; far quieter than it should

have been. Beyond the lack of movement in the hut or the yard, there was no smoke coming from the small chimney. Roeglin came to an abrupt halt, his sudden stop echoed by those behind him. When Clarinay had emerged from the side of the path and told them the claim was quiet, they'd thought nothing of it, given the early hour.

Now, though...

They all stared at the small cottage in the center of the clearing. It was close to the back wall of the cavern. The low ceiling billowed and wavered to the right before dipping toward the floor in a wall of blackness. Worst of all, the door hung open, and silence reigned.

Roeglin lifted his arm from behind Marsh's neck and stepped forward, drawing his sword.

"Wait with Zeb," Roeglin ordered, and Marsh heard the command in his voice—and the unspoken warning.

This time, she'd better not try shadow-fishing or looking for life signs around the cavern. Well, that was fine with her. She'd be lucky to keep her eyes open until he got back. She turned around in time for Henri and Jakob to slide Zeb's arm over her shoulders and make sure she had a good grip on the man's waist. To her surprise, Zeb was conscious.

"I *can* stand on my own, you know," he said, and tried to push himself upright.

"Uh huh," Marsh said a moment later when they landed in a heap on the ground. "Tell me how that works for you."

The look he gave her might have been lethal if he hadn't given up and started to smile.

"Sorry."

"Yeah. I'll keep watch; you're a mess," Marsh told him, and got to her feet...or tried to.

She really *had* overdone it, and found herself sitting on her ass beside Zeb, trying not to meet his eye. He reached over and nudged her in the ribs.

"So," he quipped, "tell me how that works for you."

Marsh opened her mouth to tell him what he could do with himself, but Roeglin emerged from the cabin, his brow furrowed with concern. He glared when he saw them sitting propped against each other.

"Honestly, I can't leave either of you on your own. Get up."

Marsh twisted her head to catch Zeb's stare, and they both rolled their eyes. In the end, it was Zeb who replied.

"We're sorry, Master Leger, but getting up is beyond us right now."

"And what were you going to do if you were attacked?"

"You were the one who thought it was a good idea to leave us out here unprotected," Marsh snapped, and Mordan gave a soft growl of concern.

"I left you with the kat," Roeglin protested. "You'd have been fine. Come on, get your asses off the ground."

He crossed to help Zeb to his feet. Marsh followed his progress as he hauled the shadow guard off the ground and bit back the urge to protest. The man had a point. She *could* damn well do this on her own...

Okay, she decided, a few moments later. *I can do this with Mordan's help.*

Roeglin led the way into the hut, half-carrying and half-supporting Zeb as he went. Marsh followed, leaning on Mordan and resisting the urge to collapse again. Tiredness weighed like lead along her limbs and the cavern spun, so she closed her eyes and used Mordan's sure progress as a guide. Even so, she was glad when Roeglin returned and helped her up the steps.

"Time to sleep," he told her, and barred the door as soon as Mordan had made it inside. "For all of us."

"What happened to the prospector?" Marsh asked, but her eyes stayed closed and her words were slurred. It was a question Roeglin answered after she had woken up and was wolfing down a shroom loaf stuffed with cheese.

She was chasing it with a cup of kaffee, hot and sweet but black as tar. Not what she wanted, but better than water—and it was waking her up much faster than she'd have managed on her own.

"So, where's this prospector?" she asked, repeating her question of the morning before, "And how long have we slept?"

"Gone, and too long," Roeglin answered. "You up for a bit of a run?"

She raised her cup and her shroom loaf.

"When I'm done here. Can we make up the time?"

"Have to. We—" Roeglin stopped, raising his hand for silence as the others around them stirred.

Outside, they heard the clatter as a bucket toppled over onto its side and then the swift skitter of claws trotting over stone. Marsh took a soft breath and slowly let it out, listening for another clue, and when Mordan raised her head, tilting it this way and that, Marsh had a better idea how to find out what sort of creatures were outside.

Closing her eyes, she drew another long, slow breath and, this time when she let it out, she sent her senses outwards with it. It was not the same as asking the shadows, but it gave her a sense of size and number, and then she asked the shadow thread to show her what creatures they could see in the darkness beyond.

Their reply made her heart sink, and she relayed it to the others.

"Joffra? Are you sure?" Roeglin asked, and it was Marsh's turn to raise her hand for silence as she shook her head.

Around them, the guards shifted their feet and then leaned against walls or seated themselves on the floor. When they were settled, Marsh reached out to the shadows, asking them to confirm what sort of creatures shared them. Only a few answered, and these stretched beneath the door and out onto the narrow porch where several of the creatures wandered curiously about, snuffing along the bottom of the door, and cocking their heads so they could see in the windows.

At first glance, they looked like oversized chickens, but that wasn't right. Their heads lacked the beak of a bird, and they had two short forearms tucked before them. None of them had feathers, either. They were either very bald chickens or lizards like the joffra, except they ran around on two legs and not four. One of them lifted its head and gave a curious chirruping call.

"No idea," Marsh said. "Never seen the lizard-chicken things before. They're not joffra."

Henri rolled his eyes.

"They're shroom walkers. We used to get them out on the farm. Death on rats and house pets, but not a threat to humans unless you were too injured to defend yourself. Guess they smelled the blood."

Roeglin picked up a dish that was sitting on a bench near a small hand tub.

"Or they were looking for scraps."

Marsh didn't want to know what was inside the bowl; what was crusted on the outside looked bad enough.

"They used to stay away from the house, though," Henri added. "Avoided humans like the plague."

"Maybe there hasn't been a human around here for a while," Roeglin suggested, looking into the bowl as he set it back on the bench and wrinkling his nose in disgust. "Pieter didn't have a lot of crockery. Doesn't make sense that he'd let things get into this state by choice."

"You think he's been taken?" Gustav asked, throwing a quick glance toward Marsh.

Roeglin looked around the cabin as though ticking things off on a list as he spoke.

"Food on the table. No resident. Nothing was stolen, not even his savings." He nodded toward a small biscuit jar on a shelf above a stove. "It sounds exactly like the waystation Marchant described."

"And Downslopes," Marsh added, and caught the looks on their faces. "Long time ago, there used to be a waystation on the hillside below Kerrenin's Ledge. Last I heard it was empty. People who set it up disappeared, but everything was left in place."

"Someone you knew?" Roeglin asked.

Marsh found a loose thread on her sleeve, pulling on it as she answered. "My parents. I was staying with my uncle when it happened."

Gustav gave a low whistle, and Roeglin put into the open what they were all thinking.

"These raiders have been around for a while, then."

Before anyone could add anything, a sudden flurry of movement erupted just beyond the door. It was accompanied by several loud alarm calls, squawks, whistles, and the sound of scattering feet.

"Marsh?"

Roeglin didn't have to tell her what he wanted to know. Marsh could guess. She tweaked the shadows, blending them in her search for the life force behind that disturbance. What she found had her recoiling from the door.

"Centipede," she whispered, and they froze. All except for Jakob, who quietly pulled the thin blanket from the bed set in the corner of the room. Crushing it into a ball, he tossed the cloth to Roeglin and pointed to the door. Outside, they heard the clatter of a myriad of hard-toed feet scurrying along the porch.

Roeglin's eyes flashed white, as though he was asking the guard what he was supposed to do with the blanket, then hurried to press it along the bottom of the door. Before he could say anything, Jakob raised his finger to his lips, and they waited. When the skitter of claws could no longer be heard, he nudged Marsh with the toe of his boot and tilted his chin toward the door.

Marsh got it. She closed her eyes and tried to sense where the centipede had gone. The shadows wouldn't answer, but she found the centipede anyway, using just her ability to search for life. It was chasing shroom walkers toward the back of the cave. Marsh let out a breath she hadn't realized she'd been holding.

"It's leaving," she said. "Chasing chicken-lizards toward the back of the cave."

"Good." Roeglin grabbed the pack he'd set on the bench at his side. "Time to go."

"We should be glad it's nothing worse," Gustav muttered, stooping to collect the pack at his feet.

Marsh pushed herself off the floor and discovered she'd been using her pack as a pillow, or someone had thought she should. She couldn't remember; she *had* been very tired when they arrived. She bent to pick it up, and a familiar cacophony of gibbering howls echoed through the cavern outside.

She dropped the pack and had her sword drawn before she finished pivoting toward the door.

"What was that?"

"You have to ask?"

"I was hoping it was my imagination playing tricks."

Something slammed into the door, and the hut trembled. Human-like footsteps stampeded onto the porch outside, and the window shattered.

"Guess they were drawn by the smoke from the chimney," Roeglin muttered. "Not as stupid as they look."

"Into the middle!" Gustav commanded, grabbing the two guards closest him and dragging them to the center of the room.

The others followed and they turned so that they stood back to back, swords drawn while the shadow monsters circled the cabin and battered against the door. When they started climbing through the broken window, Marsh, Gerry, and Jakob stepped forward to meet them.

Marsh and Gerry pulled shadow blades from the dark,

and Jakob pulled enough shadow to coat his very normal blade. Marsh wondered when he'd learned that, but then she was too busy stopping the monsters from getting inside.

At first, they held their own, but then they started to struggle—and that was when Roeglin intervened.

"Now would be the time for the shadows to come to your protection," he told Marsh. "Remember what happened at the eatery?"

Marsh did, but she didn't understand what he was trying to tell her. The shadows had gathered in the eatery because part of her had drawn them close as if they could protect her. She remembered how they had clung to the walls in a thick patina, and how the eatery's cook had told her to dispel them or she'd be doing dishes until they were gone.

The woman had meant it, too, and the laws of Ruins Hall would have allowed it to happen. Roeglin had told Marsh to tell the shadows she was safe, that she didn't need them to protect her...

Well, she damned well needed them now!

Good, Roeglin whispered. *Call them again. Ask them to cover the cabin.*

Cover the cabin? Marsh disagreed, but she didn't bother correcting him. She didn't want a sticky mess to clean up. She wanted something like the swords she called to her hands or the darts she could throw, but she didn't want them in the cabin. Oh, no; she wanted shards of shadow falling from the cavern ceiling to skewer every shadow monster gathered on the porch and in the yard beyond.

She wanted a rain of spears, lightning bolts of shadow. She wanted nothing left outside the cabin but craters. The cabin shook, but Marsh ignored it. She wanted...

"Uh, Marsh? Marchant? Trainee Leclerc?" Roeglin's voice was tentative. "Marsh? You can tell the shadows thank you, now."

At this, Gustav cut in.

"Yes. *Please* tell the shadows thank you. There are no more shadow monsters outside."

"Marsh?" She felt fingertips very tentatively poke her shoulder. "You with us?"

"Uh huh."

"You gonna tell the shadows it's all okay now?"

"You sure?"

"Oh, yes!" Gustav sounded extremely sure. "It is *very* okay out there."

"And we need to leave for Ruins Hall."

"Oh."

They couldn't do that while the lightning was still falling.

"Please tell the shadows everything's okay."

Roeglin's voice had taken on a coaxing tone, as though she was something wild and unpredictable that he didn't want to upset. Marsh wondered why, but she agreed to do as he asked.

"Okay."

She drew a deep breath, thinking of the shadows, her guardians and protectors.

"Thank you," she said. "You can return."

She pictured the ceiling from which she'd called them,

thought of it as calm and still and not roiling with power. She felt the air around her calm and heard sighs of relief.

"All good now?" she asked, and the fingertips became a palm patting her shoulder.

"All is very good," Roeglin told her, and Marsh found her own place in the dark.

9

CHOCOLATE FARMS AND RUINS HALL

"I'm sorry," Marsh blurted when she woke—and was abruptly hushed by someone kneeling hastily beside her and covering her mouth with their hand.

For a moment, she came close to panicking, but Roeglin's voice sounded in her head.

Someone's here. Please be quiet until we know if they're friendly.

Oh. Okay.

Marsh nodded and closed her eyes, listening for the sound of footsteps approaching, or voices. Voices would be better. As if on cue she heard voices, adult voices, softly murmuring, and then the frustrated yell from someone much younger, followed by an all-too-familiar piping treble that echoed off the cavern's ceiling and the cabin walls.

"Marsh!"

Marsh sighed. She knew that voice. She also knew they were in trouble when the pitch went up a notch, and her name was called again.

"Marsh! Is me! You come out. *Right. Now!*"

"Aysh!" Tamlin was clearly frustrated, and Aisha was just as clearly having none of it.

"Is too here. Rocks say. Shadows say! Is. Too. Here."

Since when could Aisha talk to the shadows?

"Aysh!" Tamlin had obviously lost his grip on his sister, again. There'd be no stopping her if she knew she was right.

What in all the Deeps was Aisha doing running with Tamlin's team? She was supposed to be in the repair team *behind* the one Shadow Captain Envermet was leading, not in the one her brother was running messages for. What had gone wrong?

Obviously, the same thought had crossed Roeglin's mind, and he stepped over Marsh, making his way to the door and through it.

"Don't shoot," he called, and Aisha gave a shriek of delight.

"Roeglin!"

Marsh struggled to get herself off the floor, grateful when Gustav helped her to her feet.

"You okay?" he asked. "Because that was quite a display you put on."

"How long was I out?" Marsh demanded, and then remembered her manners. "And I'm fine, thanks."

Actually, she felt anything but fine, but she wasn't going to admit it. Marsh made her way out the door, trying to walk straight and not weave like a drunk after a long night out. When she got there, she stopped and stared. The floor outside the cabin was pocked with small craters and scarred by shadow. She looked at the cavern's ceiling, and the shadows sat there, calm and unperturbed.

Marsh hurried over to Roeglin.

"What did I do?" she whispered and then noticed a set of very blue eyes peering at her over his shoulder. "Aisha!"

As the little girl scrambled out of Roeglin's arms and into Marsh's, a familiar figure stepped forward.

"Master Leger, we thought you'd be farther ahead," Master Envermet said.

"We had some trouble on the trail."

Roeglin gestured toward Marsh, and then the craters pockmarking the floor of the cavern.

"Our mages needed to rest."

From the look on Master Envermet's face, Marchant knew the shadow guard had figured out that it had only been one mage that had needed to rest.

"And you couldn't very well leave them behind, while you went on."

From the tone of his voice, Marsh couldn't tell if it was a criticism, a statement of fact, or a gentle dig at Roeglin's evasion. Roeglin merely nodded.

"No, Master Envermet, we couldn't."

The shadow guard leader gestured toward the cabin.

"I take it the inhabitant is missing?"

"Yes, and he hasn't returned in the two days we've been here."

Two days! Marsh stared, unable to hide her shock at their delay, but Roeglin continued.

"We were just leaving, if you need the cabin."

Master Envermet shook his head.

"No. We only came this way because the child insisted."

He indicated Aisha, who rested in Marsh's arms, her tiny hands wound around Marsh's neck as she held her close. Marsh felt Aisha stir, but Master Envermet wasn't finished.

"It seems she shares some of her guardian's traits."

Aisha lifted her head as Marsh turned to face the shadow guard master, but Roeglin cut in before either of them could speak.

"I understand." He glanced at Marsh. "We need to go."

It was both instruction and apology, and Marsh saw Aisha's face fall. She pulled the little girl close, looking for Tamlin. The boy appeared at her side as if by magic.

"Come on, Aysh. You found her, but she has to go."

"To make the trail safe?" Aisha asked, lifting her head from Marsh's shoulder, her eyes luminous with tears.

Marsh swallowed against the lump in her throat and nodded.

"Yes, so you can follow me all the way to Ruins Hall and fix the glows."

Aisha regarded her with a solemn stare.

"Fix glows," she said, and Marsh nodded before putting her lips close to Aisha's ear.

"Because I can't, okay?"

She said it like it was a secret, and the little girl smiled, placing a hand on either side of Marsh's face.

"Okay," she whispered, her voice carrying across the cavern, and Marsh set her on her feet.

"Be good for your brother," she ordered, trying to look stern.

"Always," Aisha told her, and Tamlin shot her a look of utter disbelief.

"Always!" the little girl repeated, glaring at him and stamping her foot in a clear challenge for him to disagree. Marsh cut in before an argument could occur.

"Always," she agreed. "Now, go see what Master Envermet would like you to do."

The children had taken two steps toward Master Envermet when Aisha turned to look back at Marsh.

"Brigitte no has the cookies," she said, her small voice mournful.

It was all Marsh could do not to laugh.

"Then I'd better hurry so I can buy you some more when we get to Ruins Hall, okay?"

"'Kay!" Aisha said and turned away with a smile.

Marsh pretended not to hear when Tamlin stooped toward his sister and said, "Con artist!"

"Are not!"

"Are too!"

"Are…"

Marsh left them to argue, looking at Roeglin to see what to do next. While she had been dealing with the children, the rest of her team had emerged from the cabin and set themselves by the side of the path. Once Roeglin and Master Envermet had exchanged a brief white-eyed look, the shadow mage led his team past the others.

Since when could Roeglin mind-speak the shadow captain? Marsh wondered.

Since I've been connecting through Tamlin. It made it easier, like the boy was a bridge. He sounded puzzled, but just shrugged and kept walking.

Behind them, Marsh could hear the master giving orders for them to secure the area around the cavern, and for Aisha, Brigitte, and Tamlin to find what glows needed recharging so they could secure the prospector's camp before they left. She and Roeglin reached where the cavern turned into a tunnel just as the bright purple stars winked into existence behind them.

When she thought about it, Marsh couldn't remember there being *any* glows around the prospector's cabin or on the trail, but they were there now.

"New policy," Roeglin told her. "They're making sure all trails and home-claims are marked by glows. We're hoping to slow the raiders down."

It was as good a plan as any, even if Marsh didn't think it was going to work. The raiders were as human as the rest of them, and the glows could be removed by humans. It was only the shadow monsters that seemed to have any trouble with them.

"We should have asked them to build a waystation at the junction," Marsh said as Roeglin signaled for them to pick up the pace.

"Already done," he replied. "There's a fourth...a *third* team following us—with the Masters of Stone and Beasts in charge. They'll be leaving a small team of shadow guards at the new waystation, and we'll be asking Monsieur Gravine to send a small squad to join them. The trails need to be monitored if we're to keep them secure, and the caravans will need safe points to camp at when they travel."

"I wonder how the prospector will take it?"

"He'll handle it better if we can get him back from the raiders in one piece, and he'll see the point of it. He might even tell us it was better late than never, even if he'd have argued black and blue against it before."

There wasn't much to say to that, so they walked in silence. Clarinay appeared and disappeared to scout the trail, but Roeglin told Marsh she was on a mandatory rest day after her display of power the day before. Personally, Marsh thought she was being coddled, but both masters opposed her when she argued, so she focused on the cavern around her instead.

The one time she tried to sense life forces in the area around her, Roeglin nudged her hard enough to make her stumble.

"No magic," he said. "Not unless we need it."

Again, they lapsed into silence, concentrating on moving quickly until they reached another junction. Roeglin turned and looked at the team.

"The Master of Shadows wants each side trail checked for survivors or raiders," he said, leaving Marsh to wonder when *that* particular order had come through.

You were sleeping.

She'd been doing that a lot.

Overextension will do that to a new mage.

Marsh resisted the urge to tell him to shut up as they turned down the trail.

"Who lives down here?" she asked.

"Shroom farmers."

Marsh sighed. She'd been hoping for something more exciting, but everyone was important, exciting or not. If there was any chance these farmers had survived the raiders' purge of the trail and the caverns closest, they had to take it. She followed Roeglin down the tunnel, the rest of the guards moving swiftly and quietly after them.

It wasn't long before the trail widened into a low-ceilinged chamber that swiftly extended into a larger cavern with a much taller ceiling. The floor sloped gradually upward beneath their feet, and the bands of light stretching down from the ceiling made Marsh think of bright, narrow curtains of warmth. As they moved farther in, the scent around them subtly changed.

Behind her, one of the guards gave an exploratory sniff. He was followed by another, and then a third. Roeglin traveled a few more steps down the trail, and then he stopped. Marsh stopped with him, as did the guards, their heads raised as they sniffed at the air. Gerry and Izmay were gazing around the cavern, looks of frustrated wonder on their faces.

"I smell chocolate," Izmay said, and Gerry nodded, his eyes searching the ceiling and the shrooms around them.

Roeglin smiled.

"Of course, you do," he said and started back in the direction they'd been going. "Thierry's Truffles is known for it. Where did you think Marc gets it from?"

"Ariella's," Izmay told him. "She grows the only cocoa beans in the area."

"Ah, but Thierry's has the only chocolate truffles in the world."

"How would you know?" Izmay challenged, and Roeglin grinned.

"There's a reason they call me the Wanderer." His face grew sober. "Let's see how the Thierrys are."

But the Thierrys weren't anywhere to be found, not in the neat bungalow at the center of the cavern nor in the processing shed that towered behind it, and not on any of the ladders or scaffolded walkways that took them along tunnels cut into the earth above. After seeing the truffles stacked in baskets and boxes, Marsh thought she could see something similar growing amidst the tangle of tree roots between the galleries.

Here and there, she found where someone had dug something out from in the middle of a root tangle, and, half-way along one of the walkways, she found an upturned basket. More of the ugly black fungi lay scattered over the boards, and a trowel teetered on the edge. As Marsh moved to pick it up, the vibration of her footsteps shook it off the walkway.

Down below, Marsh saw that Roeglin had stepped out of the bungalow and into the path of the falling trowel.

"Look out!" she shouted, and the shadow mage looked up.

If he'd moved, he wouldn't have had to conjure a shield to protect his head. He was just lucky he was fast enough—but he wasn't impressed. Marsh finished her search of the walkways and headed back to where he was waiting.

"Find anything?" she asked, and he frowned.

"It's just the same as the prospector's."

Around them, the guards murmured in agreement.

"We're not far from Ruins Hall," Clarinay said. "We can be there by midnight if we don't stop."

Roeglin glanced at Marsh.

"I can do it," she asserted before he had a chance to ask. She looked at Zeb. "You?"

He turned back down the trail and broke into a jog.

"Race you there," he said, but he didn't increase his pace as she fell in beside him. The others formed up around them.

They jogged all the way back to the junction and then fell into the traveling pace the Master of Stone had used to reach the shadow-mage monastery. Jogging twenty paces and then walking twenty was still hard work, but they could keep it up for ages. They traveled along the dark and empty trail leading to Ruins Hall, stopping when they arrived at the turnoff for Cleon's farm, Under-Paris Cheeses. Marsh looked at Roeglin.

"Are we going to stop, or do we need to get to Monsieur Gravine first?"

He looked torn.

"We should..." He let his words trail into nothing and looked up the road.

Jogging toward them, three abreast, was a trio of heavily armed warriors. Instead of the leather armor worn by the caravan guards, these guys were wearing tunics that looked like someone had sewn small overlapping plates of metal together. Four interlocking circles were outlined in bronze on their chests. The warriors raised their weapons as they approached.

"Halt in the name of the Four Caverns!"

Given that they'd already stopped, Marsh thought that was overkill. She tried to see if there was anyone among them that she knew, but their helmets obscured their eyes and cheeks, and she couldn't see enough of their features to be sure.

She looked around for Mordan, and was relieved to see the kat and her kits had vanished into the surrounding dark.

"Who—" she began, but Roeglin raised his hand.

"I'll take it from here, Trainee."

Right. This was official business. Marsh held her tongue, but it was hard. She was used to dealing with her own problems, and working inside a hierarchy was harder. As she waited, Roeglin stepped forward. His movement was mirrored by one of the warriors blocking the road before them.

"State your business."

"We have urgent news for Monsieur Gravine from the shadow-mage monastery."

"That trail is closed."

"We are in the process of re-opening it in accordance with the agreement we made with the founder, but we need to see him."

"You will surrender your weapons."

"I will n—" Marsh began, only to find Gustav's hand over her mouth as he lifted her sword from her belt.

"We will surrender our weapons," Roeglin confirmed. Marsh wanted nothing more than to flee.

You could run, Roeglin told her, *but it would be better if you did not.*

His voice inside her head reminded her that he could walk the pathways of other people's minds, and Marsh steadied her breath and nodded. Gustav removed his hand and passed her the hilt of her sword.

"I trust you can take it from here," he said, and Marsh's face heated even as she nodded again.

She accepted her sword and then removed the dagger from her belt, careful to hold them in such a way that she posed no threat when she walked up to the waiting soldier and handed them over.

"They will be returned when the founder orders it," the

woman assured her, and Marsh was sure she'd heard the voice before.

She couldn't put a name to it, though, so she just nodded once more and stepped back to where Roeglin and the others were waiting.

"Form a single line," the warriors' leader ordered, and the shadow monastery's emissaries complied.

The warriors formed up around them, and they headed to town.

"Keep up," was all the warning they got before the squad broke into a fast trot that took them through the town and out along the road to where Monsieur Gravine had built his mansion.

10

RUINS HALL ARRIVAL

The squad rattled their way through a pair of gates set in a high wall jutting out from the base of the cavern wall. To Marsh, it looked like the road led to a dead end, except for the wall and the gates. She could see figures walking along a balcony set inside the wall, and some stopped and glanced down at their arrival. They were armed, she was sure.

Marsh came to a halt with the rest of the squad, careful not to run into Roeglin's back. When they moved forward at a quick walk, she went with them. The soldiers who had escorted them in stayed in a tight formation around them until the outer gates were closed and a pair of heavy metal-bound doors set into the cliff opened.

By the time that happened, Marsh had a lot of questions she wanted to ask, but she didn't say a word. She also resisted the urge to look for the kat, trusting Mordan would stay close by until Marsh could find her. Instead, she followed Roeglin's lead. After all, he'd pulled the Trainee card, and he hadn't done that often. Time she trusted someone, right?

Right.

Marsh sighed.

Especially when that someone could see right into her head...

Before Roeglin could add anything to that, the inner doors stopped moving and the patrol led them through. They found themselves in an entry hall large enough to accommodate them, but not big enough to accommodate much else.

"This way."

They followed the squad leader through to a smaller room, the squad peeling away from them as the leader directed them to line up along one wall.

"Hands," he said, pulling a set of handcuffs from his belt.

Marsh stepped back. Roeglin put a fist on one hip and cocked his head.

"You want to tell me why?"

"There have been attempts on the founder's life. Cuffs make that harder."

Roeglin locked eyes with him, and Marsh caught the flare of white that told her he was checking the truth behind the man's words. After a short moment, he sighed, shrugged, and presented his hands.

"Sure," he said, but his sigh was echoed by Gustav and more than one of the guards.

"Do it," Gustav ordered, and the brief shuffling of feet stilled.

They were cuffed quickly and efficiently, then led out

the door at the opposite end of the room and along several corridors before the squad leader stopped in front of a large steel door.

"Come."

Marsh tensed. Somewhere in her journey along the corridors, she had started to worry that they weren't in Monsieur Gravine's mansion at all. That someone else awaited them, and their fate was uncertain.

You have no faith in people.

Marsh ignored Roeglin's comment. Given that her parents had neither returned nor called for her to join them when they set up Downslopes, she had her reasons.

That was a long time ago.

Marsh refrained from telling him Kearick hadn't been the best example of humanity, either.

You need to make better friends.

If he kept it up, she was going to kick him.

"Roeglin!" Monsieur Gravine's exclamation of delight brought Marsh abruptly back to the present and she blinked, but the founder hadn't finished speaking. "Get the emissary and his escort out of those handcuffs and return their weapons."

"*Oui,* Monsieur!" The squad leader snapped to, freeing them in double-time and returning their blades.

He didn't apologize, though, and the founder didn't expect him to.

"Thank you, Andres," he said. "You are dismissed. Finish your shift."

"*Oui,* Monsieur."

The founder watched his men leave, but that didn't mean he was alone. Marsh recognized the guards standing around him and they recognized Gustav, as did Monsieur Gravine. He stepped out from behind the large desk that dominated the center of the room's back wall and hurried to greet his guard.

"Gustav! I have missed you!"

"Bardin has treated you well, I trust?" Gustav replied, his gaze flicking to the man who had stayed by the founder's side.

"Yes, yes, very well." The founder echoed Gustav's glance, his lips curling with mischief. "But he is not you."

To Marsh's surprise, Gustav colored at the remark.

"I am honored to be back, Monsieur."

"As am I. Please, come and sit." This time the founder extended the invitation to everyone. "I look forward to hearing what the Master of Shadows has to say."

"He agrees," Roeglin told him, and Monsieur raised his eyebrows.

"He does? What, to all of it?"

"With some modifications."

Gravine smiled at that.

"Of course, with modifications. How could it be otherwise?" He paused as a door at the other end of the room opened and several stewards entered, bringing food and drink. "I assume you have not eaten recently?"

"Thank you, and no, founder, we have not eaten."

Marsh noticed that Roeglin did not say they had not eaten for much of the day, the excitement of meeting with Master Envermet's security force followed by their rapid journey to Ruins Hall having made them forget. Either the founder could read their silence or he'd had experience with envoys before because he waved the stewards forward.

"I hope you do not mind talking while we eat," he said. "I worked through the evening meal and am hungry. I'd be honored if you'd share this with me."

"Founder, the honor is ours."

If Roeglin's words hid a smile, his face hid it better. Monsieur Gravine waited until the stewards had served them each a thick, meat-filled sandwich, and heavy glass containing a dark liquid. Judging from the light-colored froth at the top of each glass, it was one of the local brews, and rather than speaking immediately, the founder concentrated on eating. They followed his example until their plates were cleared and their glasses emptied, the stewards appearing as soon as they were done to refill their glasses and take their plates.

"Now," the founder said, sitting back in his chair, "tell me what the Master of Shadows said in response to my request."

Roeglin cleared his throat and glanced at Gustav. The bodyguard waved for him to relay the message.

"The Master of Shadows greets you and agrees to your proposal to build a force to protect the Four Settlements, starting with the Ruins Hall cavern. He agrees to provide a place of security for your troops and their families, just as he would extend such hospitality to any in the caverns. He also suggests that eligible adults be trained within the ranks of your forces, while younger talents serve their apprenticeships at the academy."

"Agreed," the founder said, "but what did he have to say about patrolling and protecting the caverns?"

"He said he would send a contingent of shadow guards and mages to be divided between your patrols, and to man the waystations the rock wizards are building on the trade routes so that the caravans have a safe place to rest. He also agrees to his mages being accompanied by your men when they recruit."

Monsieur Gravine gave Roeglin a long and steady look.

"May I speak with him?"

"Yes, Monsieur," Roeglin replied and shifted his seat so that the founder could look him directly in the eye. "When you are ready."

His eyes flared white, as Roeglin relayed the Master of Shadow's words, and the two leaders finalized their understanding.

"I will send you the parchment by courier," Monsieur Gravine said as they concluded their business, and Roeglin dipped his chin in a very Shadow-Master-like nod.

"I look forward to seeing it."

When the white faded from Roeglin's eyes, Monsieur Gravine nudged the shadow mage's glass closer.

"Thank you, Shadow Master."

With that, the founder sat back in his chair, running his gaze over them as though he were contemplating what he might say next. In the end, it was another request for information.

"Tell me what you found between here and the shadow monastery."

Roeglin obliged, pulling information from each of them. The founder seemed most disturbed by the depopulated claim and farm and sighed.

"It is the same here," he said. "We are losing the outlying

settlements, to the point that I am on the verge of pulling the outermost people closer to the center."

"You will need to do that anyway," Roeglin added. "They have assembled a force in Leon's Deep and intend to attack Ruins Hall."

He shifted uneasily in his chair as though he'd just remembered how urgent that part of his message was.

"We had an assassin come after Marsh. Something she was carrying for delivery was of some importance to them."

The founder leaned forward.

"Did they get it?"

"No. We have secured it."

"I don't suppose…"

Roeglin shook his head and held up his hand, and the founder sat back, his lips twisting in a wry smile. "I thought not. Please. Continue."

"The Master of Shadows is repairing the glows between here and the monastery, and the road to Kerrenin's Ledge will be next. He does not believe we have the time to delay. That team is on its way, along with a security team to ensure its safety. Please let your patrols know. I do not think Master Envermet will be either as cooperative or understanding as we were."

Monsieur Gravine nodded.

"It shall be so. Continue."

"Master Envermet's security team will join you in defending this cavern, and in helping us secure and repair the route to the Ledge. His mages will bolster your forces immediately afterward until his replacements arrive.

Recruiting needs to occur soon, or you will run out of mages to distribute between your forces."

Roeglin looked at Marsh.

"Is there anything I missed?"

"I need to see Madame Monetti."

This brought raised eyebrows from both Roeglin and the founder.

"Why?"

"I believe she is working with the raiders. She is the only one who could have told them who had the artifact since she was the one slated to receive it."

"She's the addressee?"

"*Oui*, Monsieur."

The founder sat back in his chair, his expression clouded as he thought about what she had said. Finally, he straightened up and looked at her.

"Madame Monetti lives a little farther back in the cavern, not far from the tunnel leading to Leon's Deep." He drew back as Marsh got out of her chair. "I will send an escort with you."

"Thank you, Monsieur."

Marsh pushed back her chair and had stepped around it to head for the door when Monsieur Gravine raised his voice.

"In the morning," he finished in a tone that said his decision was final.

Marsh hesitated, tempted to continue walking, but she stopped. When she turned slowly around, Monsieur Gravine and Roeglin were staring at her.

"Tomorrow might be too late," she said. "We need to go tonight."

This time it was Roeglin who denied her request.

"Tomorrow will be soon enough," he told her. "She doesn't know we've arrived, and she certainly doesn't know what happened to Mikel. We have to be the first to reach the Hall since then."

He waited, and, when Marsh did not resume her seat, he sighed, putting a sense of uncompromising steel in his next two words.

"Tomorrow, Trainee."

Use rank on her, would he? Marsh gritted her teeth.

"She could get word tonight. The raiders used gates to navigate the shadow, remember? They don't need to follow the trails. She could be being briefed right now, and we'd never know it." She paused. "Shadow's Deep! She could *already* have been briefed, and we wouldn't know. We have to go, now. Tomorrow—"

"Will be time enough!" Roeglin snapped, glancing at Monsieur Gravine. "Now, return to your seat."

"You need to wait for your shadow guard," Monsieur Gravine said, picking up where Roeglin had left off. "The six men you have with you will not be enough to deal with the guards I would expect at *that* lady's mansion. I must insist you wait."

"Marsh," Roeglin's voice was softer, now, almost pleading, "Master Envermet will be here in the morning. At least wait for him."

Marsh sighed, catching the subtle shift of the guards as they moved to block the door leading out of Monsieur Gravine's office. To her surprise, the founder spoke again, doing his best to convince her of the wisdom of waiting instead of giving her a direct order.

"The cavern is not safe by night," he added. "With the glows down, packs of joffra have moved in, some from the direction of Leon's Deep and some from other tunnels. We're working on blocking those, but we're a long way from done, and the Seekers won't be happy."

Marsh couldn't imagine they would be. The secrets of the tunnels were their bread and butter, roads to wealth or oblivion for the ones who dared to walk them. Blocking the tunnels meant less access to the very routes that gave the seekers a livelihood. Monsieur Gravine carried on, oblivious of the direction of her thoughts.

"Only the Protectors move freely during the night, and that because they go so heavily armed and in squads of eight to twelve. Even the joffra prefer easier prey. You can leave when Master Envermet arrives. In the meantime, while you were gone, I had my clerk search the records in Ruins Hall pertaining to the Danet family. As you can imagine, there were very few, and the ones we do have suggest there might be documents pertaining to the Danets in Kerrenin's Ledge."

Marsh walked slowly back to her seat, noticing that Roeglin relaxed just a little as she sat beside him. Still, Monsieur Gravine wasn't finished.

"I will speak with your Master of Shadows regarding the importance of you traveling with the repair teams when they leave for the Ledge. We should do our best to connect the children with their loved ones."

From what Tamlin had said, there hadn't been a lot of love shared between his parents and their relatives, but Marsh kept that to herself. No doubt it would come out in the wash, and there was no need to air it here.

"Thank you, Monsieur Gravine."

She couldn't think of anything else to say. In fact, she was trying hard not to think of anything, what with Roeglin sitting right beside her. With his propensity to go walking through her head, she didn't want to think of visiting Madame Monetti before Master Envermet could arrive with the shadow mages everyone thought she needed to keep her safe.

It was enough to make her blood boil, being treated as though she didn't know her side of the business. If she were Kearick, she'd have had someone waiting for Mikel outside the monastery, and if that artifact was as important as they seemed to think it was, *she'd* have had a mage or two standing by to open a gateway directly from the monastery's cavern to as close to Madame Monetti's mansion as she could.

They *could* be that precise, couldn't they?

I think so, Roeglin intruded. *It wouldn't make any sense otherwise.*

And *there* was the reason she was trying not to think of what she needed to do next.

And what is that? Roeglin wanted to know, and Marsh turned her head to scowl at him, completely ignoring the sudden interest on Monsieur Gravine's face.

"Sleep!" she murmured, and it wasn't far from the truth.

The founder responded as though she had spoken to him.

"An excellent idea, Mademoiselle Leclerc. We all need to rest. Tomorrow is going to be a very long day, and with an early start, if I'm not mistaken. I will have the stewards escort you to your quarters."

Marsh blushed.

"I'm sorry, Monsieur; I did not mean to be rude."

He waved her apology aside.

"No need to apologize. You raised a good point." He made a show of stifling a yawn. "And I am tired too. I will see you all in the morning."

Whether that last was a polite farewell or firm order, Marsh couldn't tell, but she'd treat it as the latter. She *would* make sure to meet him again in the morning.

Good to know, Roeglin told her as he rose from his seat, following Monsieur Gravine's gesture to where the stewards were waiting.

"Sleep well," he said, and Marsh joined in with the murmured replies wishing him equal fortune in finding rest.

11

SLIPPING THE LEASH

Marsh ended up sharing a room with Izmay, but she didn't complain. The female shadow guard seemed friendly enough behind the veneer of distance she maintained. She lounged against the door as Marsh washed up, catching the trainee's look of unease with a slight upward quirk of her lips.

"I'm supposed to watch you until you're asleep," she admitted. "Roeglin said so."

"Nice." It wasn't hard for Marsh to sound disgusted at the idea.

Marsh decided wringing Roeglin's neck might not be out of the question. She didn't say so, though. Instead, she raised her hands in mock surrender, then shucked her armor, boots, and blades and slid between the clean sheets of the lower bunk.

"Night, Mama."

Izmay flashed her a smile and crossed over to lean on the top bunk and look into Marsh's face.

"If you were any kid of mine, I'da tanned your hide by now."

Marsh pulled a face and rolled over on her side, putting her back to the room.

"It's a good thing I'm not, then, isn't it?" she muttered, feeling childishly defiant.

I wonder if this is what it's like for Aisha, she thought, closing her eyes and letting her breathing even out. She also wondered how Mordanlenoowar was faring. The big kat had vanished into the shrooms and shadows when the squad had taken them in tow on the other side of Ruins Hall, and Marsh hadn't seen her since.

She tugged at the shadows close by, asking them for news of the kat, but not a single one of them trembled. It was like none of the shadows around her connected with the cavern outside the walls. Marsh sighed and tried to use her ability to sense life forces to detect where the kat might be, but all she got was a sense of thick walls and muffled flames, then nothing.

The very density of the walls interfered, similar to the way the cavern walls divided the outside world into compartments. Marsh sighed, thinking she shouldn't have been surprised that Monsieur Gravine's mansion walls acted in the same way. Forcing herself to relax, she listened as Izmay finished her evening's ablutions and climbed into the bunk above.

Then Marsh waited some more.

She was tired from the long day's run, but she knew she had to reach Madame Monetti while the woman was unprepared...if the woman was *ever* unprepared. Marsh's mind flitted back to her time working for Kearick. She doubted there'd ever been a time when the wily old businessman had been unprepared.

Ever.

It made it hard to stay relaxed. It should have made it impossible to sleep.

But it didn't.

Marsh woke to the sound of Izmay pulling her armor on as quietly as she could. The woman started when Marsh rolled over.

"Oh, you're awake."

"*Merde!*"

Izmay grinned.

"What? Slept in?"

Marsh scowled at her and swung her feet over the edge of the bed.

"You could say that," she grumbled, and set about getting dressed.

Izmay laughed.

"The master said you'd be unimpressed."

"Roeglin?"

What did he know about her sleeping in?

"Yeah, but he also said you needed the sleep."

He had? Wait, what had he done?

Marsh rammed her arm through her sleeve and jerked her boots onto her feet.

If that dirty mind-crawling pain-in-the-ass had *tampered* with her head, she was going to take large, hairy pieces out of his hide!

A polite knock at the door interrupted her thoughts, and Izmay gave her a cursory glance before answering it.

Good thing I'm dressed, Marsh thought.

"I'm to take you to the dining hall."

The child standing at their doorway couldn't have been any older than Aisha, and her dark eyes were wide with awe as she took in their armor and swords. Marsh could almost see the thought crossing her fuzzy little head: *When I grow up, I'm going to be just like them!*

Oh, no, kid, she thought. *Not like me. Be something better.*

But she didn't say it out loud. Instead, she focused on finishing getting herself armored and then exchanging kit checks with Izmay, aware of the child's intense scrutiny the entire while. She let Izmay lead the way out of the room and followed, ignoring the woman's glance back to verify that she hadn't tried to go elsewhere.

Marchant pulled the door to their room closed behind her and walked after the guard, letting herself drop back a little bit at a time. By the time she was ready to take a side passage, Izmay had stopped looking over her shoulder. Mourning the loss of breakfast, Marsh stepped away, taking partial cover behind a man carrying a tray laden with dirty dishes.

With any luck, he'd be heading for the kitchen, and the kitchen would have some sort of way out that would be connected with an exit to the caverns beyond the mansion. Marsh just had to move fast enough that Izmay didn't realize she'd ducked away, and Roeglin couldn't catch up with her before she made it out the gates. Maybe he'd be late for breakfast…

Marsh shook her head.

Nah. No hope for that—but he might be too *busy* with breakfast to realize she hadn't arrived with the rest, and the same might go for Izmay and Gustav.

Gustav.

Now, *there* was a more likely problem.

Marsh hurried her steps, discovering she had guessed right about where the man was heading. She found herself in the kitchen. Snatching a couple of crescent-shaped shroom pastries from one tray and a shroom roll from another, Marsh looked around, searching for another door.

One clearly led to the pantry, and she couldn't resist lifting an uncut slab of bacon from another sideboard as she passed —Mordan would be hungry—and went through another in the wake of a boy carrying a bag of vegetable scraps. *Those* had to go outside, right?

Turns out they did—and that the outside they led to was right by the stables where Monsieur Gravine kept his mules. Not that Marsh needed a mule, but she *did* need the gate leading out of the mansion's grounds. Funny how the founder hadn't thought to make this one an airlock like the main entrance.

It was something she'd point out to him when she got back. If she could find it from the inside, careful reconnaissance from the outside would reveal it, too, and given the forces they were facing, Monsieur Gravine should know that.

She waited until the stable yard was clear, then went quickly and quietly out the gate, sliding into the shadow of the wall and realizing she'd come out along a different part of the barricade. It didn't matter. Leaning on the stone, Marsh looked for Mordanlenoowar. She blended a request to the shadows with a search for the blazing life force that marked the big kat like a beacon.

It didn't take long for Marsh to find her. Mordan was

lying patiently beneath a clump of callas not far from the main entrance, and Marsh tried to let her know where she was. This far away, she wasn't even sure their minds *could* touch.

To her surprise, the big kat opened her eyes and slipped quietly away from the gates, disappearing into the shrooms and rocks without a sound. She appeared beside Marsh moments later, raising her muzzle and sniffing appreciatively at the hunk of bacon Marsh held in one hand.

"Yes, this is for you," Marsh told her, giving the kat the meat and pulling the roll from the pouch she'd stuffed it in.

When they were both done eating, Marsh bent down and leaned her forehead against the hoshkat's head.

"I need to find an enemy," Marsh said, speaking aloud even as she gave the kat the impression of her need to find her foe's lair and hunt her down inside it.

The kat lifted her lips in a silent snarl, taking the vague directions out of Marsh's head, and turning toward the trail to Leon's Deep.

"Not by the road, girl," Marsh said. "Today we hunt alone."

She caught a sense of puzzlement from the kat and pushed it aside. She had a *very* good reason why she was hunting without the rest of her pride. Yes, even for prey as deadly as this. Roeglin did not approve.

The kat hissed softly, her opinion of a male who did not care for the concerns of his mate quite clear.

"He's not my mate," Marsh protested. Mordanlenoowar flicked her tail, stalking into the shrooms.

Now, what was *that* all about?

The kat wasn't stopping to answer questions, however,

and Marsh hurried after her, giving up on using her feet normally to take to the shadows and move with a speed she couldn't have in solid form. True to Marsh's wishes, Mordanlenoowar didn't take Marsh via the trade route. Instead, the big kat cut across country, stopping when they reached the edge of the open field of one of the small farms dotting the cavern.

Marsh joined her beneath the shelter of a cluster of callas, laying an arm over the big beast's shoulders.

It is still, the kat thought, her azure eyes studying the farmhouse, *and I smell no blood. No human life and no blood.*

No human life? Apprehension formed a lump in the center of Marsh's chest. No life, and no blood. Her heart sank, and she pushed carefully out of the callas. No life meant she shouldn't encounter anyone or anything, but that wasn't what she was afraid of. No...

Moving quickly and quietly to the rear door, Marsh wasn't surprised to find it open, the signs of a struggle evident. There was overturned furniture and broken dishes as she moved through a kitchen and then into a dining room, where the table had been tipped on its side and a buffet shoved across a broken window.

Even knowing what she would find, Marsh climbed the stairs to investigate the bedrooms. They were empty, and it was more depressing being right than it would have been otherwise. She noted what had been left behind and what had been taken.

Nothing but people for the latter, and everything for the former, just like it had been at the prospector's hut. Just like it had been at the truffle farm. Just...just like her parents' place, and all the others in between. Grief formed a lump in her throat and tears blurred her eyes, and Marsh stopped, forcing herself to face reality.

People had been taken, and she had been unable to stop it. She drew a deep breath and let it out, her hand drifting to the hilt of her sword. Well, next time it would be different. Turning around, she hurried down the stairs and back out the door to where Mordanlenoowar was waiting.

Her thoughts of haste were accompanied by her own very human snarl, and the hoshkat responded with flattened ears and a snarl of her own. Marsh wasn't the only one tired of losing people to the raiders. Reorienting themselves using the scent of their target, they crossed the empty yard behind the farmhouse and leapt into the shadows of the overgrown field beyond.

Mordan's paws made no sound as she passed, although she flattened patches of shrooms. Marsh took to the dark, shedding her human shape and weight to move through the cavern's shadows, at once at one with and yet completely separate from them.

They came across the next deserted farm less than an hour later. This time, Marsh took enough time to give it a cursory look before returning to where Mordan was pacing the yard. The big kat's tail lashed as she snuffled the ground.

Not long gone, the big kat said, and Marsh got the impression that the raiders had struck while they were investigating the first farm.

It made Marsh wish she had a map of the cavern, and she realized she knew someone who did. Where was Roeglin? Hadn't she been gone long enough for him to notice she was missing? Why couldn't he be in her head when she needed him, not just when it was damned inconvenient?

It was like she'd summoned the man.

By the Deeps, I am going to kick your ass! You are the most undiscipl—

Marsh cut him off.

What's the closest farm to this one?

There was silence, and Marsh hoped he hadn't decided to ignore her.

Please, Ro, she thought. *Please, please, please.*

Why?

I need to get there before the raiders do.

By the Deeps, no.

To warn them. I need to warn them. If I can get there first, they might have a chance.

And you have Mordan with you.

It was like he was thinking out loud—and then the map was in her head. Marsh took to the shadows again, Roeglin's voice no more than a flicker as she raced through the darkness, one with the shadows as she willed them to let her pass.

Be careful.

Marsh didn't respond, all her attention was focused on reaching the farm and its people before the raiders did. She came close. From the looks of things when she got there, the raiders had only just arrived.

They'd arrayed themselves in the yard and one was standing at the door, his hand raised as though he'd been knocking. Marsh slid behind the cover of a fall of boulders and started working her way around to the back of the house. If she was quick, she might be able to slip inside and get them out before the raiders thought of checking.

Apparently, the farmer and his family had thought the same. They had just opened the back door and stepped through when the raiders rounded the sides of the house. This was clearly not the first time their prey had tried to escape the back way.

They leapt forward even as the farmer's wife tried to herd her children back through the door, two raiders grabbing the husband and the oldest girl before they had a chance to avoid them. A little boy made a break for the rocks at the end of the yard, towing his brother with him, but one of the raiders ran him down. Another grabbed his brother and lifted them both, shrieking, from the ground.

Their father twisted against the hands that held him, shouting in outrage as he fought to get free, and Mordanlenoowar roared. This was exactly what had happened to her kits, only she had not been with them to fight for them as the male was trying to do, as the female was trying to do, as each cub was trying to do. She jumped into the fray, knocking one of the raiders to the ground and snapping his neck with brutal efficiency.

Marsh looked toward the front of the house. Mordan's roar had drawn the attention of the raiders trying to break through the front door, and several of them had turned to run down the side of the house, pulling swords and crossbows as they did so.

Don't you da— was as far as Roeglin got, and Marsh had the impression he was moving fast in her direction.

Strange, since she didn't think he'd learned to shadowstep like she had, and that was the only way she could think of that would let him move as fast as he seemed to be going. Well, good, because she was going to need some help.

Get them away, she thought, sending the idea along her connection to the kat.

There was no reply, but Marsh didn't expect one. The kat was busy taking down raiders. If she took down enough of them, the farmer's family might break free and escape on their own—and what a tale they'd have to tell. All Marsh had to do was stop the dozen or so men and women racing around the side of the house to intercept them.

That was all...

She stepped out from behind the rocks she'd been using as cover, shouting to draw their attention even as she pulled the shadows toward her.

"Hey, shit for brains! You missed one!"

They shouted something in reply, and a half-dozen of them broke away toward her. It wasn't exactly what she'd hoped would happen, but it would do. Marsh spread her arms wide and then drew them in close to her chest, gathering the shadows as she did so. When she had them all together, she reversed the motion, thrusting the shadows away from her with her hands, and sending them in a wall over the raiders moving toward the back of the house. That they caught the ones moving toward her as well was an added bonus.

She watched as the shadows slammed into them, flattening men and women to the stony ground surrounding the house, the impact sending their weapons flying out of their hands. The shadow wall rolled past them and slammed into the other half-dozen making their way to the back.

Not one to waste the advantage, Marsh went after those closest her. None of them was getting up, not if she had anything to say about it. The first raider had pushed himself upright, and Marsh used a two-handed swing of her shadow blade to separate his head from his shoulders. The second one made it to her knees before Marsh plunged the sword through her heart. The third one blocked her strike.

Screams rose from the back of the house, as well as sharp, urgent cries to get into the rocks. Marsh only hoped the latter were from the farmer getting his wife and kids to safety. She knew the rest were Mordan's work, but she didn't have time to check. The raiders had picked themselves up and were heading in her direction.

All of them...with their swords drawn, and looking as pissed as any monster from the Deep.

Oh. Oops. Well, this was going to be interesting. Marsh couldn't help grinning as she went to work. She was so deep in the brown stuff she probably wasn't going to get out again, so she figured she might as well make it count. The raider who had blocked her strike counterattacked, the steel of his blade glinting in the light of the shrooms. Marsh caught sight of it in time to block it with a hastily summoned buckler of shadow and she countered, but he parried. They broke apart, circling each other warily.

If Marsh had thought the raiders would form a civilized circle around them, she was wrong. This was a raid, not some gentleman's duel, and they weren't prepared to fight fair. She caught a flicker of movement from the side and brought her sword around in time to deflect the blow.

Her opponent laughed and darted forward, forcing her to use her shield and step back and away. Before she could work out why, something solid struck her across the back, slamming into her armor and sending pain through her. Marsh lost her grip on the sword just as a second solid blow hit her behind the knees, dropping her to the ground.

All she could do was try to roll out of the way of the next hit, and when that proved impossible, curl into a ball and watch what looked like half a log coming down toward her. She didn't know whether to laugh or cry when a long, dark shadow caught the raider in the side, making him drop the log as he fell. It still landed on her, but he did not.

Even with that raider out of the picture, Marsh didn't dare uncurl. He hadn't been the only one with a stick. The second raider switched targets, turning so Marsh was behind him as he sought another opponent. Another shadow speared out of the dark, taking him through the throat, and then a third, and a fourth. Marsh decided she'd lie right where she was.

Each spear found a raider, and the rest started running. It didn't do them any good, though. More shadow spears cut the darkness, and they fell. Marsh slowly uncurled, looking for whoever had saved her. She was certain it hadn't been Roeglin. Even moving at the speed he'd been going, he shouldn't have arrived.

It was a relief to see Scout Clarinay materialize briefly from the shadows and shadow-step away toward the back of the house. She hoped he could catch the farmer and his family in time. They had to know there was a sanctuary for them. She slowly hauled herself to her feet, calling another blade out of the shadows as she did so—and glad it weighed nothing in her hand.

She hurt.

Trying to shove the pain aside, Marsh headed for the back of the house, coming around the corner to a scene of utter carnage. Mordanlenoowar had brought down every raider who had tried to harm the farmer, and then she'd started on the raiders coming around the other side of the house. Nothing moved, and Marsh continued to look for someone else to fight.

She found them at the stables. Two of the farmhands had bolted themselves inside, and several raiders were at the doors, trying to force their way in.

"Hey!" Marsh shouted, but her voice sounded weak in her ears, and the raiders laughed. One of them was shoved roughly in her direction as though she were an easy target.

Marsh lifted the shadow blade and gasped. The raiders might have a point. There might be only one of him, and he might not even know how to wield that blade he held so awkwardly, but he might still win.

"*Merde*," she muttered, doing her best to ignore the spikes of pain shooting down her arms and back.

Need a hand?

Roeglin didn't wait for an answer. He rode around from the front of the farmhouse, running his mule straight at the raider, who dove out of the way, before sliding from the animal's back and racing toward the warriors attacking the door. Seeing him call a blade and buckler from the dark, Marchant didn't know whether to laugh or cry.

12

IN TROUBLE DEEP

M arsh watched as Roeglin charged the raiders by the door, glad she didn't have to take on another one but not wanting to leave him to deal with them on his own. As she stepped toward the fight, she caught sight of movement at the other end of the barn. The raiders had a shadow mage!

Marsh turned on the spot, wishing she could alert Mordan to the mage standing at the back of the barn; the kat would take him down in no time. As it was, she could no longer feel her connection to the kat, and figured it was because she was tired from racing across the caverns and battling with the raiders.

At least Mordan had saved the farmers.

As she straightened up, Marsh saw the mage making broad strokes through the air with his hands. From this distance, it looked like he was drawing a door against the shadows.

Oh, by the Deeps, no, he wasn't!

With a shout, she pulled a sword from the shadows and

charged. She would not—could not—let him open a gateway to the shadow monsters. There had been enough destruction, and while most of it had been caused by her and the hoshkat, she was not going to let the shadow monsters add to it. She was not going to have those beasts loose in the cavern.

As she raced forward, she felt the ground vibrating under her feet and heard the thunder of hoof beats behind her, but she did not stop. She shouted again, and the mage looked in her direction. His hands did not stop moving until his eyes looked past her and widened in fear, and then they moved faster, but it was too late.

Marsh thought of shadow and thought of speed and was at his side in seconds, startled shouts rising behind her. The first glimmer of the gate's outline appeared, mapping itself over what she could see of the cavern beyond. With a scream of frustration, Marsh twisted, putting the full force of her body behind the blow and trying to slice her way through the mage before he could finish his work.

As she did, she hoped the outline would fade; that the mage hadn't already asked the shadows to part. She also hoped that the shadows needed more than just the outline to open the way between the Ruins Hall cavern and wherever in the Deeps the monsters dwelt. Pain flared across her shoulders and she screamed in defiance, her cry matching the agony in the shadow mage's voice.

Behind her, the hoofbeats slid to a stop and someone landed heavily, before moving toward her.

"Marchant!"

She knew that voice but couldn't think of any reason

why the cavern founder would pay her the slightest bit of attention, although he *did* sound angry. Marsh pulled her blade out of the shadow mage, relieved when he collapsed to the floor and the gate's outlines slowly faded. What was it her uncle had said?

Better to ask forgiveness than—she struggled to bring the saying into focus—permission. From the sound of Monsieur Gravine's voice, forgiveness might be needed. She turned, intending to ask, completely forgetting the blade in her hand.

A startled shout greeted her, and someone slammed into her from the side.

"*Merde.*"

The landing drove the wind from her lungs and momentarily knocked all thought from her head. The shadow blade disappeared, but the weight of the guard pinning her to the ground did not.

"What in all the Deeps are you doing?" Marsh managed as Monsieur Gravine spoke.

"Let her up."

"You heard the man," Marsh said when the guard's weight did not shift.

She had meant that to come out a lot stronger than it did, but it was a creaky whisper. She pushed against him until he moved, and he hauled her to her feet.

"Thanks a lot," she muttered as she turned to face Monsieur Gravine. "I'm—"

"You did well," he snapped, cutting her off, "although next time you will understand that it is much better to ask permission than forgiveness, at least with me. You are under arrest, pending disciplinary action."

Marsh stared at him, her mouth open in surprise. The guard laid a heavy hand on her shoulder.

"I haven't seen him that angry in a long time," he told her, then added, "You'd better come with me."

Marsh nodded. It wasn't like she had much choice. Firstly, because she didn't think she could make a successful break for it, and she definitely couldn't slide into the shadows, and secondly, because—

"Trainee Leclerc!"

Judging by the tone of his voice, Roeglin was mad at her.

You bet the Shadows I'm mad at you.

Well, at least she couldn't make it worse.

"Yes, Roeglin?"

"That is Master Leger, Trainee!" Shadows flew to his hand, snaking together to form a long staff. "Defend yourself."

The guard's vocabulary of curses clearly extended well beyond *merde*. He let go of Marsh's shoulder, moving to stand off to one side and out of range.

Marsh thought about asking forgiveness but decided it would be a waste of time. She pulled her own staff from the shadows, deciding she might as well get this over and done with, and then see what the founder thought was a suitable punishment for someone who—

Roeglin's staff caught her a solid blow to the thigh, then danced up to smack her on the hip, and up again to... Marsh recovered in time to block the blow and make a counterstrike to his head. He ducked under it, turning his staff side-on and stepping forward to hit her across the chest and push her off her feet.

Marsh stumbled back, regained her footing, and shifted her grip on her staff to see Roeglin spin his stick, bringing one end up toward her face. She pulled her head back, but not far enough, and the blow landed, setting her ears ringing and making her see stars. She landed on her backside, her staff vanishing from her hands.

"Next time, you will follow orders."

Uh huh, Marsh thought, *Sure I will.*

What she said was, "Yes, Master Leger."

I can see what you're thinking.

And your point is?

He rolled his eyes, letting the staff dissipate from his hand so he could reach down and help her up.

One day, you're going to find yourself deeper in the Dark than you know how to handle.

Marsh accepted his help, wincing as the results of the day's activities made themselves known.

And when that day comes, I'll be sure to ask you to help me get out of it.

"This way," he said, "I need to speak to Monsieur Gravine."

Marsh just bet he did, but Roeglin wasn't waiting, and she had to concentrate just to keep up. When the founder's guard fell into step beside her, she didn't try to move away.

I wish you'd waited, Roeglin grumbled as a second guard fell in alongside them.

Marsh didn't agree. If she'd waited, they'd be down three farming families instead of two and would have had an incursion they didn't know about until much later. No, it was better that she'd been on hand to intervene.

"Six," Roeglin said.

"Sorry?"

"We'd be down six farming families. The founder sent squads out to each farm in this sector and stopped the raiders who had escaped from making a second hit. They didn't reach the last three farms, but they had a map, and all six were marked. Don't let it go to your head."

Why had he gone after her with a staff, then?

Because the appearance of discipline is important, and hopefully you'll think twice before you cut me out of your plans again.

Right. It *was* food for thought.

Roeglin didn't answer that, but he did give a heartfelt sigh as he headed to where Monsieur Gravine was talking to the farmer and his wife. To Marsh's surprise, Mordan was standing beside the family, three children resting their hands on her brown and gray hide. The founder saw them coming and reached out to shake the farmer's hand.

"You'll be able to return as soon as the cavern is secured. In the meantime, my men will help you move your family and animals to the township."

"The crops..." The farmer waved his hand toward the nearby fields.

"I'll appoint a steward to help organize protection during the harvest for all the farms." Monsieur Gravine indicated one of the soldiers standing nearby. "This is Captain Novel, and he will assist you in your move."

For a moment, the farmer looked like he might have more questions, but then his gaze swept the area around them, taking in the fallen raiders and injured protectors, and he turned toward the captain and Monsieur Gravine.

"Thank you, Founder."

With Novel at his side, he led his family back to the house, Mordan surprising Marsh by trailing along with them.

The kat spared a brief glance in her direction, her tail lashing briefly as she let the children cluster around her. Marsh didn't know how to feel, but she understood. When the cubs were safe, Mordan would be back. In the meantime, Monsieur Gravine was waiting.

Marsh's head spun and she frowned, conjuring a staff to lean on before she fell. Beside her, the guard wrapped his hand around her arm. The firm touch was enough to disrupt her grip on her magic, and the staff vanished just as she went to lean on it. She stumbled, the guard's grip all that kept her upright, and he cursed.

"By the Deep and Shadow's Children!"

Marsh hadn't heard that one, but she liked it, filing it away for later use as the guard pulled her arm over his shoulder. Roeglin observed the interaction, his face a mask of calculated calm.

"Overdid it, did you?" he asked, and Marsh resisted the urge to flip him off. Instead, she answered with all the respect her tired mind could muster.

"Yes, Master Ro...Leger."

His lips tightened into a thin line but he said nothing, turning away to speak with the cavern's founder.

"I believe you have arrested my trainee, pending disciplinary action."

Monsieur Gravine's face was solemn.

"I have."

For a second, Roeglin waited for the founder to

continue. When it became evident he was not going to, the shadow mage spoke.

"Perhaps we can discuss the form of disciplinary action required."

Monsieur Gravine glanced at where Marsh leaned on his guard. After a moment's consideration, he replied.

"I will see you in my office when we return, Master Leger. In the meantime, I'll leave her in your charge."

Beside her, Marsh heard the soldier muffle a sigh of relief.

Just how much trouble had she been in, anyway?

A lot.

Not what she needed to hear.

Merde! Marsh thought as crushing fatigue washed over her. Just once, she'd like to make it back to safety under her own steam.

13

FROM FRYING PAN TO FIRE

Marchant woke to find herself back in the bottom bunk of the room she shared with Izmay. At first, she just lay still, slowly registering the heavy warmth and musky scent of hoshkat and realizing the great beast was stretched out beside her on the bed.

"Mordan," she murmured, pulling a hand clear of the covers to lay on the great kat's side.

A soft rumble vibrated the bed, and she realized the kat was purring. The sound was followed by a raspy tongue licking her cheek, and Marsh opened her eyes. After all, she was going to have to open them sometime.

"Finally," Roeglin said, his voice coming from beside the bed and startling her.

Marsh gasped and turned to face him, and then she yelped as the bruises from the previous day's battle made themselves known. Marsh's mind raced as she tried to remember what had happened. It slowly pieced itself together, and she found there was a lot she wanted to know.

"Has Master Envermet arrived yet?"

She was really asking if the children had arrived safely, and Roeglin picked that fact right out of her head.

"He did, but Tamlin and Aisha have to wait a little longer before you can see them. Their team got the route to the monastery up and running, and we should have shadow-guard reinforcements arriving late today."

He stopped as though waiting for her to ask him something else, so Marsh asked him the next question preying on her mind.

"Did you get to Madame Monetti?"

"Not yet." He held up a hand to still Marsh's protest. "We picked up the trail where several smaller groups had split away from the main raiding party, but they ended at a blank wall."

"Shadow gates," Marsh muttered.

Roeglin nodded, licking his lips before he continued, "Yes. By the time we worked that out and dealt with the raiders who'd survived, dusk was falling and the joffra were emerging." He hesitated. "There are a lot more joffra out there than there should be. No kats, though."

Not yet, Marsh thought, remembering Mordan's kits.

"We'll get them back," Roeglin assured her.

"We need to get *her* first," Marsh insisted. "She has to be the one in charge of this cavern."

Roeglin scowled and pushed back his chair.

"I agree, but it's not going to be you, and there'll be a guard on your door to make sure."

There was a sharp tut from the doorway, and Brigitte came in with a man Marsh didn't recognize.

"I hope you aren't aggravating my patient," he said with a reproving glare at the shadow mage.

"Wouldn't dream of it," Roeglin replied. "I was just reassuring her that everything was working according to plan and that nothing required her personal intervention."

That last was delivered with a meaningful look in Marsh's direction, and she rolled her eyes. Roeglin gave her another scowl for good measure and stalked toward the door.

"I'll check in on her later."

"Much later," the medic stressed. "She needs to rest."

"She needs a good kick in the ass," Roeglin muttered, but he was through the door and away before the medic came back with an answer.

Instead, the man sighed and came over to take Roeglin's seat.

"How do you feel?" he asked.

"Like I was run over by a stampeding mule," she admitted.

"That's a good analogy. A better one would be more like you were beaten to within an inch of your life."

Marsh tried to shrug, winced, and lay still.

"I had a fight with a couple of raiders. It happens."

The medic pursed his lips.

"You'll need to take that shirt off so I can inspect your bruises."

Marsh stilled, studying his face.

"They're on your back," he added, keeping his expression perfectly solemn, "and I can't see through cloth."

"Sorry, Doc."

Marsh got up and let the medic check her. When he

was done, and she was dressed and back in bed, Brigitte brought her something to eat and a cup of chocolate.

"You're to sleep," she said. "We'll be back to check on you before dinner. If you're up to it then, you can come to the dining hall and see the kids."

Marsh nodded, looking at Brigitte over the rim of her cup as she drained her chocolate.

"Thank you," she said, and let the journeyman settle her under her covers.

"I'll be back to collect you," Brigitte told her, and her tone of voice suggested Marsh had better be there.

Why wouldn't I be? Marsh thought, feeling tiredness gnawing the edges of her mind. She closed her eyes, as the woman left the room and pulled the door closed behind her. Beside her, Mordan huffed out a sigh.

"We'll get your cubs," Marsh murmured as she drifted into sleep.

She woke later to silence and the sense of something being terribly wrong. Taking a breath and holding it, Marsh listened, but heard nothing, either inside the room or from outside it. Beside her, Mordan lifted her head and hopped down from the bed.

Marsh watched the big kat's bulk pass over her and slowly sat up.

"What is it, girl?"

The kat gave a soft rippling snarl and turned toward the door. Marsh heard nothing and tweaked at the threads of shadow around her. To her surprise only a few answered, and these showed her that the corridor outside was empty.

So much for Roeglin's threat of putting a guard on her, she

thought, then wondered why the shadow mage thought he'd need to. It took her a moment to remember why, and she drew more pictures from the shadows stretching beneath the door.

There really *was* no one guarding her door—and she sincerely doubted that Monsieur Gravine was going to send anyone after Madame Monetti, given just how busy he was setting up defenses for the rest of the cavern. She looked at the hoshkat.

"I guess that leaves just you and me," she said, and the big kat lifted her head toward her with a silent, approving hiss.

"Do you think we have enough time to get away before they send someone to fetch me for dinner?"

Mordan flicked her tail and butted her head against the door.

"Good point," Marsh told her. "We'll have no time if I don't get my arse in gear."

She dressed as swiftly as the all-pervading stiffness of her injuries would allow and was grateful nothing had cut flesh in the last battle. If that had happened, she wouldn't be attempting to go anywhere. As it was, she was probably being stupid for attempting to leave.

Well, too bad.

Marsh pulled her armor around her, doing her best to check the buckles and straps before settling her sword belt around her hips and lifting her pack from the floor. She hissed in pain and took a moment to let her body's protests subside. Maybe the doc had something for that...except the only thing he was likely to give her was a stern lecture and orders to go back to bed.

"No time," she muttered, sliding her arms through the pack's straps and turning to the door.

Resting her fingers on the handle, she took a moment to ask the shadows to show her the corridor again. This time, she had to wait while two soldiers passed, watching as they took the stairs to the next level.

"Best hurry," she told the kat and woke the link between them, sending a desire for open gates and the shroom-forested cavern beyond.

Mordan nudged her hand and walked to the door. She knew the way, but she didn't have hands and wasn't strong enough to knock the door down by herself. Marsh solved that by turning the handle, feeling the kat's envy of her fingers and thumbs as they stepped into the corridor.

Marsh stopped long enough to pull the door closed behind them, and then they hurried down the hallway toward the stairwell. On the way, Marsh had to twice duck through doorways and wait for people to pass. At one point, she thought she heard Tamlin and Aisha in animated conversation with Brigitte—something to do with cookies and which ones Marsh liked best.

As a way of distracting the children, Marsh had to admit it was a pretty good option. It was also a great way to make her feel as guilty as sin for what she was about to do. It was bad enough having Roeglin and Monsieur Gravine angry with her without Aisha, Brigitte, and Tamlin being upset, too.

"Come on, Dan, before I change my mind and do the sensible thing."

The two of them hurried down two flights of stairs, passing through the kitchens amidst the hustle and bustle of what had to be pre-dinner preparations. Marsh hoped no one recognized her. If they did, she was toast, but despite her fears, they reached the stable yard without being called back.

Marsh was just about to turn toward the outer gate she remembered when the hoshkat surprised her by heading away from it. At first, Marsh wondered why, but the kat moved with swift certainty and she decided not to question her judgment. After taking a cautious path around the stables and a storage shed, Mordan led her to an open drain.

"You have got to be shitting me," Marsh protested, and the kat gave her a blue-eyed look tinged with scorn. Marsh sighed. "You're not kidding."

She glanced back, catching a glimpse of two guards heading toward the gate in the wall and moving a lot quicker than she'd like.

"Drain it is," she told the kat, and slid carefully into the culvert. "We're both going to need a bath after this."

Mordan said nothing, but judging by the way the kat lifted her feet, she wasn't overly impressed with the route she had chosen either. Marsh refrained from arguing, relieved when they emerged on the other side of the wall. She was even more relieved to discover herself in the middle of a tangle of hanging moss, tall callas, and tightly clustered shrooms grounded by ditch mint and grackle thorn.

At least they wouldn't be seen. Not yet, anyway. Marsh followed Mordanlenoowar to the edge of the clustered plants and fungi and peered out, searching for heat and light in the shadows nearest the wall. It took her a moment to pinpoint the gate she'd used before, and she realized the cavern founder had learned from her previous outing.

For a long moment, she watched as a team of masons worked to build a small barbican around the gate, and she wondered why they weren't waiting for the rock wizards to assist them. It was something she'd ask about, later—after she'd returned from her confrontation with Madame Monetti.

"Let's go, girl," she said. "You know where we need to be."

And so did she, she realized. She knew exactly where to go, thanks to the maps Roeglin had shared with her noting the farms' locations. Taking a moment to bring them to memory, Marsh oriented them in her mind, using what she knew of the cavern and the farms as a guide. The dot at the edge of the map, the one closest to the Leon's Deep junction, had to be where Madame Monetti had built her mansion.

It was, after all, the only marker where Monsieur Gravine had said the woman lived, and Marsh could reach it if she asked the shadows to show her the way, just like she had when she had gone after the shadow mage at their first campsite on the way to Ruins Hall. One minute she'd had a hundred yards or more to cover, and the next she'd stepped into the shadows, asking them to speed her path, and she'd been beside him.

"Sorry, girl," she said to the hoshkat, "but this is where we part ways."

Refusing to think about the wisdom of going to confront Madame Monetti without *any* form of backup, Marsh stepped out of the grove, fixing the map in her mind. Another step took her into the dimly-lit shadows of a clump of callas and she spoke to them, thinking of the distance she had to cover and the point on the map she had reach.

"I need to be there," she told the shadows, highlighting the marker and picturing the location she remembered from her arrival with Fabrice. Becoming one with the shadows, she began to run.

To her surprise, the pain of her bruises faded with the weight of her body and pack and movement became as easy as selecting the next section of shadow. Marsh wished she could go faster; she wished she could step through the shadow and find herself at the edge of the first farm, and then the second, and then at that point on the map. That one—the one near the junction.

She *needed* to be there; needed it badly.

The shadows blurred around her, her surroundings pivoting at a dizzying rate. Where she'd been skipping from the shadows beneath a grove of calla shrooms to the darkness at the edge of a stalagmite or rocky outcrop, now she slid through the cavern's perpetual night, the walls of the first farmhouse she'd visited the night before looming before her.

Marsh gasped, only to have the walls fade until she stood outside the barn of the second farm she'd visited, and then, almost too fast to register, the scenery shifted once again and Marsh stood where two roads met, their glows dark, the shadows crowding close on either side. Somewhere, in the distance, she heard a hoshkat roar with frustration.

"Sorry, Mordan," she whispered, stepping into the deeper shadows surrounding the base of a jumble of rocks.

Letting herself drift out of shadow form, she thanked the cavern dark for the speed of her journey and wished she'd remembered to pack something to eat. Her head spun and she felt a little weak, but she knew where she was. She remembered passing through the junction with a herd of moutons and a string of mules that hadn't belonged to her.

That seemed so long ago. It was hard to believe it had only been a few weeks, and only a few weeks more since she had been a courier for Kearick's Emporium in Kerrenin's Ledge. It had been even less time since her employer had sent Mikel to retrieve her commission and kill her. Anger surged through her and Marsh caught hold of it, harnessing her outrage and using it to give her energy.

Time to find out what Madame Monetti's role was in this entire debacle had been.

Marsh!

Marsh didn't have time for Roeglin's fury...or the anxious undertones she heard in that single word. She set him firmly to one side of her mind and focused on the cavern around her. The junction she was familiar with, but she knew there had to be another road—one that would take her to Madame Monetti's mansion.

Marsh!

Shut up, Ro. I need to concentrate.

You need to get your ass right back—

Marsh shut him out. Man couldn't be quiet? Man wasn't going to be allowed inside her head. And he thought he was *such* a mental magic titan...

It took her a moment to find it, but the trail was there. Marsh stepped out onto the trade route and walked back to where two tall white pillars stretched from floor to ceiling. At first glance, they looked like a squared-off stalagmite had finally met the matching stalactite reaching down from above, but on closer inspection, Marsh would have sworn the pillars had always been one, and that they belonged to something man-made; an older structure that had sent roots deep into the earth hundreds of years ago.

Roeglin's next intrusion, when it came, arrived as a polite knock on the edge of her mind. Marsh sighed and cracked the barrier.

What?

Mind if I come along for the ride?

Marsh thought about it.

I've found it.

Roeglin was silent for a moment, and Marsh got the impression he was trying to catch a glimpse of what she was seeing.

Fine, she told him. *You can watch, but not one word. You can't stop me.*

This time Roeglin sighed. It was a sound of such utter despondency that Marsh almost felt sorry for him.

Since when have I ever been able to do that?

Almost.

Point, she agreed and went back to the trail.

Having worked out that the pillars were quite solid regardless of their origin, Marsh stepped between them and followed the trail beyond. After several feet, it widened into an open expanse of white rock on which nothing grew. More pillars rose around its edges, but these did not reach the ceiling, forming a kind of ragged fringe instead.

Roeglin stayed silent and still, and Marsh soon forgot he was traveling with her, albeit only in her mind. She crossed the expanse of white flooring and entered another narrow section of trail.

I don't like this, Roeglin muttered.

Too bad. We're here. Marsh told him as the trail ended in front of two pristine white doors.

Wait for me.

He was begging.

Can't.

Not when she was already at the doors.

Marsh raised her hand and lifted the heavy golden knocker, using it to send booming echoes through what-ever lay beyond the doors. When they opened to reveal two lines of shadow mages, she realized she might just have made another mistake. To give him credit, Roeglin didn't waste time rubbing it in or scolding her.

I'm coming, he said, and Marsh swallowed hard as she took in the towering dark-cloaked figures. She swallowed again when an equally tall man in the armor of the raiders stepped out from behind them and stalked toward her.

He was flanked by two others, both wearing the same armor, the same insignia, and the same curving weapons she'd last seen being carried through Leon's Deep when she'd asked the shadows to show her what was coming. Marsh felt her skin grow cool as she paled, but the man didn't seem to notice.

"State your business!" he ordered and Marsh cleared

her throat, forcing herself to look at him. She tried not to glance nervously at the guards and mages on either side.

"I have a delivery for Madame Monetti," she said, then added, "From Kearick of Kerrenin's Ledge."

It was a bold statement to make, considering the only things she carried in her pack were whatever was left from her journey from the shadow-mage monastery. She really didn't need to hear the new voice that echoed down from the other end of the hall.

"She lies!"

It was not a voice she recognized, although the tale it told was a scenario she herself had run by Roeglin.

"I waited for Mikel and saw his body buried outside the monastery walls."

Marsh backed up a step and turned to leave, but it was already too late. Her heart plummeted at the sight before her. Four shadow mages were slowly pulling themselves from the shadows and returning to human form. Well, *merde*! She'd thought she was one of a very few folks to be able to work that trick.

They also knew the trick of using shadow weapons mixed with real in case their target could also shift form. She could tell that from the darts and crossbows they held. If they were even half-way proficient, she was done for.

"Well, *merde*," she murmured, out loud this time, and the warrior who had met her gave a bark of laughter.

"Come with me," he said. "Madame Monetti will want to speak with you."

Marsh turned side-on so she could see him, then stood very still as two of the shadow mages approached. The others were still pointing lethal weapons in her direction, and she wanted to live—at least for a little while longer.

I'm coming, Roeglin repeated, and Marsh could think of only one reply.

Hurry.

14

MADAME MONETTI

Once they'd taken her weapons, gagged her, and bound her hands, Marsh was led into a plush office lined with display cases filled with teapots. Some looked like they'd been bought recently from local sources, but others...Marsh stared. They looked really old, and not just because they were dented or missing a handle. No, there was something about their designs that felt unfamiliar.

Why teapots? she wondered, tripping over the edge of a mottled gray-and-brown rug. It dragged her attention back to the present, and she swallowed a feeling of revulsion. The rug looked like someone had skinned a hoshkat and laid it on the floor. Seeing the head still attached made her stomach roll, and she willed it to be calm.

Marsh shivered, glad Mordan hadn't come with her. She'd have hated to see her friend decorating the floor in another part of the office. She stumbled and was jerked upright by the shadow mage walking to her right.

"Watch where you're going," he snapped, giving her a none-too-gentle shake.

Marsh wanted to tell him to watch where *he* was going, himself, except that it would have been childish...and she wouldn't have gotten the words past the cloth covering her mouth. She also wanted to take her sword and run it through his middle, but this wasn't possible either, given that her hands were bound and her sword had been taken and handed to someone else for safekeeping. It wasn't' safe to try to pull a shadow blade here.

This was not how Marsh had envisioned meeting Madame Monetti, but she drew a deep breath and kept moving forward. At least she *would* be seeing the lady. For a long moment, she hadn't been sure she'd live to make it through the door. Some of the mages had wanted revenge for fallen comrades.

Some of the soldiers, too. Apparently, they'd had brothers and friends out on those raids. The gag had been their leader's decision when she'd told one man his brother might have lived if he hadn't been picking on little children and had been gutted like the pig he was. There was a good reason that man was still outside guarding the door.

Marsh started smirking.

If Roeglin hadn't been so busy trying to catch up with her, he would have been appalled...but only if she let him into her head, again. It was almost fun being able to keep him out at will. She'd have to ask him how that worked. Mirth bubbled up inside her, followed by an instant of crushing despair. She would tell him if she ever got the chance. For all she knew, this could be the last room she'd ever see.

Sucking in another breath to steady her pitching emotions, Marsh focused on putting one foot in front of the other and concentrated, trying to calm her mind. She really couldn't afford to offend Madame Monetti like she'd offended the guard outside, not if she wanted to discover what happened to the people they took.

And she did want to know what they were doing with those people; she really did. Did they live? Were they killed? Why did the shadow raiders need so many? Were they short a workforce? What sort of work would need all those people, all at once?

Why did they look for children with magical talent, yet take those without it as well? There were so many answers she didn't have, not least of which was what had happened to her parents. Yeah, that was the one thing she wanted to know above all else, no matter what promises she'd made to the others. She hadn't realized her own folks' disappearance still haunted her that much.

Movement caught her attention, and she realized she'd been too lost in thought to notice they'd reached the end of the room.

"Berens says you have a delivery for me."

Berens had said no such thing and both he and Marchant knew it, but neither he nor Marsh was about to contradict the woman who'd just entered. By the looks of her, Madame Monetti had not been raised in the Four Settlements. Judging from her height, she'd come from the surface...like Berens. Marsh stared at her, hoping the woman didn't decide to take her silence for rudeness.

Meeting Marsh's eyes, Madame Monetti wrinkled her nose and tutted.

"You might want to remove the girl's gag, Berens. She can't tell me anything if she can't talk."

"Yes, ma'am."

Berens tone was bland, as was his expression when he turned toward her, but that changed quickly enough. As he raised his hands to take the gag, Berens frowned.

"You mind your manners, girl, or I'll be gutting you myself."

Marsh's eyes widened at the threat, but she managed a nod, and he removed the cloth from between her lips and lifted a flask of water in its place. Thankful for his foresight, Marsh took a gulp of water and rinsed it around her mouth, surprised when he let her take a second to wet her throat.

The woman came closer, her long dark hair looped on top of her head in an intricate tangle of braids and clips. Marsh wanted to know how she ever found the time to do it but didn't dare ask. For her part, the woman stalked around Marsh, her dark brown eyes inspecting every inch of the prisoner. When she was done, she looked at Berens.

"She'll do. When we're finished, you'll put her with the rest." She stopped speaking, making a display of looking Marsh over and pursing her lips with distaste. "Maybe not *with* the rest. From what I've heard, she's likely to cause trouble. Have Ardhur make sure she doesn't."

"Yes, madam."

From the clipped tones of Berens' voice, he didn't like what his mistress was suggesting, but he didn't have anything better to offer. Marsh's nerves formed a knot in the pit of her stomach and sent apprehension through the rest of her body. By the Deep, what had she gotten herself into?

She waited until the lady turned her attention on her,

noting narrow features and full lips in a face that went from striking to beautiful.

"Do you know who I am, girl?"

Marsh nodded but said nothing. It was not enough for Madame Monetti.

"And?"

Oh, she really *did* want an answer to that. Marsh resisted the urge to say she was the stupid woman who'd had her tied up and came up with something else.

"You are the one Kearick said to deliver the artifact to."

"And?"

"And what, mistress?"

"Where is my artifact?" the woman shrieked, putting her face an inch from Marsh's.

Marsh started, almost falling as she backed up. Berens grabbed her before she'd gone more than two steps, his grip tightening when Marsh tried to pull away. Firmly caught, Marsh froze, staring at the woman as her breath came in fast gasps.

Madame Monetti straightened and studied her, a slow smile forming on her face. When Marsh remained silent, she reached out and curled her fingers under Marchant's chin. Marsh flinched, but when Madame Monetti spoke, again, her voice was much softer.

"So, child. *Where* is it?"

Marsh shook her head, or tried to. The lady's grip tightened, and her face became hard.

"'No' is not an option. Tell me where it is."

Marsh shot a glance at Berens, but he pointed at the woman with his free hand. Again, Marsh shook her head, and Monetti nodded.

"You'd have to take it off her anyway."

He would? Marsh shot a startled look at Berens, stiffening with alarm as he drew the dagger from his belt.

"Your choice," he said, flipping the blade and catching it in his fingertips. "I can cut the armor off you or just unbuckle it."

He flipped the knife again, once again gripping the hilt.

Tell them, Roeglin said, breaking his silence in her mind. *It's not like they'll ever find it.*

Marsh breathed a sigh of relief and looked at Madame Monetti.

"It's at the monastery."

"Where?"

It was hard not to look toward Berens and his knife, but Marsh managed it.

"In the armory in storage."

As far as she knew, that was true. The Supply Master *did* keep weapons on the wall.

"Where?"

"I don't know. They don't let trainees past the front counter."

Berens raised the knife and Marsh shrank away from it.

"Please," she whispered. "I don't know. I *don't*. I really don't."

It wasn't hard to pretend to be afraid of the knife. She *was* afraid of it, —and that much showed through. Berens looked at his mistress.

"I could start cutting," he said, "but I don't think it would do any good—and we'd miss the next shipment. If the artifact is in the fortress; we'll find it when we make the place our own. Hasn't been a hiding place yet that we can't discover."

Marsh wondered if that was true, and sincerely hoped it wasn't. If the raiders wanted the artifact that badly, that was how badly they needed not to have it.

Hang in there, Marsh.

At least Roeglin had stopped calling her 'trainee.'

Not yet, I haven't, Leclerc.

But Madame Monetti was speaking again, and Marsh knew she needed to listen.

"You know, you'd do a lot better working for us than against us," the lady suggested, and Marsh lifted her head.

She was about to retort that the last person who'd thought that, she'd gutted like a pig...and then she remembered Berens warning as they'd come into the room and decided she should not say anything. Madame Monetti stepped closer.

"What, nothing to say? I understand you're a trainee with the monastery, but the skills I've seen would put you at journeyman at the very least, if not junior master. Is that not so, Master Warven?"

She lifted her head and looked toward one of the mages standing in front of a display cabinet. He gave her a startled glance and turned his attention to Marsh.

"Ah, yes. Certainly. A junior master at the very least," he said, rushing through the words as though not agreeing was a fate worse than death. "A junior master, indeed."

Madame Monetti turned to Marsh, her expression triumphant.

"There! You see? A junior master rather than a trainee—and we pay much, much better."

"How much better?" Marsh wanted to know, and the madam named a figure five times what she was making as a trainee.

Marsh looked impressed. It wasn't hard. The amount was more than she could make in a year of running errands for Kearick. Still...

"Thank you, ma'am. That is...very generous, and while it would be good to have my skills recognized, it means I would have to be working for arseholes like you. I'm afraid I can't do that."

Marsh! Roeglin's horrified reaction was enough to crack the deadpan exterior Marsh had been trying to maintain. She ducked her head, but not quite in time to hide the smile that flitted along her lips, even if she *did* stifle the giggle before she made a sound. Madame Monetti stepped in and slapped her hard enough to set her ears ringing, and then she turned away.

"Take her," she commanded. "And give her something to remember me by, while you're at it."

Berens' backhand was delivered by a gauntleted fist and dropped Marsh to her knees, but he only struck her once before the lady intervened.

"Not in here! You'll ruin my rugs or break a treasure. Take her out with the others, and don't damage her too badly."

"Yes, Madame," Berens replied and hauled Marsh to her feet before dragging her toward the door.

Marsh went willingly, not that she had much choice. Berens kept a firm grip on her arm as he hauled out of the well-appointed office into the corridor beyond. When the door had closed behind them, he leaned close to her ear.

"You'd best be grateful. I'd beat the living Dark out of you, except that we have a ways to go to catch up with the others and I don't feel like carrying your scrawny carcass anywhere."

"I would," muttered one of the guards leaning on the wall. "Only I'd be dragging her."

Berens gave a mirthless laugh.

"Not this time, Merek." He looked at Marsh. "Although you give me an ounce of trouble and you're Merek's until I think you've learned your lesson, you understand?"

Marsh shot a sidelong look at Merek and shivered at the expression on the man's face. He was the one whose brother she'd killed. Having told him it was his brother's own fault now seemed like a very bad idea. She nodded.

"Understood."

"Good. Come."

Marsh went, following Berens into another corridor and through what felt like half a mountain before walking through a twenty-stall-wide stable with barracks above into a stone-walled courtyard in an alcove off another tunnel. Marsh tried to orient the tunnel in her head but couldn't. This was another area of the world below that she hadn't explored.

Her wrists and forearms were aching from being bound behind her back and she thought about asking to have them released, but one look at Merek, who was walking on her left, warned her that it might not be a good idea. Then again, with him that close, she'd rather her hands were free than bound. She turned to Berens, and he glanced down at her.

"No," he told her when she drew a breath, and Marsh wondered how he'd known what she'd been going to ask.

He led her to one side of the courtyard and stood her next to the wall.

"Wait here."

Marsh waited as he selected two mules and pointed to Merek and the shadow mage known as Warven.

"You know where to go. Make sure Ardhur knows he is to keep her whole and out of trouble. I'll be checking in the morning when I bring the rest of the supplies."

"Yes, Captain," Warven said, and Merek grinned.

"We'll let him know."

Berens frowned.

"*Before* anything happens to her, Merek, or you'll suffer the same fate."

Merek scowled.

"Yes, Captain."

"Good."

Berens crossed to Marsh and clipped a lead rope to her belt.

"Try to keep up," he said and pulled the gag from where he'd tucked it in his belt.

Marsh tilted her head back, but he took a firm grip on her hair and fastened the gag in place.

"You don't need to get yourself into any more trouble."

Like Hell I don't, Marsh thought, but Roeglin approved.

You might be alive by the time I get there after all, he commented, sounding inordinately relieved.

Before Marsh could think of a reply, Berens handed Merek the end of the rope and the soldier kicked his mule into a trot.

"*Merde!*"

It came out as a muffled growl, and Merek laughed.

Marsh wanted to say a lot more. Better, she wanted her sword.

Clarinay says to shadow-step, Roeglin's voice came through fast and urgent, but Marsh got it.

Shadow-step. The thought had her stifling a desire to laugh as she concentrated on keeping on her feet long enough for her body to blend with the shadows. It was disappointing that her restraints and the rope attached to her belt blended with her, but running became easier... right up until the moment Warven looked back and saw what she was doing.

"Keep riding," he said, tapping Merek on the shoulder. "I'll deal with this."

Oh, he would, would he? Marsh wondered exactly what he was going to do. It was hard to keep an eye on him and maintain the concentration needed to keep herself in shadow form, but she managed. Her heart sank when he pulled a staff of shadow from the dark and swung it in her direction.

She ducked his first swipe but wasn't fast enough to dodge the second. The blow connected solidly and Marsh stumbled, temporarily losing her focus. For a moment her steps were as heavy as lead, then she fought her way back into the shadows...or tried to.

Warven struck her again, and Marsh got the impression he'd done this before. This time, before she could regain her concentration, a low growl rumbled out around them, causing the mules to buck and shy. Warven lost his grip on the staff and Mordan roared.

"No!" Marsh cried, and almost choked. She also fell out of shadow form and tripped over her own feet as she twisted, trying to see where the hoshkat was.

No, she repeated more quietly down the link they had between them. *Let them take me to the others. Let them take me to the cubs. Come for me then.*

She sent the imagery of what she was hunting, what she was *hoping* to find, and made it clear she thought of the two men as deer leading her to a watering hole where the real game gathered.

Hide, she ordered. *Follow, but let them live—for now.*

With a lingering growl, the kat moved farther away, letting out a frustrated screech so that Marsh knew exactly what she thought of this plan.

Sorry, Mordan. Human games. Marsh tried to comfort the kat, but the big beast was having none of it, sending the equivalent of an open-pawed swat down the link between them.

Marsh was still trying to work out how to respond to that when the line at her belt drew tight and she was dragged along the ground.

"Aagh!" Marsh shouted, trying to catch Merek's attention—and then she realized she already had it and the soldier was immensely satisfied with hauling her along the trail.

She tried rolling so that the thicker armor on her shoulders and hips would take the brunt, but the lead kept turning her around so she ended up on her front.

Merde! Merdemerdemerde!

Marsh put one foot down and used it to lever her body around and up, her knee complaining at the pressure. It was a relief when it held long enough for her to make it to her feet, not so much of a relief when she found herself limping, the pain too much for her to find the focus to return to shadow form once more.

It was a poor consolation when Warven refused to let Merek ride any faster.

15

STONE-WRAPPED

By Marchant's calculation, the journey took the better part of two hours. On top of a day of magic and fighting, it was too much, but not too much to keep her from recognizing the place they stopped. She'd only seen it once before through the shadows, but she knew it.

This was where the raiders had camped the night she had hidden from them with the children. This was the place the people of Leon's Deep had been held, and she hadn't even guessed. She'd left them, too intent on taking Tams and Aisha to safety to think that the others might not be traveling of their own free will. She'd just let them be taken.

When the mule stopped, Marsh stopped too. She dropped to her knees, leaning forward as she dragged air into her lungs in ragged breaths. This was easier when Warven peeled the gag out of her mouth and held a flask to her lips.

"I'll stay with her while you fetch Ardhur," Warven said

as Marsh drank greedily, taking as much as she could before he pulled the flask away. Merek spat.

"Fine," he answered, making it sound anything but.

Marsh listened to him walk away and felt a faint sense of relief. While she might not be exactly where she wanted to be, it was good that she hadn't been left there with Merek. It was also good that Warven didn't speak, but left her to her suffering and pain-filled thoughts.

All too soon Merek returned, and he was not alone.

"Here she is," he said, landing a boot in her ribs and tipping her onto her side.

"Deep's misbegotten son," Marsh managed. She grunted as he landed a second kick.

He might have tried for a third but Warven pulled him away, calling a junior mage over to attend the mules while he found the pair of them something to drink. Marsh cracked an eyelid to watch them go. As she did so, she noticed the heavy leather boots standing not two feet from her head. By the Deep, she hoped that this guy didn't feel like sinking the boot in as well.

She rolled slightly so she could get a look at him and decided Ardhur was descended from giants.

He was a big man; tall, but also broad. His shoulders and thighs were heavily muscled, and he had a body like a solid block. From this angle, it looked like he had a dark red beard in twin plaits, but it was hard to tell. He might just have been wearing some kind of furry shawl. He lifted his foot and prodded her with the toe of his boot.

Marsh gasped, expecting pain, but it was no more than a nudge, and she blushed at her panic.

"Get up," he said, stepping back to let her work out how to obey.

Once she got started, it wasn't as impossible as it had seemed, and she stood in front of him, trying not to sway. By the Deep, she was tired.

"Merek says you need to be caged in stone."

Marsh felt her face pale and the man cocked his head, bending to look down at her.

"Boy says you're a shadow mage. Is he right?"

Marsh thought about lying, but he read it on her face.

"So you are," he said, and she hung her head.

"She shifted to the shadows at the trot." Warven had returned, and he hadn't finished. "After a day of fighting and running."

Marsh didn't want to know how he knew that, but she refused to look at either of them. This worked until Ardhur crooked his finger under her chin and lifted her head so he could study her face.

"I'd ask if what he said was true, but you'd likely lie, wouldn't you?"

Marsh shook her head, making the effort to lift her chin and look him in the eye. If she was going to be this far in the shit, she might as well earn every inch of it.

"It's true," she said, and tried to fade into the shadow to prove a point.

She succeeded a little better than she expected, only to have Warven knock her back to human form with a well-aimed blow from a hastily conjured shadow staff.

"Then you're coming with me."

Like she had a choice.

"Not going anywhere else," Marsh managed, her words slurring with fatigue.

Ardhur shook his head. "No, you're not." He picked her up and threw her over his shoulder, carrying her to the other side of the pool and into a chamber whose entrance was hidden behind an overlap of rock.

The chamber wasn't empty, and Marsh's spirits lifted at the thought she wouldn't be alone. They plummeted just as fast, and for the very same reason. How in all the Deeps was she supposed to free all these? It turned out that Ardhur had that covered—and she wasn't.

He put her down just inside the doorway on her side, placing the splayed fingertips of one hand on her shoulder and the palm of the other hand on the wall. "Be still."

Be still? Marsh was about to turn her head to look up at him when she felt something creeping off the wall and over her side and back. It was like a tide of lukewarm honey was flowing off the stone wall to cover her. She tried to twist around, but Warven knelt quickly beside Ardhur and pinned her legs and hips.

Whatever was crawling over her flowed just a little faster.

Marsh felt it cover her hair and ears, then run down across her forehead, and realized it wasn't sticky. Not honey. Not insects. Where it touched it solidified, cooling, blocking all sound from her ears. It weighed on her legs as Warven took his hands away, and then placed them on top of it, and Marsh felt it flow around her calves. She noticed that it didn't drip like honey, but shaped itself around her, encasing her from both sides until its edges touched.

Where it touched her cheeks and solidified, it cooled, and Marsh knew exactly what it was.

Stone!

She pushed against it, her breath coming fast with fear, but she couldn't move an inch. When her whole body was covered, Ardhur lifted his hand from her shoulder, letting the stone fill the space it had occupied.

"Close your eyes," he said, and, when she hesitated, brushed his palm over them, a thin veneer of stone following his downward stroke.

"No!"

Some of the stone cleared away from her ears.

"Steady, girl. You can still breathe. You can still breathe, see?"

It took Marsh a couple of minutes to understand that he was telling the truth and she *could* still breathe. She wasn't being crushed, and the stone both held and supported her body. She couldn't move, though, and couldn't do anything to help herself.

"I'd sleep if I were you," Warven advised. "There's nothing else you can do."

The thought left her feeling hopeless, but he was right. As much as her mind raced to try and find a solution to her problem, she couldn't see one. Sure, she could melt into shadow, but the only holes in her prison were the ones for her nose and mouth, and she couldn't see how she might fit through them. She tried to imagine how to make that work and failed.

"Please…" she whispered, and felt the warmth of a hand laid lightly over her mouth.

It rested there just long enough for Marsh to worry that

he'd cover her nose as well, and then it was lifted away. Gulping back a sob of panic, she forced herself to take a deep breath. They hadn't gone to all the trouble of encasing her in stone, just to kill her. She swallowed. Maybe.

"I'll let you loose in the morning," he said, "and this will keep you out of trouble in the meantime. Get some rest, girl. There's a long day's travel ahead."

Oh, there was, was there?

Marsh really hoped Roeglin was coming. She hoped he'd be able to follow her in spite of the distance she'd traveled under the rock. Did mental magic have a limit to how far it could reach? Could he work out where she was just by being in her mind? *Would* he come?

Sadness welled up inside her, and Marsh panicked by the thought she might cry. If she did, her nose would run… and she had no way to wipe it. Not only were her hands encased in solid rock, but they were still tied behind her back.

"*Merde,*" she whispered. "*Merde. Merde. Merde.*"

Fingers trailed over her lips and she gasped, trying to pull her face away from them and getting nowhere. Again the stone shifted around her ear, and sound flooded in.

"I will be here. Now, sleep."

Whether Ardhur meant that to be soothing, Marsh couldn't tell, but she pressed her lips tightly together, unable to nod and not trusting her voice. She was well and truly trapped, and her heart was beating like a moth against a lantern. In spite of her fatigue, it felt like forever before she could convince her body to sleep.

Marsh woke with a start to find her body still trapped.

Air moved against her mouth and nose and then stilled, but not a smidge of sound made its way through the rock now sealed close over her ears. She tried to open her eyes, but Ardhur knew his work, and the stone held them closed. Panic ran along her arms and legs, and Marsh tried to wriggle free of it, only to find movement impossible.

Somewhere in the back of her mind, she became aware she was screaming, then fingers laid themselves over the slit above her mouth. She stilled, breathing hard as the touch made her fear fade. This time the stone above her ears did not thin, and no sound made it through. When her breathing had calmed, the fingers went away.

She must have made some sound of protest because they returned, resting lightly on the stone, where she could feel their warmth but not their touch. Marsh hated herself for needing them there; hated the fact she couldn't escape the confines of stone. Couldn't...

She drew a deep breath.

Aisha could talk to stone and blend her body with it, and Tamlin talked of a traveler who claimed everyone could do magic. And then there'd been Lennie with her need to heal. There was no reason Marsh couldn't do the same.

Except that she couldn't. She tried talking to the stone but the hand covered her mouth, and, when she persisted, it pinched off her nostrils. It had been brief, but Marsh had gotten the message: no talking. Her next attempt was made without the use of words, and it failed, too.

She couldn't imagine how Aisha could get the stone to do her bidding without talking to it and tried to remember another occasion when she'd seen someone manipulate rock. The Stone Master had, but she'd used her hands—and even *she'd* spoken as she'd worked. Marsh sighed and tried to wiggle her fingers. Maybe she could convince the rock encasing them to move aside, even just a little bit.

She tried, but it was like recharging a glow. The effort of trying to will the rock to do her bidding was exhausting. Marsh kept at it until her body trembled with fatigue, then let herself relax. If she wasn't going to be able to talk to the rocks, then she was going to need to be awake when she was free of it. She had to be rested if she was going to be able to take advantage of the next opportunity.

16

CAPTIVE JOURNEY

Marsh was woken by the feeling of stone slithering away from her limbs, and pushed away from the wall in a panic just as soon as she was able. A large hand grabbed her hair as she tried to slide around a horribly familiar pair of boots, and Ardhur dragged her to her feet.

"And where do you think you're going?"

"Latrine?"

He sighed and handed her to one of the female guards. The woman didn't ask what was required but took Marsh where she needed to go, helping her get through her morning ablutions without undoing her hands. Twice, Marsh tried to ask. The first time she was met with a scowl, and the second time she received a fist to the gut.

She didn't bother asking again; the answer was clear. When she arrived back where Ardhur was waiting, most of the other prisoners were eating small shroom-bread rolls and drinking water from a shared flask. The guard deposited Marsh beside the rock mage with a sour glare.

"Tell her how it works," she snapped before wheeling around and stamping away.

Ardhur turned his head and held up a roll.

"Hungry?"

Marsh nodded but kept her eyes on his face rather than the roll.

"Best eat fast, then," he said, and dropped the roll at her feet.

Marsh dropped to her knees after it but stopped. There was no way she was going to chase after it with just her mouth. She glanced up and caught the look on his face, then she glanced across at where a small knot of guards had gathered and was waiting in eager anticipation.

"You are one set of sick shroomies," she said, looking up at the rock mage and sitting back on her haunches.

Ardhur's lips tightened and he set his foot on the roll, grinding it under his heel.

"Maybe that will help," he said, but Marsh got her feet under her and stood.

"I'm not *that* hungry," she declared, although her stomach rumbled loud enough to give away the lie.

Ardhur smirked.

"Suits me," he said. "Less you refuel, less trouble you'll be."

Man had a point, but not enough of one for her to try eating the mushy smear of crumbs that should have been her breakfast. She watched as he lifted a flask of water to his lips and took a long swallow, and was not surprised when he waved it toward her.

"Thirsty?" he asked, and Marsh gave him a single nod, wondering what he'd do next.

To her surprise, he placed the bottle against her lips and tilted it.

"Wouldn't want you dying of thirst, now would we?"

Marsh rolled her eyes, but she didn't stop drinking until he took the flask away. When he held up the gag, she took a step back, but he snaked out a hand and grabbed her by the scruff of the neck before she could move too far. He soon had the filthy cloth in place.

"There'll be no speaking to the dark for you," he said, and Marsh glared at him.

She didn't need to speak to the dark; she could just step into the shado—

A staff slammed into the middle of her back, jolting her back into the real and knocking her back to her knees. This time her attempt to stand was stopped by the end of the staff resting between her shoulder blades.

"You'll walk like the rest of us," Warven told her and poked the staff into her back.

Marsh gasped and bowed her head. It looked like she'd have to work out another way to get free. She *really* hoped Roeglin would catch up to her, soon. As much as she dreaded what the master was going to say about her sneaking off again, she didn't care. She needed to see him. She couldn't just disappear into the caverns.

Her mind drifted to her uncle. It would be just like her parents all over again, and that was if it wasn't already like that. After all, he couldn't know she'd escaped the attack on the caravan. He might not even know there had *been* an attack. All he would know was that the trade route to Ruins Hall was closed, and there'd been no news of her since.

She had to get to him. She *had* to let him know everything was all right.

Marsh gasped as Warven poked her again. Honestly, when she got free, she was going to take that stick and...

Except it was shadow, and would bleed into nothing the minute he let go of it.

"Get up!"

For real this time? she thought, remembering that he'd been the one to put her on her knees in the first place. The staff struck her once more, harder this time. Fine—for real. Marsh struggled to her feet and got into line with the rest. It didn't help that she was at the back, the worst place to be in any caravan, just like she'd been the last time the shadow monsters had attacked.

Only this time, she was in a caravan of slaves run by the very people who'd summoned the shadow monsters. Maybe this time, she'd be safe from that. She could only hope, especially since there were plenty of other things she should be worried about. She sighed, and Ardhur stepped in close and fastened a collar around her throat.

As if that wasn't bad enough, he clipped three ropes to it. One he fastened to the collar of the person in front of her, the second he passed to Warven, and the third he tied to his own saddle.

Huh, Marsh thought. *Looks like they don't want me to go anywhere.*

Trying to think of a way to do exactly that kept her mind occupied as the raiders got them moving. It also stopped her fretting over Roeglin's absence from her mind or testing Warven's vigilance. So much for "walking in the dark like the rest of us." the shadow mage was riding a mule to one side of her, while Ardhur rode on the other. Talk about a statement of power.

As they left the campsite, Marsh wondered where this trail led. It seemed well traveled despite not having any glows, which begged the question of where it went and just how long it had been in use. Her questions were only partially answered when the trail came to an abrupt end in a tunnel that had been constructed in the time before the world went mad.

Marsh swept her gaze over the walls, wishing she could reach out and touch the ragged chunks of manmade gray stone that clung in random patches between clusters of shrooms, toadstools, and moss. The ground beneath her feet showed two dull and rusty strips of metal, and she wondered why it hadn't been mined, and just how long it had taken for the dirt and debris to fill the gap between them and be packed into the hard trail beneath her feet.

Overhead, the tunnel formed a perfect arch, and she twisted her head, following its curve. Despite her situation, she was in awe. It was no wonder Mikel brought in the best artifacts, and a wonder he'd brought them to Kearick at all. It puzzled her as to why he would when he could access Madame Monetti on his own. Why go to the dealer instead of directly to the customer?

Marsh chewed that over, almost missing when the folk ahead of her slowed and a low moan of despair rode back along them. The sound made her look to the front, even as the guards up front poked and prodded the reluctant leaders forward into a much more open space. She had almost reached the point at which the first of the prisoners had balked when Mordan crashed into her head.

I am here. I follow. I can take the stragglers. Marsh had a clear impression of Ardhur on his mount and the swift desire to see him fall between her sharp teeth and claws before leaping over Marsh's head to snap the neck of the "little one in black."

No, Marsh thought, answering the kat even as she jerked to a halt, looking around to see where Mordan was hiding. *Stay hidden. Follow, but please stay hidden. No hunting.*

Warven's staff slammed into her. Once. Twice. A third time, flattening her to her knees, her head ringing even as Ardhur's line stayed taut and she choked for breath. A low snarl rumbled down the passage, and the mules shied and danced.

Marsh tried to send soothing thoughts to the kat, but she couldn't think straight. Couldn't breathe, couldn't... Warven hit her, again and she curled over her knees, waiting for it to stop. She was glad when Mordan remained silent, even though she could feel the kat's disapproving presence in her skull.

"Up," Ardhur commanded, jerking on the lead when his mule had settled down.

"Up," Warven repeated, jerking on his lead and prodding her with the staff.

Marsh "upped," thinking of what she'd like to do to them, staff and mules included. Ahead of her, the man she was linked to also rose, as did the one in front of him and the woman in front of that man. Watching them, Marsh saw there had been more consequences to her beating than she had realized.

"I'm sorry," she tried to say, and choked on the gag.

Warven's staff nudged her forward, and the whole line

started to proceed once more. She closed her eyes and let her mind drift to the link she had with the hoshkat. Behind her, in the dark, Mordan stalked them, keeping her scent in range and assessing the essential prey keeping Marsh captive. This time, Marsh refrained from saying anything. She just kept putting one foot in front of the other.

As she did, her thoughts turned to Roeglin and the annoying presence he usually was. Curious to see if he was still in her head, Marsh sought him in her mind, but he was nowhere to be found. She tried to reach out to him but couldn't, and fatigue spread through her limbs. She stopped, trying not to think of how much she would miss it if she never heard his voice again.

Her thoughts were brought to an abrupt halt when she ran into the back of the man in front of her. He gave a soft oomph and stumbled forward, just as Warven and Ardhur pulled their leashes tight. Marsh's eyes snapped open, and she backed up a few steps. She was mumbling apologies behind the gag when Ardhur slipped from his mule and took the two paces needed to reach her.

As he raised his hand toward her, Marsh flinched away, but he merely unclipped his lead from her collar.

"We're here," he told her, unclipping the rope that linked her to Warven's mule. "Follow the others—and behave. We'll be watching."

With a shift of his eyes, he indicated the two closest guards and Warven. Marsh followed the look and then looked back at him, but Ardhur wanted an answer and gripped her shoulder.

"Understand?"

Marsh repeated the track her eyes had taken over the

guards and Warven, taking in the staves carried by each. This time when her eyes returned to Ardhur, she nodded. There was no point in trying to say anything since he'd left the gag in place.

To her surprise, he pulled his dagger and stepped behind her, cutting the ropes binding her wrists and forearms. The pain as her circulation returned brought a whimper to her lips. Marsh stifled it, rubbing her arms until the pain subsided. When she didn't reach for the gag, Ardhur slipped it from her head.

"It's hard to eat with this," he said. "You can have it back later."

As if she'd want it, but Marsh didn't reply. She just nodded, again; it was safer that way. Seeing she understood, Ardhur swept his hand toward where the line was moving into a large cavern. The trail ran between two islands of slightly raised stone that looked like they had been tiled a very long time ago. The shrooms had been cleared as far back as she could see, and the loam covering the cavern floor had been scraped back to reveal more of the tiled floor.

It meant they'd be sleeping on something harder than earth, but cleaner, too. Marsh wondered what Ardhur was going to do for stone. It wasn't like he could encase her in ceramic…or could he?

She let her gaze drift around the cavern, taking in the walls, and the people. By the Deep, so many people! They sat in rows, starting at the farthest wall and reaching halfway across the nearest tiled platform. Something in her recoiled at the sight, and Marsh stopped. All she wanted to do was run.

Unfortunately, she was still clipped to the man in front of her, and he had no intention of running. When the rope drew tight between them, he stopped too. This time he turned and looked back. Taking one look at her face, he reached out and took her arm.

"Come on," he said. "You don't want to get into any more trouble than you're already in."

He had a point, and Marsh let him draw her forward, noting that the nearest guards relaxed as she followed his lead.

"Thank you," she murmured, and one of the guards shook his staff in her direction.

Marsh flinched and looked away, but not before she caught something familiar in the cast of her companion's features. He kept hold of her arm until they were settled in a line in front of the nearest row. Once they were all sitting, one of the guards came along the row, dropping a roll into each of their laps. This time Marsh was quick to catch hers.

She was about to raise it to her lips when the man beside her covered her hand with his own.

"Wait," he said, and she realized the guard was watching her with a predatory look on his face.

When Marsh rested her hands in her lap, he cast his gaze down the line and then nodded.

"You may eat," he said, and this time Marsh waited until her companion lifted his roll and took a bite before raising her own.

As Marsh did, however, the guard stepped forward and laid his staff across her forearms.

"Except for you," he said. "You can wait."

Marsh lowered her hands but kept her eyes on the guard's face, refusing to look at her meal. After a long pause, he nodded.

"*Now* you can eat."

"Thank you," Marsh whispered, her stomach lurching as she took a bite.

The guard did not reply, but his mouth tightened with distaste, and he looked back down the line.

"Water!"

Water was given from several shared canteens, and Marsh was grateful there was any left in the bottom of the one that reached her. She drank and waited for whatever was coming next. She was not expecting Ardhur, but she knew what he was there for.

The thought of being encased in stone sent her heart plummeting, and her eyes filled with tears. She still hadn't been able to get any sense that Roeglin knew where she was, and she still hadn't figured a way out of her predicament. She knew there was one; she just hadn't found it yet.

Part of her wanted to beg not to be put back into the stone, and part of her wanted to thoroughly deserve having to go there. That second part might have won if her traveling companion hadn't laid his hand on her knee.

"I will be here," he said even as his face asked the rock mage for permission to fulfill that promise.

Ardhur caught the glance and nodded.

"And you will be responsible if she gets up to anything tonight."

The sudden responsibility didn't deter the man.

"Agreed."

He took Marsh's hand as Ardhur called the rock from

the earth beneath the tiles, keeping her steady when she thought about fleeing. As the stone flowed up her throat and over her head, he added one more thing.

"I'm Patrik, by the way."

It was the last sound Marsh heard until morning, but she felt the weight of his arm on her shoulder and caught the warmth of his hand near the holes beside her nostrils and mouth, and it was enough.

17

COMPANY IN CAPTIVITY

It was a relief when the stone melted away from Marchant's face the next morning. She was stiff and sore when she was finally freed, and no closer to working out how she could escape the stone casing, not that she'd tried very hard.

"Patrik?" she asked, not sure she had heard correctly the previous night.

He nodded, casting a wary glance at the guards. Marsh followed his gaze but kept speaking.

"Fabrice's husband?"

He turned abruptly to face her.

"Yes. Do you know her? Is she okay? Did she—"

He grunted as two of the guards crossed to where they were sitting and drove a staff into his stomach.

"Silence in the lines!"

"Quiet!" added the other guard, striking him a second time.

Marsh reached out and grabbed his staff.

"Hey! I'm as much at fault as—"

It was a mistake. Curling up under the rain of blows that followed, Marsh reminded herself that there were times when she really needed to keep her mouth shut.

But that was not one of them, she told herself. That wouldn't have been fair—and she *had* taken their attention off Patrik. That was good, since Fabrice wouldn't thank her if she got her husband beaten to death just when she'd found him.

She stayed curled up for several long moments after the blows had stopped, waiting until one of the guards nudged her with the toe of his boot. Her hiss of pain must have reassured them that she was still alive because they moved back to their positions by the wall. When she was sure they had left, Marsh uncurled, stifling a groan of pain as she did so.

Patrik gave her a look that said he might be about to offer her sympathy, but Marsh raised a finger to her lips and pulled herself upright.

'I'm fine,' she mouthed, not saying a single word out loud.

His mouth twisted in an expression that said he didn't believe her, but he didn't reply. Marsh wished she could take that haunted look from his face, but knew she couldn't afford to speak the words it needed. She settled for resting her hand on his knee instead. After a minute, he rested his hand over hers, and they sat like that until the guards made their rounds.

After they'd been fed and watered and taken to the latrines, they were settled back in their lines and ordered to silence. Marsh watched the guards, wondering when they'd move them out. She wished she had something to do or that they were allowed to talk, but she knew better than to push that boundary again.

It wasn't long before she discovered what was going on, since the guards were under no obligation to keep quiet.

"When do you think they'll arrive?" one asked as they walked past, making a cursory check of their prisoners.

"Word is they're expected late in the day."

"So we'll be here one more night, then?"

"Just one."

Another shipment? Marsh huffed out a long sigh and tried to calculate how many hours had passed since she'd woken. It was too depressing to think about.

Her sigh drew the attention of the two guards, and they turned to regard her. Marsh looked right back and was unnerved when they exchanged secretive smiles and strolled away.

"Do you think she knows?" one asked.

The other shook his head.

"Not a clue."

They kept walking, leaving Marsh to wonder what they were talking about. She resisted the urge to shout after them and concentrated on the tiles between her feet. There wasn't much else she could do. She still couldn't contact Roeglin, but she didn't think she had tossed him out of her head again. This time, it was more like he hadn't been there to begin with.

Her boredom continued until mid-morning, when there was an outraged screech and yowl, followed by shouting. The sound had Marsh on her feet—and jerked back off them just as fast when Patrik grabbed the line joining them together and pulled her down. He caught her hands when she reached up to unclip the leash, stopping her before she could start.

It wasn't enough to keep her out of trouble, though.

Four guards were on them in the blink of an eye. If Marsh hadn't known any better, she would have said they'd been waiting for her reaction, and they took great satisfaction in adding another layer of bruises to her hide. That wasn't the worst of it, though.

Patrik also bore the consequences of her actions, and they were both left panting and bleeding at the end of the row.

"Told you we'd hold you responsible for her actions." Ardhur had come to stand just in front of them.

Patrik spat blood and rolled himself into a sitting position.

"*Oui*. You did."

Beyond tilting her head a fraction so she could see Ardhur's boots, Marsh didn't try to move. Truth be told, she didn't think she could. Everything hurt, from her skin to her soul. All she wanted was to be back at Monsieur Gravine's mansion, facing whatever disciplinary action was coming her way. It couldn't be any worse than this.

She worked at staying as still as she could, and decided she was okay right where she was. After all, she'd found Patrik, and she'd be willing to bet that the young man casting anxious glances from beside him was the Raph who had saved Eveline by dumping a pile of dirty washing on her head. He didn't speak, however, just regarded his boss with brown eyes dark with concern.

Ardhur, though, knelt beside Marsh and unclipped the rope linking her to the rest of the line.

"I think it would be better if we did not give her the opportunity to cause you any more pain."

To Marsh's surprise, Patrik disagreed.

"I don't think she'll do that, again," he said. "You can leave her with me."

Ardhur snorted and pivoted on his heels to look at the man.

"I'll meet you halfway," he said. "I'll leave her with you, but I'll make sure she can't cause any more trouble."

He paused, then pulled Marsh out of her ball, setting her on her side and then putting her hands under her head as though she was sleeping. With one hand on her shoulder, he called the stone, but, to Marsh's surprise, he didn't cover her head, stopping the stone once it had flowed over her legs and shoulders, trapping her hands to the floor.

"Before I tuck you in for the night, there is something you need to see," he told her and turned slightly to direct her attention toward the tunnel.

As much as she didn't want to, Marsh followed the turn and felt her heart sink with despair. Mordanlenoowar came into view, dangling upside down from a pole carried by four shadow mages. The big kat's eyes blazed with azure fire, and her lips were lifted in an angry snarl.

Marsh tried to go to the kat's aid, but the stone locked her to the floor. Catching sight of the movement, Ardhur stared down at her, letting her watch as a cage was rolled into view. From the sound its wheels made on the tiled floor, it had been drawn from a chamber beyond the last line of prisoners. Marsh watched as the kat was loaded into it and saw her roll to her feet as soon as the poles were slid free of her bindings.

I will get you out of there, she said, knowing her eyes flared green and not caring.

Or I will free you from there, the kat replied, curling up on the floor of the cage.

"As touching as this reunion is, I think you've seen enough," Ardhur said, blocking the kat from view by crouching between them.

Fear coiled through Marsh as the stone flowed from her shoulders to her neck and then over her head, but she refused to beg. He would let her out of the stone soon enough, and by then she would have a plan.

18

A STEP THROUGH THE DARK

M archant didn't have a plan. She'd lain for hours in what felt like a soundless, viewless coffin. Her mind had ranged from near panic to fatalistic calm. She couldn't work out how to escape and was too tired to manage more than a brief attempt at turning to shadow.

That was the easy part, but when it came to filtering herself through the narrow gaps that made up the holes for her mouth and nose, she froze. She could *feel* the stone squeezing around her, but couldn't work out how to lose the shape she usually had in order to extricate herself from her prison's confines.

And she still couldn't talk to the stone.

She tried, but it was the same as when she tried to charge the glows. The stone wouldn't speak to her, and the effort left her exhausted. When she was trembling with fatigue from the effort, Marsh let herself relax. She'd only meant to rest for a moment, but it was much later when she woke to the feeling of the stone slowly parting around her.

Except that this time it was different.

When Ardhur freed her in the morning, the stone flowed off her in the exact reverse of how it had flowed on. What she was experiencing now was more like the stone was being peeled away like clay from around a stone. Marsh came to with a gasp and a hand was clapped over her mouth, one finger gently tapping her lips in a request for silence.

She would have nodded her understanding, but her head wasn't free. She had the oddest sensation that a small pair of hands was pulling the stone away from her, less like clay and more like paper. What in all the Deeps was going on?

When enough had been cleared to expose her shoulders, another much larger set of hands wormed their way under her arms and pulled.

It wasn't enough and she got caught in the folds of stone, muffling a cry of pain as it grated against her skin. The pulling ceased, and the small hands went back to peeling it away from her body. Only this time, they concentrated on her head, clearing the rock blocking her ears.

Once that was done, the small hands reassuringly patted her back, hesitating when Marsh gasped with pain.

"Gently," came Patrik's voice. "They beat her pretty badly."

"Typical," Roeglin replied, keeping his own voice soft. Marsh couldn't tell whether it was typical of her to need a beating or typical of the raiders to deliver one.

Both, Roeglin said. *Now go into shadow form.*

Shadow form? Okay.

Marsh focused on blending with the darkness around them, willing her body to become one with the shadows yet separate from them. As she did so, Roeglin slipped his hands under her arms and pulled. This time, her body bent and flowed enough for her to slip free of the shell.

"And back," Roeglin said before turning to the person who'd freed her.

"Marsh is hurt," he said, pausing when the little girl gasped, but Aisha didn't need any instruction.

"I fix," she said, and Marsh winced as she felt two small warm patches of pressure settle against the back of her armor.

Before long, she felt much better and was able to stand up without wanting to cry out in pain. The sick feeling that had dogged her every move had faded, and she bent down to wrap her arms around the child.

"*Merci.*"

What she wanted to do was pick the little girl up and race her clear of the prisoners and their guards, but Aisha flashed her a smile, her teeth glinting in the dark.

"Who next?"

We're freeing the prisoners, Roeglin said, *while the founder and his men keep the raiders busy.*

Which explained the sounds of battle coming from the other end of the ancient hall.

"We have to get Mordan out of the cage."

"Me do." and Aisha slipped out of Marsh's grasp before she could stop her.

"Wait!" she called, throttling her shout to a whisper as she caught sight of guards emerging from the far wall.

She ducked, but they raced toward the battle without

appearing to have heard or seen her. Breathing a sigh of relief, she looked around for Roeglin and saw him moving steadily down the line, unclipping neck lines and quietly rousing prisoners.

Get the kat, then lead these guys down to the next junction. He flashed a map into her head. *You know the one?*

Marsh *did* know the junction. It was the one she'd passed through not two days ago.

Good. Get them there. Henri and Jakob will walk them clear.

Without waiting for any more instructions, Marsh hurried after Aisha. When she got back to the mansion, she was going to strangle Roeglin. He had no right to put the child in this much danger.

She snuck out after us. You and I are going to talk about the examples you set.

This was *her* fault? But Marsh didn't have time to be any more outraged than that. Aisha had reached the cage, her eyes flaring green as she talked to the kat.

Marsh looked around for Scruffknuckled and the kits, but didn't see them. Again, Roeglin was quick to answer.

She left them behind under the covers so everyone thought she was still in bed. It gave her time to catch up with us... on the mule she'd "borrowed."

Little brat, Marsh thought, but Aisha made a small sound of frustration and caught Marsh's eye.

"I not talk to metal," she said, sounding very much like she was sulking.

"I'll get it," Marsh said, relieved when she saw that the raiders hadn't bothered locking the door with more than a bolt.

"Arrogant sons of the Dark," she muttered, and heard Aisha gasp.

"Dat's rude."

"*Oui*," Marsh told her, pulling the bolt clear and opening the door. "It really is."

Aisha giggled and raced around to meet the kat as she came out. Marsh swung her off the floor, and set her on Mordan's back, ignoring the kat's muffled grumble of protest.

"Later," she said. "For now, you need to get my cub to safety."

To her relief, Mordan seemed to understand what she wanted; the big kat turned and headed for the junction. Marsh was about to follow when she remembered Roeglin's instructions and looked back at the prisoners he'd been freeing. They'd gathered a respectful distance from the cage, but now they moved toward her.

Marsh gestured toward where the kat was carrying Aisha down the tunnel.

"Follow the kat," she said, searching their faces for the one she most wanted to return with.

It took her a few minutes to find him, but when she did, she realized Patrik was moving in the wrong direction. She moved against the tide of men and women intent on following the kat and finally caught up to him.

"I have to find the boys," he said when he saw her. His eyes scanned the cavern. "I have to…"

Marsh grabbed him by the arm.

"We're moving everyone back to the founder's mansion. *Everyone*," she emphasized, shaking his arm. "I'd hate for them to make it and you be recaptured."

"But I'm their father," he said, gesturing helplessly at the people moving past them. "I'm supposed to be looking after them."

"Then get yourself to where they'll be going."

"You don't understand!"

Marsh remembered how she'd felt when she'd seen Aisha in the tunnels and knew how she felt, now, letting the little girl lead a bunch of strangers up a tunnel to where her friends were supposed to be waiting.

"I think I do," she said, "and Fabrice will murder me if I let you get caught again."

She shook his arm again.

"If they're not there, I will find them. You are not the only ones I've promised to find. Please."

She was thinking of asking him not to make her drag him out of there but didn't have to. Roeglin joined them.

"That's everyone," he said, then scowled. "What are you still doing here? You're supposed to be leading so Henri and Jakob don't kill anyone."

"I've got Aisha doing that. I think they'll recognize her and the kat." She indicated the farmer at her side. "Patrik's looking for his sons."

"Well, they aren't behind me. I've cleared the cavern. They'll be with the rest..." He paused and then shook his head. "Come on. We'll sort out who we've got when we've got them to safety. We still have to get them past the Monetti place."

That got Patrik moving, although whether it was because of the danger of the raiders gaining reinforcements from Madame Monetti or because he hoped to find his children among the prisoners who'd headed back up the tunnel, Marsh didn't know. As they started back, there was a shout from the other end of the cavern—the end where Roeglin had said Monsieur Gravine and his men were battling the raiders.

Roeglin stopped, his eyes flashing silver, and Marsh pushed Patrik in the direction he needed to go.

"Tell Henri and Jakob Marsh says go."

"Don't worry, I've told them." Roeglin had come out of his head in time to hear her instructions. He glanced back toward where the sounds of battle had ended, and from where they could hear the sound of running feet. He grabbed Marsh's hand and ran back down the tunnel, Patrik keeping pace beside them.

"What is it?" the farmer asked, and Roeglin glanced over his shoulder once more.

"The raiders called for reinforcements. I'm going to need Aisha's help to seal the tunnel."

"I'll fetch her," Marsh said, trying to pull her hand free of his. He didn't let go, though, gripping more tightly to prevent her from leaving.

"I've already called," he said, and glanced at Patrik. "You'll have to come with us."

To give him credit, the farmer did not argue; he merely came back to Roeglin.

"What do I need to do?" he asked as the hoshkat arrived carrying Aisha on her back.

They stepped aside at the rumble of mulish hoofbeats, and Monsieur Gravine and almost twenty riders swept past them. As soon as the last mule had vanished into the darkness, Roeglin began running.

"We need to close the junction," he cried. "We can't stop what's coming."

Marsh wanted to ask what exactly *was* coming, but she didn't need to. She could already hear it.

Clawed hands scraped over stone, and voices screeched in gibbering howls that sent tremors up and down Marsh's spine before dancing over her skin like a thousand taloned fingers. Hoshkat and humans fled as one. No wonder the mules had been moving so fast!

Although the junction wasn't too far from them, by the time they'd reached it, the sound of hunting shadow monsters was too close for comfort.

"Bring it down, Aysh!" Roeglin ordered, plucking the little girl from the hoshkat's back and placing her at the edge of the tunnel opening.

Marsh was relieved to see he didn't take his arms from around the little girl's waist. Seeing Aisha close her eyes, she stepped around them, pulling a sword and shield from the surrounding shadows and preparing to defend them if she had to. She heard Roeglin's protest in her mind as she stepped into the tunnel on the other side of the arch.

Don't!

Behind her, she heard the rumble and crack of rock and started to take a step back toward the opening, knowing she was going to be too slow.

"Marsh!"

Aisha's shrill cry was followed by startled shouts from Patrik and Roeglin. Their cries were accompanied by the roar of falling rock and then Mordan was beside her, Aisha dangling from her jaws like a runaway kit.

"*Merde*! You two are supposed to be on the other side of that!"

"Bad Marsh!" Aisha started, but Roeglin had no time for arguments.

Run! he shouted from the other side of the barrier, pushing the order through her mind with a mental shove for her to do exactly as he said. Marsh was bolting down the corridor before she was aware her legs could move that fast.

Mordan ran beside her, a white-faced Aisha still in her mouth.

Marsh took the child from the kat's grip and turned her around to put her back on the kat's shoulders. *Now* the little brat should have a chance.

Run, Mordan! Get the cub to safety.

Run with the shadows, Mordan told her, sharing the mental image of a shadowy Marsh running after her through the cavern.

Marsh didn't stop to argue. She sent an agreement through the link between them and focused on becoming one with the shadows.

Mordan roared in her head and leapt away, and Marsh realized the kat could always have paced her as a shadow, except for when she'd transported herself through... the... shad...

Marsh stopped.

Mordan!

She almost sobbed with relief when the kat skidded to a halt, circled, and came racing back.

Come with me, Marsh told her burying her hand in the ruff of Mordan's neck.

The Deep help me, she thought, picturing the tunnel beyond the junction in her mind. She didn't think it mattered what direction she was running in as long as she knew exactly where she wanted to be. She only hoped she could take the kat and the child with her.

"Hold onto me," she ordered Aisha, lifting her from the kat's back and turning on the spot.

If this didn't work, she was coming right back here to defend them from the pursuing horde. All she could hope was that it wasn't going to come to that; that the kat and child would be considered extensions of herself as she moved from human solidity to part-shadow.

Run with me, Marsh commanded, showing the kat what she was doing.

The hoshkat obeyed, running beside her, careful not to tear herself free of Marsh's grip. As they leapt into the darkness, the shadow monsters screaming in their wake, Marsh focused on becoming one with the shadows and taking Aisha and the kat with her—and then she thought of a distinctive stalagmite and rock cluster she'd passed when she was Ardhur's prisoner.

There! They were going to step from here...to...*there*, through the shadows and the dark from one point to another, because the shadows were connected just like the caverns were.

Her foot hit the ground and she stumbled, and then she remembered to open her eyes and ran smack into the rock formation she'd been picturing in her head. It was like running into a cavern wall; *exactly* like running into a cavern wall. Marsh heard Aisha give a squeak of protest as she bounced off the rocks and dropped like a stone.

Beside her Mordan twisted mid-stride, breaking Marsh's grip, and hitting the formation side on before landing on all fours.

"Bad Marsh!" Aisha muttered, pulling herself free of Marsh's arms. "Bad, bad Marsh."

When Marsh didn't reply, the little girl hesitated and then moved over to touch Marsh's face. Marsh tried to get up, but couldn't find the strength. She felt as wrung out as a wet dishcloth.

"Give it a minute, kid," she said, her voice slurring with fatigue as she tried to get Aisha to come into focus. "I need…"

What did she need? Her head spun, but Marsh fought it. She needed to be away, by all the Deep.

"I help," Aisha said, laying her other hand on Marsh's forehead. "Ouch."

Yeah, kid. Ouch. Marsh thought as Aisha's touch sent echoes of agony ringing through her head. Even the emerald glow coming off the kid's hands was painful. Why did she have to *glow*? Her irritation turned to concern when the glow shuddered and then went out.

"All gone."

Not quite, Marsh wanted to say since her headache was still there, but she heard voices and knew they had to move. She had to get them under cover. They hadn't come this far only to be caught again.

Again, Marsh tried to get to her feet, but again her body refused to cooperate—and Aisha was no help. The kid had settled across her chest and was a dead weight. Marsh wanted to tell her there wasn't any time for cuddles, but she figured there wasn't any time for *that*, either. Instead, she reached out to the shadows.

"Cover us," she said, hoping Mordan had either curled up close enough to share their blanket of shadow or found her own hiding place nearby.

The shadows rippled, but they would not come. Marsh's head pounded with effort, and she tried again. Maybe asking nicely?

"Please cover us."

But the shadows would not listen, and the two figures, one in the dark armor of a shadow mage and one looking more like a caravan guard, saw them. Marsh's spirits sank, and then the shadow mage let out a shout of surprise and ran toward her.

"Marsh!" He turned excitedly to the man with him. "Patrik! She made it! They made it! They're here!"

For Shadow's sake, he didn't have to sound so surprised. Of *course*, she'd made it, and just what was he doing here, anyway?

"Roeglin?"

Marsh couldn't figure out why in all the Deeps he was so excited, and she couldn't stay awake to ask. Fatigue rolled over her and sucked her under as he reached her, his look shifting from excitement to frustration.

Just how much trouble was she in, anyway?

And why in all the Deep did he think she needed him?

19

THE MISSING

"Of all the bone-headed, bone-deep stupid, idiotic, infuriatingly—"

"You done yet...*Master*?" Marsh asked, spraying Roeglin with crumbs.

She was starving, and he'd split the supplies he'd been carrying between her and Aisha. Of course, he'd refused to give her the cookies until she'd eaten the shroom-bread and cheese. He didn't seem to care how much faster they'd have restored her energy.

On top of that, she already *knew* just how dumb she'd been; she didn't need him to tell her *again*! If he kept it up, she wasn't going to feel sorry about it; she was just going to get Mordan to eat him.

She saw Roeglin's eyes flash white.

Nice. He still didn't sound happy, but at least he'd stopped trying to yell at her and whisper at the same time.

"We're going when you're done," he told Marsh, handing Aisha a cookie.

"Hey!"

"She's finished her roll."

Aisha waved her cookie and took the biggest bite she could stuff into her tiny mouth.

"Showoff!" Marsh muttered when the child grinned at her through a mouthful of crumbs.

But she finished off the second roll that Roeglin had insisted she eat and then stuck out her hand. Smirking, he placed two cookies in it.

"Hey!" Aisha wasn't impressed, but Roeglin turned to her, one finger upraised.

"She had two rolls, so she gets two cookies."

He was trying to sound reasonable, and Patrik snorted.

"It's like dealing with *my* kids," he remarked. "Same old, same old."

Marsh stopped chewing. It was hard to protest with a mouth full of cookie crumbs, so she glared.

"If the shoe fits," Roeglin told her, catching her look. She turned her glare to him.

Smart ass.

I can hear you, you know.

So he could. That had possibilities. Marsh wondered what she'd have to think about to discourage him from looking inside her head...and then she wondered if she really wanted to stoop that low.

You could try, he said, *but later. Right now, we have to move.*

Marsh stood up and dusted cookie crumbs out of her armor. As she did, she caught a whiff of herself after three days of exertion and no bath. Oh, by the Dark. How could Roeglin even stand being that close to her?

He didn't reply, just picked up his pack, set Aisha on her feet, and glanced at Mordan. The hoshkat got to her feet and stretched, yawning to show an impressive set of fangs. Patrik stared at her, and kept staring as the kat padded over to Aisha and nudged her. The little girl turned to Roeglin.

"Up," she demanded, patting Mordan's back. "Dan says up."

Roeglin obliged, setting Aisha on the kat's shoulders. Once she was settled, the five of them started moving back down the trail Marsh had taken just a few short days before. At least this time her hands weren't tied. The journey seemed to take a lot less time, and soon they were moving past the grotto where Marsh had spent her first night of captivity. She was glad when they didn't stop.

The way she calculated it, they had at least a day's journey ahead of them, and the next part of it would take them through the junction not far from Madame Monetti's mansion. And that reminded her...

"Did you get a hold of Madame Monetti?"

Roeglin shook his head.

"No. We tried when you disappeared. Monsieur Gravine sent a squad down to look for you, but she swore black and blue that you hadn't been there and there was nothing to prove otherwise. They searched but didn't find the passage leading to this one, and then Madame Monetti kicked them out. Said she was insulted by the way she was being treated, and that the founder would be hearing about it. Without proof, they had to leave."

"But you *knew* I'd gone there..."

"And I was held up interrogating the raiders we'd managed to capture." He looked torn. "I'm the only mind mage in the caverns, Marsh. I go where I'm most needed, and I don't always get to choose. Monsieur Gravine decided he needed me to question them."

"And you couldn't say no?"

"I asked him to wait, but he didn't, so I came after you, as soon as we were done."

From the shudder in his voice, "done" hadn't been pleasant. He shook it off, though, and continued.

"She said she'd never heard of you, hadn't seen you, and asked if you were a courier for Kearick. Apparently, he should choose his people better and ensure he makes his deliveries on time. I told Monsieur Gravine she was lying, and he had us search the junction and the trail rather than press the point. It also gave him an excuse to station a squad at the junction near the Monetti place, but that was the best he could do without evidence. She's still respected in Ruins Hall."

"She *was*." Patrik sounded grim, his voice making Marsh jump. The big farmer had been traveling in silence up until that point. Now his voice was hard with determination. "I'll make sure folk know exactly what she's done. Her lines of supply will dry up, and she'll have no choice but to run to the raiders or admit what she's done and make amends."

Given those options, Marsh was pretty sure what the woman would do.

"And we could catch her when she ran."

Roeglin shook his head.

"We've got you. We don't need any other evidence, because I can pull the memories from your head at the trial."

"And what then?" Patrick asked.

"Then she'll be executed," Roeglin said, the utter calm in

his voice coming as both a shock and a relief to Marsh. "We don't have the people to spare to guard prisoners, or the resources, and we can't let them go, knowing they'll come back and do more harm."

The reality of it made Marsh feel just a little bit ill, but she couldn't think of a real alternative. Roeglin was right; they *didn't* have the resources to allow themselves the luxury of imprisoning someone who wanted to do the community harm, and the idea of letting them go so they could return with stronger forces and use their knowledge of the caverns against everyone was ludicrous.

Patrik had no such qualms.

"I'd say dispense with the trial for any of them," he said, and Roeglin laid a hand on the man's arm.

"Trials and questioning help us find out if there are any worth saving."

"They're not the ones who need saving."

Privately, Marsh agreed with him, but she didn't say so out loud. Roeglin had to have a reason for what he was saying. If he did, though, the shadow mage didn't bring it up. He just patted Patrik on the shoulder and kept them moving down the tunnel.

They were an hour's walk away from the junction when Mordan stopped, curling her lip in a warning snarl. Marsh looked down the tunnel, moving to the cover of the shadows at the edge of the tunnel before crouching, and asking the shadows to show her what was coming. Roeglin mirrored her actions, dragging Patrik into the shelter of a cluster of shrooms standing tall on the other side of the path.

When he'd dragged the man into their shelter, they

faded from view, and Marsh realized the shadow mage had called the shadows to cover them. Before she could think to do the same, the shadow threads answered, bringing her pictures of a heavily armed and armored group riding down the tunnel. Marsh held her breath.

Just how many raiders *did* Madame Monetti have holed up in her mansion, anyway?

She tweaked the threads, wanting a closer look at their faces, and gave a shaky sigh of relief. She'd seen their leader before, but not at the head of a group of raiders. She'd seen him leading the charge against the raiders at the farm, coming in behind Monsieur Gravine to take out the raiders trying to beat their way into the barn.

The man beside him had helped the farmer and his family out of the shadows at the back of their house and been the first to lay a hand on Mordan's head in friendship. The woman beside him had been one of the guards to greet her when she'd first arrived at the mansion.

Marsh slowly rose from behind the rocks, signaling Roeglin to do the same, and calling the hoshkat to her side.

"Friends," she said, walking forward.

Mordan stuck close to her side, dividing her attention between Marsh and the road ahead. If Marsh hadn't known any better, she would have thought the big kat was nervous.

"Stay close," Roeglin told Patrik. "We're about to meet some Protectors. They'll help us."

"I'm glad to hear it," came a voice on the path behind them, and they whirled to face it.

At first, the woman's shape was an indistinct outline, but as they turned, it became clearer, the outline firming into flesh. The first thing Marsh noticed was the crossbow aimed at the center of her chest. The second was the way the woman released the tension on the string and lowered it.

They stood, staring at one another for a long moment, and then the woman smiled.

"I was hoping we'd meet you. Monsieur Gravine said we should look for you on the path."

He had?

"The raiders summoned shadow monsters to cover their trail. We blocked the tunnel to make sure they did not follow."

The woman's smile faded.

"That is good to know. Monsieur Gravine said the raiders got away with some of the prisoners. We're going after them."

As she spoke, Marsh heard the sound of hoofs on the trail behind them. Turning slightly, she saw the riders the shadows had shown her. Roeglin followed her look.

"Captain Orelia," he said. "I am glad to see you."

"And I you," the man boomed, sliding from his mule and coming to greet Roeglin with outstretched arms. "I thought we'd lost you."

"Did you get them all away?"

The man's face darkened.

"It's as Petrine says; the raiders escaped with some of their catch." His eyes shifted to Patrik. "At least they have one less than we thought."

As if on cue, Patrik closed the distance between them.

"Tell me," he said. "There were two boys. They were with me in the field when the raiders came. One would have been sixteen, the other twelve. They would have asked for me..."

His voice trailed off as the captain shook his head.

"There were several youngsters, but they were all claimed by their parents. I'm sorry. You're not the only parent to be missing children. It's why we're going back."

As he spoke the last sentence, he turned back to the mule and swung into the saddle.

"Monsieur Gravine says we must hurry."

He turned his attention to Roeglin, leaving Patrik to stare at him in disbelief.

"What did you say about shadow monsters?"

"They must have released a score or more into the tunnel behind us." Roeglin gestured toward Aisha. "The girl brought down the entrance and blocked them out. I don't know how you're going to get through."

The captain gathered his reins and glanced over his shoulder.

"A contingent of rock wizards arrived while you were out chasing your gi—" He caught sight of Marsh and cleared his throat. "Trainee! We brought two of them with us, along with a half-dozen of your shadow-mage friends."

Roeglin looked past him, but the mules were lined up two abreast, and he soon returned his attention to the captain.

After a moment's silence, the captain continued. "We'll go after them hard to try to get everyone back," he said, digging his mule in the ribs and starting forward, "and we'll take out the shadow monsters on the way."

Marsh remembered the chorus of howling noise that

had assaulted her ears back in the tunnels and hoped Roeglin's estimate of a score or more was still accurate.

Don't worry, he assured her. *I can see your memory. It's close.*

Marsh could only hope it was close enough to not get the patrol killed.

Give me a little credit.

But he didn't say it out loud, taking Patrik by the arm instead and leading him to the side of the path.

Mordan followed the movement, eyed the mounted squad, and moved off the trail too, taking herself behind a clump of rocks despite Aisha's protests that she couldn't see. Marsh followed them and stood in front of the rocks, hoping her scent so close to the kat's would help calm the mules. She glanced back at the scout who had confronted them on the trail and saw the woman shift back into shadow and vanish into the dark.

As the captain drew alongside them, Patrik darted out onto the path, frightening the mule and causing it to shy. The captain gave a startled yell, cursing as he brought the animal back under control. Roeglin hurried after Patrik, trying to grab his arm, but Patrik shook him off.

"I'm coming too," he said. "They're my sons. My responsibility."

Steadying the mule beneath him, the captain shook his head.

"I'm sorry, but no. You're not equipped and not armed."

"I can borrow a sword. I know how to fight."

The captain dug his heels into the side of his mule, nudging the animal past Patrik.

"No," he said.

"You can't stop me following you," he said, shaking Roeglin's hand loose, and turning to walk alongside the mule.

The captain ignored him, apparently content to have the farmer walk beside him. Patrik did not notice when the scout slipped out of the shadows behind him, but he crumpled beneath the blow from her staff. The captain drew the mule to a halt and glanced back at Roeglin.

"Will you be able to manage him?"

Roeglin looked from the fallen man to the captain and shrugged.

"We have help coming."

Marsh did her best to keep her expression neutral. Help? That was the first *she'd* heard of it, but she nodded when the captain glanced her way, watching as the scout melted into the dark. After giving the pair of them a very doubtful look, the captain shrugged.

"As long as you're sure you can manage," he said.

They both nodded, and Marsh noticed that Roeglin's face was a blank as hers.

The captain frowned but nudged his mule into a walk and then a trot.

"Safe wanderings," he said, not looking back, and the double column of soldiers trotted by.

Marsh caught sight of the rock wizards as they passed, and the darkly garbed shadow mages, but neither group acknowledged them, and she didn't recognize anyone among them.

20

IN SEARCH OF MADAME MONETTI

Marchant waited until the last of the soldiers and mages had passed them and continued out of sight down the tunnel before she turned to Roeglin.

"We have help coming?" she asked as Mordan crept out from behind her pile of rocks.

Aisha slid from the big kat's back.

"Do they have cookies?"

Roeglin sighed and bent down to haul Patrik's unconscious body over his shoulders.

"Not really, and no," he said, answering both questions.

"It's bad to lie," Aisha scolded and started walking the way they'd been going when they met the patrol.

Marsh walked after her, tilting her head and raising her eyebrows at the shadow mage as she passed.

"You hear that, Master Ro? It's bad to lie." She didn't wait for him to respond, but kept walking, listening for his footsteps as she went. Her mind worked furiously over what the captain had told them: the raiders had gotten away with some of their captives. The younger ones, people's children…

It made her sick, and she forced her mind to think back over what she'd seen in the muddled events of their escape. She remembered the shadow-mage shadows she'd seen sliding along the wall when she'd been getting Patrik and the kat free. At the time, she'd thought they'd been going to join the battle, but now she realized they'd been going for the prisoners held closest to the walls—the children that had been separated from their parents, presumably as a means of keeping the grownups under control.

A lump formed in her throat, and she glanced over her shoulder in the direction the riders had gone. People's children, their families…and she'd promised Patrik that they'd gotten them all, that his children had gone ahead—

"Don't beat yourself up over it," Roeglin told her, clearly reading her thoughts, and answering them aloud. "You're the reason we got any of them back at all."

Like that was supposed to make her feel any better. She'd just been lucky things had gone so very wrong when she'd gone to confront Madame Monetti.

"That's one way of looking at it," Roeglin snarked, but he didn't sound very happy about it.

Marsh waited for him to have another go at her about being stupid and boneheaded, but he surprised her with a short bark of laughter.

"I wouldn't dare," he told her, and shot a look at where Mordan was walking beside Aisha. "I don't want to get eaten."

Marchant's cheeks colored. That had been a private

thought, one borne of frustration that he was both right and very, very wrong.

"No wrong about it, trainee, and when we get back to the mansion, the founder and I are going to talk to you about consequences."

And this day just kept getting better...but he *had* reminded her that he could speak to the founder.

"I don't suppose you could have a little chat to him about helping us so that meeting can happen faster," she snapped. "The suspense is killing me."

Behind her, she heard Roeglin take a breath as though he was going to tell her how boneheaded *that* idea was as well, but he didn't.

Instead, there was silence, then he spoke. "Done."

She stopped. "Really?"

"Really, and thank you; I should have thought of that before."

Yes, he should, but she wasn't going to rub it in.

"Uh huh." Marsh sighed. It wasn't her fault that he was dumb enough to go looking inside her head.

"And there you go, calling your master dumb again."

"That was the first time..." Marsh protested, hoping it was true since she couldn't remember if she had or hadn't called him that before.

He snickered.

"Keep walking. They're not far off."

"Do they have cookies?" Clearly, Aisha had been listening to a lot more than she appeared to be. Marsh made a note to be very careful what she discussed when the child was around.

Noted.

At least Roeglin was paying attention to the important things, as well as stuff he'd be better off keeping his nose out of. There was nothing to say after that. Aisha insisted on walking, even though Mordan stayed right beside her.

"I walk," she said when Marsh asked her if she wanted to ride. "Kitty tired."

The kitty gave a brief yawn and lashed her tail in what Marsh took to be frustration. She wasn't the only one worried about the little girl's well-being, even if it wouldn't hurt the child to walk.

"They're here," Roeglin called as Mordan grumbled out a warning.

The big kat wasn't alarmed, though. She tensed, then sniffed the air and relaxed, padding forward until Marsh picked out the heat and shapes of a group of people moving toward them. This time she didn't bother tweaking the shadow threads; Tamlin's shout of recognition was enough.

The boy raced out of the gloom ahead, and Aisha ran to meet him. Marsh recognized Brigitte's familiar form as the female journeyman followed him.

"Cookies!" Aisha cried, catching sight of her, and Roeglin and Marsh echoed Tamlin's embarrassed groan.

"No cookies for you," Brigitte snapped back, but Aisha remained undaunted, flinging her arms around the shadow mage's waist.

"I love you, Jurman Brij."

Marsh had to smother a smile as the woman knelt and hugged the child back.

"I love you, too, Apprentice Brat."

Aisha giggled and grabbed Brigitte's hand, turning to offer her free hand to her brother.

"I crashed a wall," she told them as Brigitte led them to the edge of the path and proved that there were indeed cookies, and that some of them were Aisha's.

Marchant glanced at Roeglin, and he moved up beside her, one hand keeping Patrik steady as the leader of the group stepped forward.

"Master Leger?" he asked, continuing as he shifted his gaze to Marsh. "Trainee Leclerc?"

"*Oui*," they answered in chorus, and Marsh glanced at Roeglin, directing the man's attention that way. He indicated Gustav, who had hurried forward to greet them. "Captain Moldrane will escort your charges back to the manse, but the founder respectfully requests that you accompany me in the arrest of Madame Monetti."

"Do you have a spare mule?" Roeglin asked, indicating Patrik's unconscious form.

Gustav stepped forward, signaling for one of his men to take Patrik from Roeglin's shoulder.

"Let me guess—he's got family with the ones who got away and insisted on trying to tag along with Orelia's squad."

"*Oui*."

"We'll keep an eye on him."

"It's Patrik, Fabrice's husband," Marsh said, and Roeglin turned to stare at her.

She shrugged.

"It didn't come up before."

Gustav looked from one to the other of them.

"Monsieur Gravine wants to see you once you get back."

"We'll be there."

Roeglin answered for both of them and Marsh gave a cursory nod, her eyes tracking to where Tamlin, Aisha, and Brigitte were sitting together, talking animatedly. The desire to go over and join them was like a physical ache in her chest, but the sudden weight of Roeglin's hand on her shoulder shook it away.

"Let's go, Trainee."

She waved, catching Brigitte's eye but following Roeglin before either of the children looked her way. Seconds later, she was dragged to a halt as two sets of arms wrapped around her.

"Bye, Marsh." Tamlin's farewell was gruff, and he held his sister's hand so Marsh could go.

"Bye," Aisha echoed as her brother pulled her gently away,

Marsh managed a shaky smile.

"Bye," she said. "I'll see you when I get back."

It was a good thing Tamlin led Aisha back toward Brigitte because Marsh didn't think she'd have been able to. What surprised her was when Tamlin left Aisha with the journeyman and came racing back across to her.

"Bri...the journeyman said to give you these," he told her, pressing two large cookies into her hands.

He didn't wait for a reply but raced away, leaving Marsh to stare after him as he scooped his sister into his arms and started to move back along the trail, Brigitte by his side. The suddenness of his return and the abruptness of his departure had left her stunned.

"Trainee," Roeglin said, but his command was softened by a compassion that matched the sadness forming an unwieldy lump in Marsh's throat.

She tried to shake it off as the squad split into two groups, Gustav leading Tamlin and Aisha back toward the Founder's home and Roeglin following the other teams' leader to the pillars marking the turnoff to Madame Monetti's mansion. Marsh fell in beside him, forcing herself to focus on the terrain around them as she handed him one of the cookies.

She remembered how the shadow mages had come out of the dark behind her and searched for them now. Swallowing the sadness at leaving the children behind again, Marsh drew a long, slow breath and then let it out. She needed to be ready for anything.

The cookie was gone by the time they crossed the strange expanse of white rock fringed by partial white pillars. Marsh took another breath and closed her eyes. When she opened them again, she requested to see what stood in the shadow. She wanted to see the things that were one with the shadow yet stood apart from them. She wanted to see what life forces beat along the shadow threads.

Laying a hand on Roeglin's shoulder so she wouldn't be left behind, Marchant opened her eyes and scanned the cavern around them. Heat and light met her gaze and the shadows spoke too, showing her what and who lay in wait around them. Men and women had blended with the shadows, standing next to the pillars or crouching beneath the sheltering caps of half-grown callas.

Marsh frowned. Even two days ago, she couldn't recall

there being callas, and the shrooms didn't grow that fast, not that she'd ever heard. It was a puzzle for another day, however, as she dragged a dart from the shadows and flung it at the mage standing near the pillar closest the path leading to Monetti's front door.

Roeglin had done his usual thing in pulling the images from her mind and mirrored her movement by casting a second dart and taking out the mage next to her target. He must have been doing something else too because the squad leader shouted an alarm.

"Incoming!"

Incoming? Well, Marsh guessed he could call it that, because she could sense the shadows trembling. She knew that somewhere a mage was opening a gate and calling in shadow monsters. Even as she thought it, it occurred to her that they could be opening a gate for another reason.

Madame Monetti might be looking for a way to escape.

"We need to get to the door!"

She and Roeglin turned to the path leading to the mansion's entrance, and Marsh realized they were surrounded.

"Sorry," she said, wishing she'd thought to use her powers before.

"Just do something about it!" Roeglin snarled, stepping away from her as he pulled twin blades from the air.

Her warning had ruined the surprise attack the raiders had planned and they emerged out of the shadows now, pulling blades and staffs as they came. It was better than being skewered by a dozen arrows or darts, but not by much. Once they closed in, her people would be outnumbered, and Marsh already knew the raider mages were battle-hardened. They were certainly harder than the Founder's makeshift army of guards.

There was only one thing to do.

Marsh raised her hands, pulling the shadows toward herself, and then she pushed her hands forward and the shadows exploded outwards, knocking the raiders back. After that Marsh called the darkness, raining ink-black spears onto them before they could stand and concentrating her fire on the half of the cavern she could see.

Somewhere in the back of her mind, she could hear Roeglin shouting, but he wasn't shouting at her, so it didn't matter. Marsh hammered the ground to her right until nothing moved, and then she turned and wove her way through her allies, making a circular movement with her hand to direct the lightning around the edges of the square.

Roeglin kept shouting and the soldiers surged around her, moving so that they stood behind her. Once she got a clear view of the other side, Marsh saw that some of her own people were still engaged with the enemy, whether because they hadn't heard Roeglin's warning or because they couldn't break away, it didn't matter. They were still there, and she couldn't rain the shadows down.

But the shadows were waiting, dark lightning hammering the perimeter, and she wasn't sure she could consolidate it into a single solid strike. Instead, she walked it forward, taking out anyone who didn't move out of the way but careful to keep just beyond combatants on her side.

As the shadows lanced down, combatants from both sides fled. The founder's soldiers parting to let their comrades return, using deadly force to stop any raiders who followed them in an attempt to escape the raining dark.

Instead of pulling it after them, Marsh slowed the lightning, calling on the shadows to be calm, assuring them that she was no longer in any danger. When they had settled and dark spears no longer pounded the ground around them, she looked at Roeglin.

"We need to get inside," he said, and the soldiers formed up around them, heading for the door at a run.

This time, Marsh felt enervated rather than drained. Shadow soared through her blood and sang through her mind, inviting her to be a part of its perpetual chorus. Marsh stretched a hand toward it, only to have Roeglin snatch her fingers out of the air and press her hand to his chest.

"No one's ready for you to leave us yet," he said, and she got the impression he spoke more for himself than any collective of children, soldiers, and traders.

That didn't change the fact that Madame Monetti was planning on leaving and had to be stopped. Marsh watched as the men charged up to the door, slamming into it and bouncing right off. She tugged at the shadow threads that slid between the door and the wall and discovered what was preventing them from breaking it down.

"We can't get through," she shouted, seeing the stone column acting as a drop bar on the other side.

Roeglin saw what she did and shared the image with the captain. Guillemot? It was another new identity she had to learn, but Marsh didn't care. The man had as good a vocabulary as her instructor when it came to cursing, and neither of them knew what they were going to do to get past.

Marsh did. The shadows had shown her that the hall beyond was empty, and she knew it would only take the two of them to lift the bar; they wouldn't be alone for very long. She reached out, wrapping her hands around the straps of each of their packs before leaping from the stairs and taking them with her. She might have laughed at their startled shouts if she wasn't concentrating on where she wanted to go as the shadows closed around them.

The darkness parted seconds later to drop the three of them in the foyer on the other side of the doors, and Marsh let them go. Before Roeglin could gather himself to say anything, Marsh was racing back into the shadow. She didn't have to remember which halls and corridors to take; she only had to think of one thing.

The teapots. Display cases of teapots, a hoshkat-skin rug, a white marble floor, and a large stone desk made of dark marble…

Marsh landed hard and tripped over the hoshkat rug's head, sprawling across the floor.

"*Merde*," she muttered, her hands and knees stinging from the impact.

Picking herself up from the floor, Marsh pulled a blade from the shadows and called a buckler to her arm. She scanned the room for Madame Monetti and was disappointed to find it empty. Advancing through the space, she noticed that the display cabinets were bare and that wisps of shredded sponge shroom were scattered across the floor. Madame Monetti had packed her teapots?

In the midst of all the mayhem she had caused, the

madame had taken the time to make sure the damned teapots were packed?

"Where are they?" she snarled, tangling her hand in the strands of shadow around her. "Where?"

Because where the teapots were, Madame Monetti was sure to be also. What had she called them? Her treasures? Treasures, indeed. If Marsh got hold of any of them, they were going to be glistening shards on the stone.

The shadows had no answers, and Marsh could hear the sound of feet pounding through the corridor beyond the door. Well, Roeglin was getting faster at finding her.

I'm going to fit you with a collar and bell, he snarled. *Just as soon as I work out where in all the gods-forsaken Deeps you are.*

Marsh might have laughed and pointed out he wasn't carrying either, but she couldn't be sure, and she had more important things to do. She had to find Madame Monetti, and the Deeps-forsaken shadows didn't have a clue. Not a single thread responded to her request to find the teapots, and none of them knew where the madame had gone.

That left the three doors at the end of the room, because Marchant was sure she hadn't gone through the one leading to the entry. She was dead certain the woman was making her way through the rear of the complex toward whatever escape route she had planned.

Maybe she'd sent the teapots on ahead. Maybe that was why the shadows couldn't find them.

I don't give two shits of a mule's backside about the Darks-be-damned teapots, but you need to wait for me.

Marsh smirked.

"Catch me if you can, Shadow Boy."

"I'm going to put you on a leash and hook it to my belt, and not let you out of my Shades-cursed sight ever again."

His comment drove all light-heartedness from her as she remembered being leashed by Ardhur and Warven.

"Not in all the Deeps with all the armies of the Dark!" she snapped, and swept her hand, palm up, toward the door that was opening behind her.

It slammed shut, and she heard Roeglin cry out in pain as he ran into it. A leash! Would he dare? She'd see about that! In the meantime...

Marsh looked at the three doors, turning them over on the map in her mind. There was the one she'd been taken through when they'd wanted her to join the caravan, but she was pretty sure Madame Monetti wouldn't be leaving that way. She had to know the fate of the last caravan and its slaves.

Instead, Marsh chose the door opposite it, aware of the door to the corridor opening—cautiously. Roeglin stayed silent, and she hoped he was thinking about the stupidity of his last suggestion.

I'm sorry?

His voice intruded in her head as she set her hand on the handle of the door she'd chosen, and the one at his end of the room continued to slowly open. Marsh was tempted to slam the door in his face again. That thought was followed by footsteps moving hastily into the room and over the rug.

She thought about warning them about the hoshkat rug's head but was far more interested in getting the door in front of her open. If she hadn't taken some of her seeker training into her own hands, it might have been a problem.

As it was, she was at a loss as to what to use until she remembered she could draw darts from the darkness.

The one she needed was smaller than the darts she threw, but it was just as easy to select. The shadows seemed to be waiting for her to ask. Calling a long, narrow needle to her hand, Marsh fitted the shadow tool to the lock and worked it carefully back and forth. Before long, the lock gave, and she opened the door.

The room beyond was lit brightly enough to make her eyes water and she winced, adjusting her vision so she could see. It took a minute, but Marsh kept moving, ducking low and sliding to the left as she listened for a crossbow bolt or axe to smash into the wall beside her head. Neither object came, and her eyes adjusted.

Marsh glanced around the room, scanning for danger; for shadow mage or shadow monster, and for Madame Monetti herself. To her surprise, she found none of them. The room was completely and utterly empty save for its furniture.

Marsh stared. The woman hadn't done anything by halves. The display cabinets in the other room had been white marble and glass-fronted, and worth more than Marsh could imagine earning in her lifetime. The bed dominating the center of this room was several grades higher than that…and the glows!

It might have answered where the glows taken from the trade routes had gone, except these were the wrong color. Marsh stepped closer to the nearest one. It wasn't purple, but a single clear crystal blazing with pure white light. She stretched a tentative finger toward it, only to freeze as Roeglin hurtled through the door.

"Don't!"

Keeping her finger poised, Marsh turned her head to look at him. His dark hair was tousled, and his hazel eyes reflected gold in the light. He cast her a pleading look.

"At least wait until we can test it outside. If it explodes in here…"

He waved his hand to indicate the room and the other strange glows, his worry clear. It was the first time Marsh had ever considered the chances of a glow exploding, or setting off a chain reaction of other glows.

"We just don't know," he said, pausing to catch his breath. "Guillemot is checking the other room."

Marsh nodded, and lifted her hand away from the glow, pretending not to hear his sigh of relief. She indicated the room.

"What do you think?"

"I don't think we have time for sleeping," he replied, and Marsh realized she'd pointed at the bed. As an answer, it could have been worse, and her face heated with embarrassment.

"The *room*," she growled. "What do you think of the room?"

He looked around, taking in the lavish wall hangings, the marble wardrobe and dresser, the mirror made of polished mica, its edge dotted with small blue and purple stones, and the bed. He walked into the middle of the room, and paced his way around it, noting the corner posts that rose almost to the ceiling, the delicate glistening fabric hanging in white and gold curtains, held back by thick gleaming sashes.

When he'd made a complete circuit, he came back to stand beside it.

"I think this would be the perfect place to hide a secret entrance."

Looking around and taking note of the clutter, Marchant had to agree. The problem was that she had no idea of where to start looking.

21

MADAME FOUND...AND LOST

Marsh and Roeglin surveyed the room, letting their eyes travel over the expensive furnishings. Marsh noted that the display cabinet was empty and wondered if Madame Monetti placed as much importance on her garments as she did on her "treasures." With that in mind, she crossed to the wardrobe.

Apart from satisfying her curiosity about Madame Monetti's priorities regarding clothes, the hefty chunk of marble would also be the ideal front for a secret door. It was empty, and nothing Marchant did revealed a hidden panel or caused its solid sides to shift. She was beginning to wish she'd brought Aisha so the little girl could ask the rocks to reveal their secrets when Roeglin gave a victorious shout.

"Found it!"

Marsh shook her head. Trust him to find the secret door.

"Not a secret," he said, closing a divider that had been

arranged to obscure a perfectly unconcealed and ordinary door. "Just a privacy screen."

He paused, his palm resting on the handle.

"Do you want to do the honors?"

"Oh, no. You found it."

Nerves crawled through her stomach and Marsh stretched out her hand, as he turned the handle.

"Stop!"

Roeglin was in the middle of pushing the door open when she shouted, and by then it was almost too late. Howls split the air, and the door was yanked out of Roeglin's hand. Calling back the sword and buckler she'd discarded when she entered the room, Marsh leapt forward to rescue him, and was surprised when the first hands to claw their round the edge of the door were human.

Roeglin didn't hesitate. He wrapped his fingers around the slender wrist he saw and yanked the woman through to safety. He was too slow to grab the door before it swung fully open, but he dragged Madame Monetti into the room and then turned to pull her across it.

"Run!" he shouted when he saw Marsh advancing with her blade. "Run!"

"You run!" she shouted in return, because there was only one person who could close that gate, and he would be lurking close by, probably in whatever room lay beyond.

She had no choice. If she was to stem the flow of monsters, she had to destroy the man or woman who'd opened the gate for them to pass through. Without the mental connection willing the passage between places, the gate would close, and the monsters would be thwarted.

Marsh ducked around the woman and under Roeglin's reaching hand.

"Sorry, Ro," she said, sliding through the door, and catching the edge of it with her fingers as she passed.

With a flick of her wrist, she got it traveling back toward the doorframe, but that wasn't what she was watching. The thing that caught her eye dominated the rear wall of the room, and she was sliding right toward it!

She could only hope she could... Marsh saw the legs of a cabinet sweep past and lashed out with her sword hand, releasing her blade to grab it and stop her slide toward the open maw of the gate before her. Shadows swarmed in the darkness beyond the edges, and red eyes turned in her direction when she gasped in pain.

The cabinet rocked as she jerked to a halt, but Madame Monetti's love of heavy furniture saved her, and it stayed upright. Marsh heard another unhinged scream break the silence, and someone just beyond the cabinet cursed. She scrambled back, pulling herself to her feet and recalling her sword from the shadows.

Another scream broke the stillness, and the hooting gibberish of a dozen ever-hungry mouths rose from the darkness beyond the gate. Cloth rustled, and Marsh didn't hesitate. She lifted the sword in a two-handed grip and swung around the edge of the cabinet, putting herself side-on to it and sidestepping far closer to the gate than she ever wanted to be.

Marsh felt something catch the end of her blade, and the mage hiding on the other side of the cabinet cursed again. This time his voice was ragged with pain. Marsh didn't let that, or the approaching howl of a hunting shadow monster, break her focus. She pulled the blade back toward her, adjusted her aim, and thrust it forward, shifting her hand to the pommel to give herself more leverage as she drove it into the mage's chest.

He gasped but didn't have time to scream, and the gate snapped shut beside her. Another unearthly scream broke the air as it did so, and a dark limb tipped in ivory claws thumped heavily onto the tiles beside her. Marsh glanced down at it, watching the ebony flesh start to steam in the light, and then she looked at the now-solid back wall and listened to the absolute silence that had descended on the room.

For a minute she just stood and stared, and then she remembered the dark-haired woman Roeglin had towed into the bedroom beyond and turned toward the door. As she did, she scanned the room, looking for a second mage. The Deeps knew there had been two of them every other time she'd seen a gate opened.

After a cursory search showed that no one was hiding in the large bathtub that stood to one side or in the alcove between the cabinet and the wall that the first mage had been standing in or behind the door leading to the privy, Marsh stepped back into the bedroom, but she did so slowly, searching for Roeglin and Madame Monetti.

It took her a second to register the clash of blades, the two figures in black raider armor, and the way Roeglin fought to keep himself between Madame Monetti and the dark-clothed intruders. With a shout, Marsh jumped into the fray.

The flash of darkness lashing out at her from beside the doorway came as a surprise, and she felt metal slide across her armor as she turned to face it. She managed to parry the dagger that followed, but only just. Even though she didn't want to turn away from the two men attacking Roeglin, she couldn't afford to ignore her ambusher, so she turned, blocking a second strike with her buckler as she brought her sword across her attacker's gut in a vicious swing.

He choked out a cry even as Marsh used her buckler to block a second strike, pulling her sword back before thrusting it into the man's chest. When she jerked her blade free, he dropped to the floor and didn't move. Seeing he was down for good, Marsh turned and took in the situation across the room.

Roeglin was still holding his own, and still successfully blocking their path to Madame Monetti. As long as the woman stayed behind him, she'd be safe, but the lady clearly had her doubts about Roeglin's abilities. As Marsh moved to help the shadow mage, Madame Monetti made a break for the door leading to her office. Her movement pulled Roeglin's attention away from his opponent for just a heartbeat, but it was enough.

He dropped his guard enough that the raider swept his blade across Roeglin's shoulder, slicing through the armor and flesh, and making the shadow mage's dagger fall. As it dropped from his hand, dissipating into darkness, the other raider broke from the melee and went after Madame Monetti.

Marsh didn't need to be told what to do. She darted after Madame Monetti, trying to reach the raider before he could reach her. It was going to be a close-run thing.

Madame Monetti made it to the door, yanking it open

and darting through before the raider could reach her. Marsh raced across the room and slid to a stop, bringing her buckler around before striking out with her blade.

The raider caught her arrival from the corner of his eye and turned, just managing to parry the blade swinging across his body. He glanced back at the door and Marsh struck out again, forcing him back a step before catching his blade in a parry as she rammed her buckler into his chest, knocking him back against the wardrobe. Finding herself too close, Marsh shuffled two hasty steps back and readied her next strike.

As the raider pushed himself off the wardrobe and back onto his feet, Marsh thrust forward, driving her blade through the center of his body before pulling it back out. Seeing the raider fall, she turned for the door, hurrying to catch up with Madame Monetti. There were three ways out of her office. Who knew which route she'd take?

To Marsh's surprise, Madame Monetti hadn't left the room. She was standing in the center of it, facing a dark-cloaked figure.

"Take me to—" she began in clear tones of command, but the figure wasn't listening.

It took a single swift step for him to cover the distance to Madam Monetti's side and thrust a dagger through her throat.

Marsh gave a shout and sprang forward, but the figure stepped away from the dead woman to disappear through a slender slit in the shadows. The gate was so narrow that Marsh hadn't seen it. She bounded forward, but light flared in a wavery vertical line and her reaching hands found nothing. The assassin was gone, and he'd closed the way behind him.

Marsh stepped back and cast a quick glance down at the woman she'd tried to save, but it was clear she was dead. That made Marsh's next decision easy; she pivoted and ran back through the door to see how Roeglin was faring. It didn't take her long to see he was in trouble.

His opponent had the shadow mage backed up against a wall. Roeglin's injured arm hung limply by his side as he parried dagger thrusts and sword swipes, and it was clear he couldn't hold out much longer. Marsh didn't bother shouting. She figured the raider had noticed her entry, and, if he hadn't, it didn't matter. He was going to die all the same.

She did not hesitate, but thrust her blade into his back, stepping back to let him fall before lashing out to cut deeply into his neck. The man was dead before he'd made it all the way to the floor, but Marsh was already moving toward Roeglin. He looked at her and gave her a wobbly smile.

"Help me out of here?"

The sword faded from his hand, and Marsh released her weapons back to the shadows as she came alongside him. Sliding his good arm over her shoulder, she helped him reach the main office as Captain Guillemot led his squad back in from the third door in the room.

"You found her, then," he said, taking in Madame Monetti's body, and then he noticed Roeglin. "What happened?"

"There were raiders," Marsh answered. "I took out one,

but an assassin got through and killed Madame Monetti before I could get to her."

"Four," Roeglin said, his voice thready and weak. "She took out four. I just kept them busy."

Then he slid sideways, his full weight almost pulling Marsh off her feet. She lowered him to the ground and looked at Guillemot.

"I need bandages," she said, and he glanced at his squad.

Before he could say anything, one of his men shouldered his way to the front and knelt beside Marsh, inspecting the wound and pulling a threaded needle from the large satchel at his waist.

"Ilias," he said. "I try to keep them alive. Let me see him."

Marsh moved back, helping when she was asked and doing her best to keep out of the medic's way otherwise.

"Help me lift him," she said when he was done and Roeglin's shoulder was bandaged, but Ilias shook his head.

"I've got my own packhorses for that," he told her, and Marsh couldn't help but look past him at the squad.

He smiled when she frowned, puzzled because she couldn't see the mules he was referring to.

"Jonas," he said as a stocky young man with a shock of dark hair and even darker eyes made his way out of the group and stooped to lift Roeglin from the ground. He was followed by an equally stocky woman with red hair and brown eyes. Ilias included her with a gesture of his hand. "And this is Lilian. She'll take over when Jonas needs a break. I believe we have a journey before us."

As he said it, he straightened up and looked at Captain Guillemot.

"Ready when you are, captain."

Guillemot spared Marsh a moment as he passed.

"We're camping at one of the abandoned farms. We can't stay here. Couldn't hold off an attack if we did, and I can't be sure we got them all. Monsieur Gravine will be sending an escort tomorrow. We'll meet them on the road."

He didn't say anything else, just led everyone from the Monetti mansion out to the road, stopping briefly to speak to the small squad guarding the junction as he passed. They melted back into the shadows as Guillemot led his squad away, and Marsh was surprised at how well they'd vanished when she looked back.

She was relieved when Mordan joined her, padding silently out from beneath a stand of calla shrooms. Marsh stayed close to Jonas, her hand resting lightly on the kat's neck as they walked. She was glad of the big beast's presence on a road that seemed suddenly empty without Roeglin's companionship.

2 2

POISONED BY SHADOW

Marsh woke to the sound of hurried, quiet movement, rolling out of the bed she'd been given at the farmhouse on the way to Monsieur Gravine's mansion. Silently she pulled a sword and buckler from the shadows, then hit the floor in a crouch and scanned the room.

It was empty, but the corridor outside was not. Strangers passed her door as she cracked it open, and lamplight cast a golden glow in the hall beyond. It was the lamplight that made her relax enough to let her sword and buckler return to the dark, glad no one had seen her, even if the activity had her concerned.

The strangers were all wearing the uniform of Monsieur Gravine's Protectors, and she realized they weren't strangers after all. She'd walked with them the day before, even if she didn't know their names, and there weren't that many, only two. Marsh stepped into the hallway behind them as they turned into the room beside hers—the one she'd watched them set Roeglin in before she'd been ordered to rest.

She hurried to see what was going on and arrived in time to hear the medic speaking.

"...going to need golden gleams, yellow moss, and lava weed," he ordered, and Marsh stepped hastily aside as the two Protectors she'd followed hurried out of the room.

One of them started when he saw her, and the other had her sword half-drawn before she recognized Marsh. Neither of them stopped to apologize, but rushed toward the stairs leading to the ground floor. Marsh waited until they were clear and then stepped into the room.

Ilias had a basin of hot water beside him and was dipping a cloth into it. He looked up when he caught sight of her and nodded, wringing out the cloth and wiping Roeglin's shoulder.

"Raiders use shadow poison on their blades," he said. "I didn't know."

The man sounded disgusted with himself, but Marsh shook her head.

"It's my fault, too. I didn't know, either—and I didn't notice."

"That makes two of us."

Ilias dipped the cloth again, rinsing it out before laying it over the wound. Roeglin groaned, and Marsh remembered how she'd felt after being hit by shadow claws.

"We need Aisha," she said, wondering if the little girl would be strong enough to deal with the poison on her own.

Ilias looked at her.

"She looks too young to be a trained healer."

Marsh shook her head.

"She's not; she uses magic to heal."

Now she had his attention.

"Magic can heal?"

"Yes." Marsh wished she had scars to show him from her own run-in with a shadow monster, but the magical healing she'd received from both Aisha and Lennie hadn't left any. Apparently, when a healer thought about how someone should look uninjured, that was pretty much how they ended up...and she hoped Aisha never realized the implications.

"How?"

Marsh hung her head.

"I don't know."

"You've never tried?"

"No."

"Why not?"

It was a good question. After all, wasn't she the one who'd asked why a shadow guard had never tried to fix the things he broke? She stared at Ilias, and he stared back. Roeglin moved restlessly in his sleep, his face flushed, and Ilias gestured toward him.

"Even a little bit would help."

Marsh sighed, trapped by her own thoughts—and haunted by the Master of Beast's revelation: "Not everyone can do every kind of magic." She'd already found it was true for her and charging the glows. Ilias nudged her.

"It's okay if you can't."

Marsh shook her head.

"It's not that. It's just that I don't know if I can."

"Only one way to find out."

And there he was, pushing her. Marsh scowled. He was also right. She hated it when the folk giving her a shove were right. Hated letting them down even more.

"No doubts..."

It was more a whisper than anything else, but Marsh heard it echoing through her mind.

"Won't work...with doubt."

They both turned toward the bed. Roeglin's eyes were glowing with faint wisps of white, and sweat sheened his forehead. As they watched, the white faded and his eyes drifted closed.

"Try..." was barely a sound, but Marsh heard it clearly in her head.

Ilias looked at her, and Marsh drew a deep breath and let it slowly out.

"Let's do this thing," she said, injecting as much confidence into her voice as she could. "You want ta give it a whirl?"

"Me?"

"Sure, why not? You've never done magic before?"

"Never thought to try."

"It's easy, like opening a gate. Someone once told me that everyone had the ability."

"But how?"

"Take a deep breath, understand that you can, and let the magic know what you need it to do."

"I don't know if I can."

Marsh gave him a feral grin and used his own words against him.

"You won't know until you try."

There's my girl.

It worried her that this time she only heard Roeglin's voice in her head, and even then, it still sounded thready, but the pride she heard there... The absolute confidence...

She turned to Ilias.

"We can do this," she told him, and together, they looked at the wound.

For a moment Marsh thought she might be imagining things, because it looked much worse than it had when she'd watch Ilias bathe it a few moments ago. The medic caught her look.

"Shadow poison," he said. "Once it takes hold, it's very difficult to defeat."

There was something she hadn't needed to know before trying a brand-new kind of magic.

Quit stalling!

For a man as sick as he was, Roeglin was awfully chatty. *Fine.*

Marsh made herself take a good close look at the deep slice the raider had made in his shoulder.

"We need to pull the poison out of that, right?"

"*Oui.*"

"I'll start with that. It comes from the shadows, and I can talk to the shadows, so *this* part I should be able to do."

"And what do I do?"

Marsh thought about what Aisha and Lennie had both said.

"You know how that should look when it's healthy. Picture that in your mind and ask the magic to fix it."

"Just like that?"

Marsh thought about scolding him but figured he didn't need to know that his doubt could stop him. Instead, she

257

gave him a nod. When she replied, she offered him absolute confidence.

"*Oui*—just like that. Ready?"

"*Oui.*"

Ilias looked down at the wound, but Marsh was already reaching into the shadows. If she was honest with herself, she didn't have a clue what shadow poison might look like, but it was killing Roeglin, which meant...

She had to be the biggest idiot in all the Deeps!

Dropping the shadow threads, she pulled on the magic that helped her sense the life around her, but this time she focused it on Roeglin's life force. She didn't just want to see if it was there; she already knew that. She wanted to see...

Marsh hesitated. What *did* she want to see? She felt the magic waver in her grasp and scrambled for an answer, wishing she had someone to guide her. But she didn't, and Roeglin needed her, so... What was it she needed to see?

The poison. And how did seeing a life force help with that? Ha! Because the poison weakened it, nibbled at the edges, and she'd know what to ask the shadows to help her find. She'd also know when she had a grasp on it because she'd be able to see it when it left the wound.

Finding her focus was easy when she knew what to look for. Looking at a life force this way was different than just finding out if one was there. It was more...intricate, like looking at a map of the caverns—and the poison was everywhere.

There were thin tendrils of it spreading out from Roeglin's shoulder down into his chest and up into his head. It was a wonder he could talk to her. Marsh concentrated, feeling the rush of power as she reached for the shadow she could see within the poison. Shadow, right?

The wound connected the shadows in Roeglin's blood to the shadows in the room. Marsh wondered what it would be like to wield a blade of poisoned shadow, to call all that deadliness to her hand. What would it be like to have it protect her instead of threatening those she loved?

If she could pull the shadows to her hand...

Marsh focused, her heart thundering as she called the shadow poison out of Roeglin's body. She held her hand out, watching through a blend of shadow and life as the dark threads inside the shadow mage wove their way out of his head and away from his heart until they made it back to his shoulder, then flowed through the air to her hand.

She remembered one very important thing at that moment.

Shadow poison was a poison, and it harmed on contact!

"*Merde!*" she whispered as the darkness she had called coalesced into a short, thick-bladed dagger. She realized she couldn't release it to the shadows around her or it would harm anyone who came into the room.

She should have just left it to pool. It was poison, right? It came out as a liquid, a sticky substance. She could just wipe it off. Looking around the room, she saw nothing she could use, except for the clean blanket on Roeglin's bed. Marsh hesitated. Who knew what it would do to the blanket?

The skin on her palm started to burn, and Marsh decided the blanket was a better place for it than her flesh. She leaned over and dropped the blade on the bed, dismissing the shadows she had called from the room and commanding the shadowed poison to find a home among the blanket's threads.

All of it, she insisted when some of it wanted to cling to her hand. *All.*

It left, settling onto the blanket, which was whisked away as soon as the last of the residue had flowed from her palm. She could still feel the burn of it and she felt mildly ill, but it didn't matter. The poison was gone, and Roeglin breathed easier. Beside the bed, Ilias sat, staring at his own hands and looking at the clean, whole skin on the shadow mage's shoulder.

"How did you know?" he asked, catching Marsh's eye.

"Know what?"

"That I could do that?"

Marsh gave him a long look, thinking about how to reply. In the end, she decided to go with the truth.

"I didn't."

Ilias' jaw dropped. "You didn't?"

"No, but I knew the stories, and I hoped, because you're a medic for a reason, right? You chose it, didn't you?"

Ilias nodded.

"I always wanted to heal."

"So, a big part of the magic seems to be that the person *wants* to wield it. The other part is that they have a need to." She indicated Roeglin, who now slept, the sweat drying on his face and his color returning to normal. "Tell me, could you have saved him without it?"

Ilias' face reddened, and he looked down at the floor.

"No," he admitted. "Never have been able to save anyone poisoned by the beasts. First time I've ever seen it delivered by a blade, though."

Anger burned through Marsh, and she sat on the end of the bed. Before she could say anything, Ilias spoke again.

"How did you do it?"

Marsh explained what she'd done with the shadows; how she'd sensed the life force and then read it, and how she'd called the poison out of the wound.

"It's not shadow, you know?" he said when she'd finished, and Marsh felt her skin go pale.

"Not even a little bit?"

Her voice sounded plaintive even to her, and a small smile curved the medic's lips.

"No, but if that's what you needed so you could see it and pull it out of there, I'm glad you did."

"Not shadow?" Marsh's voice shook. "Then what is it?"

Ilias shrugged.

"You'll have to ask one of the rock mages," he said, "or an apothecary; someone who knows medicines and poisons." He paused. "I'll do it the next time I talk to one of mine."

Marsh was glad she was sitting on the edge of the bed because she didn't think her legs could hold her. What had she done?

"Found another kind of magic." Roeglin's voice was weak, but amusement lurked in its depths. "And then blended it with shadow magic to make it work. Tell me, how do you feel?"

Marsh looked at him, puzzled as to why he would ask— and he repeated the question.

"How do you feel?"

It took Marsh a moment to realize that she didn't feel as

fatigued as she usually did. She felt more alive and awake than ever.

"I feel great," she said and Roeglin smiled, turning his attention to the medic.

"And you, Ilias?"

"Good."

"Energized?"

"Yes! Like…I don't know… Like I've had a good night's sleep."

Marsh put her hand on her hip and cocked her head.

"When was the last time *that* happened?"

Ilias laughed.

"Not for a very long time, young lady. A *very* long time. It was like the magic came from around me, good, clean energy that healed what it touched. I just imagined what the injury would look like whole, and the magic came." He sobered, his face growing serious as he fixed her with a thoughtful look. "You said anyone could do magic?"

Marsh swallowed. She wasn't about to tell him she'd lied.

"*Oui…*"

"So, my people, my staff—they could do this, too?"

Marsh bowed her head, biting her lip as she realized she really *would* have to tell him the truth. She raised her head to look him in the eye.

"*Some* will be able to do this, but it's like singing or fighting or running. Some folks are better at it than others, and some can do one kind of magic better than they can do others, while some struggle to do any at all."

Ilias stared at her in shock.

"You're joking." He glanced down at Roeglin. "Tell me she's joking!"

The shadow mage shook his head.

"No, but she couldn't exactly tell you that *before* you tried or the magic might not have come at all. The main thing you need, even if you *can* call magic, is the belief that you can do it. No doubts."

Ilias opened his mouth, angry color suffusing his face, but Roeglin kept talking.

"The way you feel now means you have found the magic that best suits you." He glanced at Marsh. "Or one of them."

Marsh returned his glance. One of them? Did he mean to make it sound like she was one of the few who'd learned to wield more than one? She caught his slight nod that indicated that was exactly what he meant, but Ilias still had questions.

"How do I know which of my people can heal? Or what they *can* do?"

"You'll just have to ask them to try," Roeglin told him, and a look of sheer mischief crossed his face. "Much like you did with my trainee here."

Ilias looked shocked, and his face flushed.

"Master Leger, I...I'm sorry. I didn't mean..." He stopped when Roeglin laid a hand on his arm.

"You did nothing wrong," he said. "Sometimes a master misses the potential simply because he hasn't thought of it."

"All the same, I—"

Roeglin cut him off, again.

"How often has magic been seen in these caverns?" he asked. "Think about it."

The medic stilled. He was quiet for a moment, but Marchant knew he was thinking the same thing she was. Until recently, magic had only been used by the shadow mages and the rock wizards, although very few knew of them and they'd been particularly secretive in the last few years.

"Not often," Ilias replied. "There have been one or two, but they've either joined the monastery or...or they've left."

"Yes," Roeglin told him, "and now I have to wonder where they went."

It was a matter they'd have to pursue another time, because Marsh heard the clatter of hooves in the yard outside, and Roeglin swung himself out of bed. He caught Marchant's blush as she turned away.

"I'll need some clothes."

"And I'll check downstairs," Marchant added, hurriedly thinking of an excuse to leave. "See if Captain Guillemot has anything he wants me to do."

Her face flamed as she left, Roeglin's smug chuckle not helping.

23

ORELIA'S RETURN

When Marsh arrived downstairs, Captain Guillemot was standing behind a chair at the dining room table, his attention drawn by the arrival of his men. Around him, another half-dozen members of the squad were on their feet, their attention divided between him and the sounds outside. The captain spared a glance for Marsh and returned his attention to the Protector who had beaten her through the door.

"Who is it?" he demanded.

"Captain Orelia sends his regards, sir, and requests your hospitality."

Captain Guillemot replied as surprise sent shockwaves through Marsh. Orelia had been the name of the captain who'd gone after the raiders and the missing slaves. That he was back so soon didn't bode well for his success. As hard as it was, she forced herself to silence, waiting for the captain's reply and not missing the glance he threw her way.

"I'll go," he said and headed for the door.

"Come with me," he added, speaking to Marsh as he passed her, and then he looked a little beyond her. "You, too."

Marsh turned her head and saw Roeglin coming down the stairs. He was alone, and Marsh wondered where Ilias was.

"I'm not his only patient."

Ah, well, that explained it. Marsh waited until he came alongside her before following Captain Guillemot. The captain didn't wait, nor did the four men wearing the insignia that indicated they were higher in rank than most of the others.

Lieutenants, Roeglin provided. *They'll go to see what changes with Orelia's arrival, and then they'll take his orders to the rest.*

Marsh studied the insignia, hoping to remember it the next time she saw it. Roeglin tapped her on the shoulder, and she realized she'd stopped.

"You're holding up the party, Trainee," he told her, and she resisted the urge to slap his shoulder in return.

Decorum, right?

And discipline, Roeglin added, like she needed reminding, then, catching her thought, he added, *You mean you don't?*

Marsh felt her cheeks color but didn't dignify his quip with an answer. There were other things she had to pay attention to.

If Roeglin had any thoughts on that, he kept them to himself, and they hurried after the captain, catching up as he addressed the new arrivals. Captain Orelia had remained mounted, as had his men, even though they were clearly exhausted.

Rules of hospitality, Roeglin explained. *He's making sure he's welcome.*

What would he do if he wasn't?

He'd keep riding until he reached the next farm.

Looking at the troops, Marchant wasn't sure they could. Their mules' heads drooped, and the animals' hides were covered with dust and sweat. Every line of their bodies was etched with exhaustion, and so were their riders. The men sat slumped in their saddles, although those closest to their captain were doing their best to sit upright and look alert.

They succeeded, but their tiredness was apparent. Captain Guillemot's reaction showed he understood the situation. Marsh assumed there was some sort of traditional dialogue expected between the two captains, and that Guillemot skipped it.

"Welcome, Francis. If you and your men will follow Lieutenants Gier and Solange, they'll show you where to sleep. Lieutenants Bairdie and Dieter will see to your mules."

"You are too kind," Orelia began, "but—

His fellow captain cut him off.

"But nothing, Captain. Unless it will affect our security, you can brief me when you've eaten and rested."

Captain Orelia subsided.

"I have nothing of immediate note to report, and place my men in your care," he said, and slowly swung himself out of his saddle. "Thank you, Captain."

As if his reply and movement were a signal, the men

riding with him followed his example. To their credit, Lieutenants Bairdie and Dieter had already sent runners to fetch help, and it didn't take long for the riders to hand the reins of their animals to the men coming to get them. Roeglin and Marsh watched as the beasts were led to the barn and the men to the barracks that usually housed the farmhands.

"Captain, may I speak with the captain?" Roeglin asked, and Guillemot nodded.

"Do not hold him up or keep him long."

"I understand."

Marsh had wondered what the captain had meant and how Roeglin was going to speak with Orelia without holding him up, but it soon became clear. The captain had stripped off his armor and clothing and was standing at a trough of water in the barn. The other men and women of his squad were standing alongside him, doing their best to wash the road dust from their skins. None of them were wearing anything, and Lieutenants Gier and Solange had set a watch around them.

"Halt," ordered one as Roeglin went to pass the line.

"I have Captain Guillemot's permission," Roeglin replied, but he didn't try to move past the man. "I can wait while you send someone to check."

To Marchant's surprise, the man signaled to one of the others and he came over.

"I need to make sure," the soldier said, and Roeglin nodded.

"I will wait."

"He says he has the captain's permission."

The other soldier did not wait for more instructions

but hurried back toward the farmhouse, returning with confirmation a few moments later.

"Thank you," Roeglin said when the man gestured for them to go through.

The shadow mage did not let the others' state of nudity slow him down, nor did he check to see if Marsh was following. He just swept through the line of guards, expecting her to follow. Orelia had moved away from the trough and was rubbing himself dry with one of the towels provided as they approached. His face broke into a smile when he saw Roeglin.

"Roeglin! Come." He finished with the towel and passed it to the next trooper, not even glancing at her as she thanked him. Moving swiftly to where packs were lined up along the walls, he pulled a fresh shirt and trousers out of one and put them on. "I take it you want to know how it went?"

"I know you don't need to report to Guillemot, but if you wouldn't mind?"

Orelia cut straight to the chase.

"We didn't catch up with them if that was what you were hoping. The trail ended at a solid stone wall. I know that because Derschanel spoke with it." Orelia paused as though remembering, and his voice took on a tone of wonder when he continued, "He said he pulled images of what had happened from the stones. The raiders opened a path and led our people through before closing the way behind them."

Again, he paused. This time there was genuine puzzlement in his voice when he continued.

"He said the rocks couldn't show him where the people

went because they weren't connected with the stone on the other side. How is that possible?"

"They create gates through the shadow," Roeglin told him, "but this is the first time we have heard of them parting the rock as they do so. It's not good to know the rock wizards working with them are strong enough to do that."

"Those wouldn't be the first," Marsh muttered, remembering Ardhur encasing her in rock, and Roeglin turned to stare at her.

Orelia gave a tired chuckle and patted Roeglin on the shoulder.

"They promised us breakfast," he said, indicating the soldier waiting for them. "She can debrief us as we eat."

Oh, she could, could she?

"Yes, *she* can," Roeglin agreed, tucking his arm through Marsh's and adding, "before I have to kick her tail for not doing it earlier."

"We were a bit busy, and then you weren't well."

"This is true," Roeglin admitted, but Orelia had picked up on what Marsh had said.

"Not well?"

"Some of the raiders use shadow-monster poison on their blades. The Deeps know where they get it from, or how."

They arrived at the large downstairs room that served as both dining hall and meeting room, and Captain Guillemot greeted them.

"Sit," he told Orelia, gesturing to a table in the corner. "I'll join you. If Master Leger is badgering you for information, I might as well save you from having to deliver it twice."

Orelia followed Guillemot to the table and waited until his host had seated himself.

Guillemot has seniority, Roeglin said when she wondered why Orelia was acting like Guillemot was in charge when they were both captains.

Ah. She'd been thinking it was because Orelia was the guest, Guillemot being the first to make the farm his base of operations.

That, too. Now, be silent and listen.

Marsh resisted the urge to roll her eyes and took her seat at the table, aware of more than one of the soldiers glancing toward them. Anyone would think this was a big deal.

It is. Civilians don't get to sit at the captains' table.

Since when were they civilians? They had as much at stake in this battle as the rest, *and* they were working for Monsieur Gravine.

All true, but we are not officially part of the Four Settlements Protectors, and that sets us apart.

Oblivious to their conversation, Captain Orelia started his report, telling them of his entry into the caverns Aisha had blocked.

"It took Derschanel almost an hour to clear that mess. Whoever made it did a really good job of it!" he declared. Marchant made a mental note to let Aisha know, although she didn't know how the little girl was going to react when she found out her handiwork had been undone.

Orelia continued, "We made a gap, drawing the shadow

monsters to it until we'd killed them all. It wasn't very sporting, but there's sporting, and then there's making sure my men come out alive. Nothing a medic can do when it comes to shadow poison."

Roeglin stayed quiet, and Marsh followed his lead. She wasn't sure why he hadn't chosen to share that they might have found a way to deal with the poison, but he'd have his reasons.

They'll be more careful if they think they're going to die.

But they'll fight more bravely if they know they have a chance

So far we only have three who can do it. Two if you consider that we can't use Lennie until her child is born, and only you have been able to remove the poison from a wound, although I'll have to ask both Lennie and Aisha what they did with you. Until then, it's better these men fight smart than die thinking some-one's going to save them when we can't. Besides, you aren't always going to be in this cavern.

"What?"

Shh.

Marsh shushed but made another mental note to ask him what he meant when they didn't need to focus on listening to a military report. Roeglin had no comment about that, so she settled down to listen to the rest of what Orelia had to say.

He'd moved on from clearing the caverns of shadow monsters to tracking the raiders and their prisoners to the wall. Marsh listened as he again described Derschanel's frustration with the stone, sitting up a little straighter when he moved on to what the shadow guards had done next.

"I had your Master Finlay go over it, asking the shadows what they knew, but all he could get them to reveal was that there were two who opened the gate. One was the rock wizard, and the other some shadow mage. They worked together, combining their powers to part both shadow and stone. He said one of the prisoners tried to make a break for it, but he was grabbed and thrown through to show the rest it was safe. He said the mages were the last through, and the gate closed shortly after."

"Did you see what was on the other side?" Captain Guillemot asked the question to which Marsh most wanted the answer.

Orelia shook his head.

"No. Finlay said they couldn't show him what they weren't connected to, and couldn't hold the memory of what they had touched once the connection was broken."

Marsh frowned. There had to be a way. If the shadows could hold the images of what was past, why couldn't they hold the images of what was past when they didn't touch the space anymore? They *had* already touched it, hadn't they?

What if the person asking them the question could open a gate to the...

Roeglin touched her arm and Marsh blinked, coming out of her thoughts with a jolt and looking straight into Captain Guillemot's curious eyes.

"What were you thinking, Trainee?"

"I was trying to work out why the shadows couldn't hold the images of places they'd once touched but didn't touch anymore. I'm sorry; I didn't mean to interrupt."

Captain Orelia brushed her apology away with a wave of his hand.

"You didn't interrupt. I was done."

Marchant looked at Guillemot, but the captain relaxed back in his chair.

"If you manage to work that one out, Trainee, make sure you pass it on."

"Yes, Captain."

Guillemot pushed back his chair and looked at Orelia.

"Get some sleep when you've eaten. I'll have you woken in enough time to join us if you wish."

Marsh was guessing that by "you" Guillemot meant Orelia *and* his men, most of whom had filed into the dining hall and been served. As if Guillemot's words were a signal, one of his soldiers came over, balancing three meals in his hands.

"I would appreciate that," Orelia replied. "My men won't keep you waiting."

It was as much an order as a promise. Marsh saw that the men seated nearest their table all wore the insignia of lieutenants and that they had all paused to listen to their captain's reply. Even so, it wasn't until he'd settled to his meal that they returned to theirs. Marsh followed suit as Guillemot left the room, pausing to speak with his stewards on the way.

If she wasn't much mistaken, the farm was going to be scrubbed to within an inch of its life before the troops left. She wondered what she would be doing, and Roeglin answered.

You're going to debrief me on exactly what you did to remove the poison from my wound, and then you're going to try to show me how you did it. After that, we're going to work on your communication skills.

Her communication skills? Marsh wondered. What was wrong with *those*?

24

FORWARD PLANNING

It was mid-afternoon by the time Monsieur Gravine's escort arrived. Roeglin was able to warn Captain Guillemot in time for him to alert Captain Orelia and have both squads waiting by the time the escort arrived in the yard.

"Captains," Gustav began. If he was surprised to see Orelia and his men, he did not show it. "I apologize for the delay. We were needed."

He did not expand on that, and the captains did not ask.

Instead, Guillemot replied, "Can I offer you and your men refreshment?"

Gustav shook his head.

"Thank you, Captain, but we need to return as quickly as we can. Monsieur Gravine's orders." He glanced at Orelia. "And he will be most anxious to hear Captain Orelia's report. I apologize for the hurry."

Oh, he did, did he? Because from where Marsh was sitting, he didn't look either very sorry or anywhere near apologetic.

Roeglin nudged her in the ribs.

It's a formality. He no more expected hospitality than Guillemot expected to give it, although Guillemot was ready to if it was needed. Everyone knows the cavern founder needs us back. Madame Monetti's assassination was unexpected, and now we have no way of knowing what's coming next.

We need to close the connection to Leon's Deep.

"Is this a private conversation or can anyone join in?"

Both Roeglin and Marchant started, coming back to the present to see one of the lieutenants standing two steps away from them. Marsh blushed, glad that Roeglin was the one who had to answer.

"Sorry, Lieutenant. We didn't want to interrupt the captains."

"They are waiting. Captain Moldrane brought extra mounts. If you'll follow me."

They followed, Marsh feeling properly chastened and Roeglin showing no sign of embarrassment. If Marsh hadn't known any better, she would have said Roeglin considered the lieutenant's behavior normal. In fact, she *didn't* know any better, so maybe it was.

Shortly afterward, he had them settled toward the front of the formation, although being placed slightly behind and to Gustav's right was a little unexpected. Once they were in place, Gustav wasted no time in explaining why they had been situated where they were.

"Master Leger, I need your trainee's ability to sense life and your ability to communicate with the founder if we run into trouble."

They had over forty men behind them. What could possibly cause them trouble?

Gustav answered that question as well.

"The joffra are stirring earlier each cycle, and there are many more of them." He glanced at Marsh. "Ask the hoshkat to stay close."

"Yes, Captain."

Marsh sought the connection she had with Mordan and impressed on the kat her wish for the big animal to travel close. She pictured hordes of joffra and a sense of concern for the kat's safety, as well as respect for Mordan's ability to take care of herself.

The kat rumbled a low complaint, but she stepped out of the shrooms closest to the road and came to stand beside Marsh's mule. The animal snorted and sidled, but Marsh laid a hand on its neck and sent it a sense of calm, telling it that Mordan was not a threat but a source of protection. Roeglin let out a low whistle of appreciation as the animal settled beneath her.

"You're getting good at that," he said, and Marsh realized what she'd done.

Up until that point, she hadn't known she *could* speak to mules and she hadn't really tried. She shrugged.

"Thanks," she replied, sounding anything but thankful.

"Trainee, we will begin when you're ready." Gustav's voice commanded her attention and Marsh looked at him.

Taking a breath, she focused on the cavern around them, concentrating on her desire to see the lives sharing the dark around them. She started with the column she was part of, then slowly expanded her awareness, thinking of herself like a stone dropped in the center of a pool, her consciousness radiating outwards.

"Hold on," Roeglin told her, and Marsh paid enough

attention to keep a grip on her reins and move her hands to the pommel of the saddle.

She shifted as the mule moved forward, but she held her focus. The captain was relying on her to see any joffra and warn them before a hunting pack could swarm them, or to see any shadow raiders or monsters in enough time to reach shelter or prepare. She could do that.

The journey became timeless, as the mule moved steadily forward and Marsh focused on the living factors of the world around them. She gradually felt less like a stone dropped in the center of a pool and more like a fish being dragged through a lake at the end of a lure, except they weren't trying to attract anything.

They did succeed in gaining the attention of two packs of joffra by the time they reached the gates to Monsieur Gravine's mansion, but neither pack was large enough to take on the double squad of men and beasts. Not alone, and they hadn't noticed each other, yet. If they had, and if they decided to team up...

"We need to hurry."

Marsh was relieved to hear Roeglin's voice give Gustav warning. It meant she could focus on keeping watch for...

"There's a third pack of joffra coming in."

Again Roeglin plucked the images from her head, although when he'd gotten so adept at reading the map of life signs, she didn't know. Deciding to ask him later, Marsh kept watch on the three joffra packs and looked for any more. The image faded as the mule was led through the gates of the recently completed barbican leading to the stable yard. She lost the image completely when the gates closed behind them.

Marsh let the images go and opened her eyes. Her fingers were still curled around the pommel, and Roeglin had clipped a lead to the chin strap of her mule's bridle. He glanced at her as she drew a sharp breath and looked around.

"When did this happen?" she asked, inspecting the stone walls and ceiling encasing them.

Roeglin glanced at the walls before answering.

"Rock wizards finished it two days ago. The shadow monastery is a good place for the troops' families, but the founder decided he needed somewhere safe for the troops themselves to live and train in. Took them four day-cycles, and that was with the masons finishing things off. We can house around a thousand now."

A thousand? Were there even that many people living in the cavern?

The question must have shown on her face because Roeglin gave her a fleeting smile.

"Founder figures on rounding up two thousand soldiers by the time we've been through the closest caverns, but that's only if we get to folk before the raiders do. We've already lost most of those in Leon's Deep, and a hundred more from the farthest farms. We need to seal this cavern, save for the road to Kerrenin's Ledge and Ariella's. When those are safe to travel again, we can slowly open things back up. Let folk go home as we secure their caverns and can protect them."

It was a nice thought, but Marsh wondered when they'd reach that point...and if they ever would. She was tired, like she'd run all the way from the farm to the mansion. The enormity of what they were facing dragged at her spirit, and the loss of the prisoners she'd been traveling with pounded her soul. All she wanted to do was curl up in a corner and weep.

And she couldn't; she had to find Patrik and tell him… What? she wondered. That we didn't get to his sons in time? That we saved him, but his kids are gone?

For a moment, she was grateful that Fabrice had rescued the three she had, but the loss of the others when they'd been so close to being safe tore at her. How…

"You're not telling him anything," Roeglin said, his voice cutting through her thoughts. "That news is for others to break."

"But I promised," Marsh protested, and Gustav turned in his saddle to look at her.

"Your master makes a good point." He indicated the men ahead of her. "The captains will break the news, and Captain Orelia's men will spend time with the parents to talk to them and calm them down. It will give you, the founder, and your master time to work out how you're going to go about getting them back."

"I *will* find them," Marsh told him, flinching at the stubborn edge to her tone.

She sounded like Aisha at her most difficult.

Roeglin snorted and reached over to lay his hand on her knee.

"*We'll* find them," he corrected. "Together. The two of us and whatever team we're assigned. Okay?"

Marsh nodded, not trusting her voice. They *would* find them, wherever they had been taken, whatever situation they were in. She drew a deep breath, feeling the tiredness of using magic for too long trying to roll her under.

"Stick around," Roeglin ordered. "We've got to see Monsieur Gravine before you can flake out on me, and tomorrow, you and I will be speaking to the Master of Shadows about your traineeship."

Marsh felt her heart sink at his words.

"Have I done something wrong?"

"No, but there are matters we need to discuss. Okay?"

"Okay."

They rode forward with the rest of the troops and worked to settle their mules into their stalls before Roeglin offered Marsh his arm.

"You ready?"

"When you are," she replied, taking his arm and leaning on him a lot more than she wanted to.

Sure, she could have insisted on making her own way up, but that would have meant weaving across the stable yards like a drunk and probably falling up the stairs rather than making it to the top.

"You're not that bad," Roeglin protested.

"Want to let go of my arm and see?" Marsh challenged, and was relieved when he didn't take her up on it.

"I'm not that mean."

Marsh thought really hard about how to respond to that, but in the end, she decided not to say anything. She really *didn't* want to end up on her ass on the floor.

"I've asked Brigitte to bring cookies and chocolate," Roeglin told her as he raised his hand to knock on Monsieur Gravine's office door.

"Oh, good." Before Marsh could say anything more, Monsieur Gravine's voice boomed out from beyond the door.

"Come."

He was standing behind his desk, and he was not alone. Brigitte had already arrived, and a tray of cookies and a decanter of chocolate awaited. Marsh noted there were cups for all of them and enough cookies that even Aisha would have been sated. Well, maybe.

"Sit," the cavern founder ordered, lifting the plate of cookies, and holding it out. "Eat."

Surely she didn't look that bad?

"Eat," Roeglin agreed, "and don't think with your mouth full."

What? But Marsh didn't argue, snagging a second cookie before Monsieur Gravine set the plate back on the desk. He surprised her by tossing her another one while she wolfed down the two she had in record time. She was relieved when the dragging fatigue faded enough that she didn't feel like she was about to fall asleep in her chair. Having finished the third cookie, Marsh was contemplating a fourth when Brigitte handed her a large mug of chocolate.

Monsieur Gravine watched the whole procedure with a bemused look on his face.

"Is it always like this when magic is used?" he asked, and it was Roeglin who answered.

"It depends on the wielder and the magic they use. Some find certain forms of magic more draining than others. Marchant's strength lies in shadow magic, so she finds some of the nature magic more difficult to wield. Not to be rude, Monsieur, but it would be better for her to give her report quickly."

"Or what?" Monsieur Gravine looked mildly alarmed.

"Or she'll fall asleep where she sits."

Marsh blushed to the tips of her ears and did her best to keep a neutral expression on her face. Roeglin was only stating things as they were, even if she wished he hadn't been quite so candid.

He's working with mages on a daily basis, Roeglin told her. *It is best if he knows how to look after them. You are merely providing a very apt training aid.*

Well, if he put it that way… Marsh closed her eyes.

Don't you dare!

"Wouldn't dream of it," Marsh replied, but her words were slurred, and she had to force herself to sit upright and her eyes to open. Catching Roeglin's eye, she looked toward the waiting founder and added, "I'd better begin."

It took her the better part of an hour, another dozen cookies, and a carafe of hot chocolate to get through her report. Her voice caught when she described how Ardhur had imprisoned her in the rock and Roeglin stiffened beside her, even though he'd heard it that morning. Monsieur Gravine looked both intrigued and horrified.

"And you could not get out?" he asked—a little too eagerly for Marsh's taste.

"No, Monsieur, although it is something my master has suggested I work on."

A look of mild disappointment crept onto Monsieur Gravine's face.

"I have a theory," Marsh told him, "but I don't know if it will work, and my master can't say what the chances for success are either."

"Let me know how you do," Monsieur Gravine told them. "It would be good to have a way of containing shadow-mage raiders until we can question them. At the moment, it is more expedient to terminate them."

Terminate...before they'd had time to question them. Marsh was both relieved and appalled. On the one hand, the raider didn't have time to change sides, but on the other, he had no time to feed them false information or escape to do them harm, either. She sighed. There were times when she wished she lived in a better world.

You and me both, Roeglin said, *but we can work toward it.*

"Hey," he said out loud, laying the palm of his hand on her shoulder and giving her a gentle push that rocked her in her seat. "Hey, it's okay. It's going to be okay."

"What is it?" Monsieur Gravine sounded alarmed, and Marsh resisted the urge to give a single bitter laugh. After all, it was *his* fault. Somewhere between facing the reality and comparing it to...to how she'd like things to be, fatigue-driven tears had welled up and were running down her face.

Of all the stupid...

She sniffed and dashed them from her face.

"It's nothing. It's stupid. I'm sorry."

The founder's face became grave.

"Marchant Leclerc, it is never stupid to grieve the unnecessary loss of life no matter what that life has been used for so far, but thank you for understanding. One day, we will be able to give people the chance to choose a better path. Right now, we cannot afford the risk of losing what will be lost if they choose otherwise."

Marsh nodded.

"Exactly."

This time, she was relieved to discover that the tears did not renew—but the founder had not finished.

"Your time as my emissary to the Master of Shadows is over, and I need you to think about the role you will play next. There will always be a place for you with my Protectors, but I feel you and your master might be better used."

He turned to Brigitte.

"And you, Journeyman... Even with your responsibilities, I will be asking if you and the children can stay on a while longer. The girl can hone her stone-shaping skills with the rock wizards and masons, and the boy can further his studies with both you and Master Envermet." He glanced at Roeglin. "With your master's permission, of course."

Marsh caught the look Roeglin exchanged with Brigitte and the brief dip of her chin as the journeyman agreed.

Roeglin turned to Monsieur Gravine. "I agree to these arrangements for my journeyman," he answered, "pending the Master of Shadow's approval."

He made a point of looking at Marsh before turning his gaze back to the founder.

"I believe you wish contact to be made with Kerrenin's Ledge?"

"Yes, although I was going to attempt to reach Ariella's Grotto first."

Roeglin shook his head.

"If you will forgive me, I think we need to ensure our path to the surface world is kept open." He drew a breath. "And to ensure the people living at its end remain our allies."

He stopped and waited, not taking his eyes from the

founder's face. Marsh mirrored him. Monsieur Gravine considered what Roeglin had said, his eyes taking on a faraway look while he thought. Finally, he looked directly at the shadow mage, sweeping his gaze over Brigitte and Marsh as he did so.

"Agreed. You will be my emissaries to the Council of Kerrenin's Ledge. Tell them what is happening in the World Below, and ask them if they will work with us to secure the trade route. The Deeps know they need us as much as we need them."

For a moment, Marsh had her doubts about that, but as she thought about it, she realized it was true: the Ledge *did* need the Hall, since most of its food supplies came that way. Trade from the surface was sporadic at best and had been almost non-existent since she was small. Since, if she thought about it, her parents' waystation had been cleared of all human life. It gave her pause, and then the realization hit her. Sixteen years ago... The raiders had been working at isolating the Four Settlements for *at least* sixteen years.

That spoke of... She wasn't sure what it spoke of, but it was devious and sinister enough to send a shudder down her spine.

Indeed, Roeglin said. *Pay attention.*

Marsh sat up straighter and listened to what Monsieur Gravine was saying.

"...of us can afford to be isolated. We need each other if we are to survive the times ahead. For that matter, we need each other if humanity is to survive. We cannot be four tiny communities forever. There are others out there. We can help those who are smaller than we are, and we can ally with those who are further along in rebuilding—but we can do nothing except fall if we try to stand alone."

As a speech, it was an insight into what had motivated the man into building an army—and a relief to know he didn't intend to build an empire, but to join hands with others and stand beside them. She only hoped it remained that way.

The founder sighed.

"But you don't need an old man to dream," he added. "You need him to put his money where his mouth is, and that means you do, too."

He turned to Marsh.

"You need to go to Kerrenin's Ledge to see what records exist of the children's family. I know you have promised to find their parents if you can, but in the meantime, we need to ensure they have a chance to know what family they have left."

Marsh refrained from asking what would happen if the children's' remaining relatives didn't want to know *them*, but Monsieur Gravine didn't notice her reticence as he continued.

"You're more likely to be given access to those records as my emissary than not, and your experiences will lend authenticity to my request. I take it you will require some rest before leaving?"

Roeglin nodded.

"At least a day," he said. "Perhaps two."

Monsieur Gravine frowned.

"Make it three," he said. "I'd like to have the junction to Leon's Deep and the raiders' trail sealed before you go. That way I can do as the Master of Shadows did and send three teams to restore the route to Kerrenin's Ledge, with you and your trainee acting as forward scouts in the first team, Master Envermet and Tamlin in the clearing team, and Aisha and Brigitte following in a third team with a mix of shadow mages and rock wizards to light the glows and seal any junctions linked to the trail. Once that is done, the children and your journeyman will return here. Is that acceptable?"

Roeglin met his eyes.

"I will speak to the Master of Shadows tomorrow and see if he has any adjustments he would like to make, but I believe this may be acceptable as it stands." He looked at Marsh. "Do you agree, Trainee?"

Marsh agreed, and she very much disagreed. It was just the same as when they had left the monastery for Ruins Hall. It was logical, and for the best. It also had the potential to put Aisha and Tamlin in danger. She leaned forward and rested her elbows on her knees, putting her head in her hands. She really was too tired for this...

"Trainee?"

"Agreed," she said, and could not keep the exhaustion from her voice.

Silence followed, then Roeglin stirred.

"Monsieur Gravine, if we could leave this until tomorrow when I have spoken to the Master of Shadows?"

"Yes, that would be best. Thank you all for what you have done for us already. I look forward to speaking with you after lunch. I will send someone."

Roeglin pushed back his chair and curled his hand through Marsh's arm.

"Until tomorrow, Founder."

25

A CHANGE IN STATUS

Roeglin woke Marsh in time for breakfast and led her to a small room set off the training ground so that they could speak with the Master of Shadows after they had finished eating.

"Are you ready?" he asked once they'd seated themselves on opposite sides of a small table, and Marsh nodded.

"As ready as I'll ever be."

"Good." He held out his hands, taking her fingertips in his and closing his eyes.

Even as Marsh mirrored him, she felt the link between them open to include a third; it was like they'd entered a room to stand before the Master of Shadows. He was seated at his desk as he usually was and looked up as they entered.

"Ah, Roeglin. I was wondering when you'd call. I've been waiting."

"I hope I have not kept you waiting for too long, Master."

"No." The Master of Shadows smiled. "I've had Monsieur Gravine send me runners. He said I should expect some kind of contact from you from today onwards. I am glad to see he was accurate."

"He keeps a close eye on what is happening in his world."

"I'm sure he does. What did you wish to speak to me about?"

"I believe Marchant has surpassed the skills of any instructor we can provide and should be recognized as a mage in her own right."

As an opening statement, it was a showstopper. Marsh felt her jaw hit the floor and struggled to keep silent as she closed it. He *what*?

"She can already call weapons and shields from the shadows, cloak herself in shadow, shadow-step, blend with the shadows, and speak to them. In fact," Roeglin continued, "she is now posing questions for me and teaching me things I had not thought to try. There is very little more I can teach her. I'd like to promote her to shadow master."

He stopped, and the Master of Shadows looked from him to Marsh.

"Show me," he said and Roeglin did, pulling the memories of what Marsh had done from her mind and laying them out before their master. When he was done, the Master of Shadows was nodding.

"Agreed. She is beyond what we expect of a master, both in capability and control, *but* she still needs guidance in the way of the monastery and how we expect our mages to operate. I will make her your junior partner—an apprentice master or junior master, whatever you would like to term it—and I will draw up a new contract to supersede her trainee contract."

He turned to Marsh.

"You can sign it on your return, but it will be dated to start today. Agreed?"

Lost for words, all Marsh could do was nod.

"Very good." The Master of Shadows turned back to Roeglin. "What else do you have to report?"

Marsh listened as Roeglin repeated the discussion they'd had with Monsieur Gravine the day before. When he was done, the Master of Shadows nodded.

"I agree. Be his emissaries to Kerrenin's Ledge, but be mine also. Forge a second alliance between them and the monastery, and seek their feelings on an alliance with the rock wizards. Magic is growing stronger, and there are more folks showing the ability to use it. Alliances will lead to acceptance and more help for those just learning their abilities."

"Agreed."

"Also keep an eye out for any who show promise at calling the shadows, but do not recruit them yet. If they wish to come with you, that is fine, but do not ask them. I would like such requests to come through Monsieur Gravine or their own leadership. We wish to operate as differently from the shadow raiders as possible."

Again Roeglin nodded, and the Master of Shadows moved on.

"Please pass my gratitude to Monsieur Gravine and ask for his assistance in manning a waystation at the monastery junction to Ariella's Grotto as well as the prospector's junction. We need to hold the Ariella junction until the glows can be re-lit, and I do not want to block it completely in case someone tries to reach us for help."

"Yes, Master of Shadows. Is there anything else?"

The man rubbed his eyes with one hand and shook his head.

"No, save Fortune's Deep follow you and smile on your safe return."

"Thank you, Master of Shadows," Roeglin replied, and walked himself and Marsh out of the wizard's head and back to their own.

Until that moment, Marsh hadn't been aware of leaving her own mind, but now she was.

"What was that?" she asked as she opened her eyes, and Roeglin smiled.

"Something you shouldn't have been able to do without access to mental magic. We'll explore it later, but you, Mistress Leclerc, are only beginning to scratch the surface of what you can do. I look forward to being around to see you explore it further."

Marsh frowned.

"Fine. Keep your secrets, but if you're going to be around while I explore my potential, you can at least promise to help me learn how to harness any new magic I might find."

Despite the sharpness of her tone, Roeglin grinned.

"*That* I can do."

He might have said more, but they were interrupted by a polite knock at the door, followed by Gustav looking in.

"Monsieur Gravine wants your company," he said, then held up a plate containing two small pies. "I also brought you lunch, given that you missed it. You can eat while you walk."

Taking their pies, they followed him into the corridor and to the cavern founder's office. To their surprise, he accompanied them inside and closed the door. This time Brigitte was not present.

"I did not want to delay sending the teams to seal the caverns," Monsieur Gravine explained. "They left just after breakfast."

While we were speaking with the Master of Shadows, Marsh thought and frowned, but Monsieur Gravine ignored her expression and turned to Roeglin.

"Tell me, what did your Master of Shadows have to say?"

"He agrees to us being your envoys, but we must also represent the monastery."

"Very well, and?"

"And he requests reinforcements for the waystation at the Ariella's Grotto/monastery junction and the prospector's junction."

"It shall be done. I'll have them on the road in the morning. Is there anything else?"

"Yes. Marchant Leclerc is no longer a trainee, but a shadow mage in her own right, and my partner in monastery undertakings."

Marsh noted that he left out her junior status and felt strangely elated.

"Well, congratulations, Shadow Mage Leclerc!" The cavern founder stood and offered her his hand. "Well-earned," he said when she accepted it.

Seating himself again, he nodded to Gustav, who was standing to one side.

"I have the paperwork for your task to Kerrenin's Ledge."

He reached over and accepted the thick sheaves of paper Gustav had lifted from one of the shelves closest him.

"If you will sign here...and here...*and* here," he said, indicating where he meant.

Gustav handed Marsh and Roeglin hollowed-out joffra claws filled with ink and they read, then signed where the founder wanted. Marsh noted that the contract said nothing they hadn't already agreed to. She'd give the man this: he was thorough.

As soon as they'd signed, he lifted two small cloth bags from beneath the desk and set them down in front of them.

"Payment for being my envoy to the Master of Shadows. You'll need something to trade when you reach Kerrenin's Ledge, and it won't hurt them to remember what they gain access to by allying with us."

Marsh mirrored Roeglin as he reached for the bag and cautiously peered inside. Seconds later, he was staring at the founder.

"It's too much!"

The founder shrugged.

"I added a bonus for your assistance in defeating the last shadow raid, assisting with Madame Monetti's arrest, and your rescue of Ruins Hall citizens. There is also compensation for your injuries. I can give you an itemized list of the value if you insist, but the payment is fair for the dangers and discomforts you have faced in my service."

This last was delivered with a long look at Marsh, and Marsh returned it with a cool look of her own.

"I also have unfinished business in Kerrenin's Ledge," she said, and the founder propped his chin on his hands and gave her his undivided attention. She was surprised when Roeglin didn't intervene. Nice to see he'd made the adjustment to partner so fast.

I don't think either of us adjusted to you being a trainee, he told her, his amusement quivering through her mind.

Marsh frowned and looked back to the founder.

"Trader Kearick may be working with the shadow raiders, and I will be investigating this. I'll start by asking him why he tried to have me assassinated, and why he tried to retrieve a delivery scheduled for Madame Monetti."

"I have no objections to you following this inquiry to its conclusion," Monsieur Gravine told her, "and it lies well within my interests for you to do so. If you'll agree to report your findings to me, I'll pay you for the information. Further, should you discover that Kearick *is* working for the shadow raiders, I will pay a bounty to have him neutralized, and more for any details you retrieve regarding his business partners and dealings. Agreed?"

It was more than she had hoped for, and much more than she had expected. Marsh swallowed hard. "Agreed."

Once that was settled, she and Roeglin chatted a little longer with Monsieur Gravine and then took their leave.

He let them get to the door before he called to them. "There *is* just one more thing…"

They stopped, Roeglin taking his hand from the door handle before he turned back. Marsh followed his example. "Yes?"

"You'll take Gustav with you—as an independent party overseeing my interests alone."

"Agreed."

"As of now, he will accompany you."

Roeglin sighed.

"Very well. Will that be all?"

"Yes. Thank you. You can have two more days for preparation, and then the other teams will be free to follow you to clear and repair the route. Is that enough time?"

The tone of his voice said it had better be, and Roeglin smiled.

"More than enough, Monsieur. Will there be anything else?"

"No, that will be all."

He bent his head to the paperwork in front of him, and Gustav crossed the room to join them. The bodyguard looked at Marsh.

"Just like old times," he said, looking far too pleased with the idea of going with them.

Marsh smiled in return. "That it is, *Dear* Man."

He blushed but laughed, remembering Fabrice using that term the last time he'd left Ruins Hall with Marchant. It didn't take him long to recover, though.

"You have to provide pancakes and croissants to call me that."

26

INTO THE DARK

Three days later, Marsh, Roeglin, and Gustav said goodbye to Marc, the owner of the eatery on the main street of Ruins Hall. They were followed by Henri and Jakob, as well as Gerry, Zeb, and Izmay, all of whom had enjoyed their last hot meal before Kerrenin's Ledge. They'd be moving fast and light, hoping to cut the two- to three-day journey to just over one. Any nerves about the road ahead had been channeled into good-natured teasing.

"I don't think there are enough pancakes in the world to let you call me 'dear man' one more time," Gustav grumbled, and Marchant held up a chocolate croissant.

"Well, in that case..." he began, and Marsh laughed and handed it to him.

"I think you've been 'dear manned' enough. This one's for the road."

"The road is not getting a single crumb," Gustav told her through a mouthful of croissant.

Crumbs sprayed as he spoke, making an instant liar of him, and they were still laughing as they swung into their saddles and turned their mules away from the rail. Roeglin joined them as he led the way out.

They made it to the edge of Ruins Hall and then to the cavern, their good spirits from the morning meal evaporating as they neared the entrance to the tunnel leading from Ruins Hall cavern to Kerrenin's Ledge. Marsh remembered what had happened the last time she'd come down that path and wished she hadn't.

Taking a deep breath, she tapped the mule's sides and rode into the darkness, aware of the hoshkat pacing the shadows before them. She slowed to a halt and looked at Roeglin.

"You ready?" he asked, and Marsh passed him the lead rope clipped to her mule's bridle.

"I've got this," she said. "Let me know when you want to camp for the night."

He caught the lead and waited until she'd taken a good grip on the pommel.

"I'll let you know if there's anything we need to be aware of. Is Master Envermet coming?"

"He left the fortress this morning. Tamlin's not happy with you, you know. He thinks Aisha should be going back to the monastery and not gallivanting around the caverns looking for trouble."

"She's only charging glows!"

"Yeah, well, you know Aisha. She's more like you than you realize. When *isn't* she looking for trouble?"

Marsh didn't dignify that with an answer. It wasn't something she needed to be thinking about. She had enough on her mind as it was.

Besides getting to Kerrenin's Ledge and hunting

Kearick down before the little weasel got wind that she was in town, she had to think of what she was going to say to the Kerrenin's Ledge council to convince them to make a formal alliance with Monsieur Gravine.

And then there was her uncle...

As much as she was looking forward to letting him know she was okay, she was dreading their next meeting, too. So much had changed between them, and then she'd changed. Now she could call the shadows, and...

It'll be fine, Roeglin reassured her. *Besides, you've got to get there first.*

Reminding her there was a good chance she mightn't.

"Thanks, Ro. Thanks a lot!"

But he had a point. The trail from Ruins Hall to Kerrenin's Ledge stretched ahead of them in the dark, and it hadn't been traveled in weeks. Who knew what cavern denizens and tunnel crawlers had come to reside along its length, or what shadow monsters remained?

Marsh sighed and stretched her magic into the dark, blending her desire for the shadows to reveal those hiding in their depths with her ability to sense the life forces of the creatures ahead. She could trust the folk around her. She knew that.

Even Gustav, for all his loyalty to Monsieur Gravine— or perhaps because of it.

She could do this. She *had* to do this.

Once she'd wanted to be a seeker, finding treasures from the past in the hope of making the future better. She still wanted to be a seeker, but not of the secrets of humanity's past. She wanted to be a seeker of shadow raiders, and when she found them, she'd destroy them all.

The end game was almost the same, except instead of just making the future better, she was hoping to ensure that humanity *had* a future. After that? Well, after *that* she could see about making it better.

First, though, there was going to be a journey through the caverns' dark.

Again, many thanks for taking the journey as Marsh tries to sort out the mess and menace stalking the porous underside of a devastated Paris. I hope you've enjoyed the story, as much as I enjoyed discovering it, because, outlines aside *some* characters have minds of their own.

As I write these notes, I can hear the dulcet tones of Penfold and Danger Mouse wreaking havoc in an imagined London, and I'm reminded that the podling needs to go to bed... or she'll turn into the muck monster by tomorrow morning. I *did* promise her she could watch the end of the cartoon, however, and I'm desperately trying not to get suckered by the silliness, too. I've always enjoyed the humour of that cartoon. It's quirky, and reminds me to look at the world in a whole different way.

It reminded me of Michael picturing elves on his dad's shoulders while being told off, or when I was a kid running over the red earth a few miles south of The Gap just south of Alice Springs. It was a dangerous place out there.

I hunted alien smugglers, human traitors, and my

cousins... with paddy melons. I taught myself how to move across the hot ground in bare feet without leaving tracks – and while avoiding the bulls-head and goats-head burrs – how to keep my head down while keeping my prey, er, cousins in sight, how to plan a rapid paddy melon bombardment, and then execute an escape over rocks and rough ground... and the occasional inch ant nest...– and to return home at dusk and dinner time when the grown-ups were too busy getting dinner and doing other grown-up chores to remember to tell me off.

And, if I was very lucky, I'd get to catch an episode of Doctor Who on the only television channel we had – the good old ABC. Tom Baker was the Doctor back then, and he remains my favourite today. That series, and that character, has been a major source of inspiration and hope for much of my life and my writing.

Because I wrote, back then, too.

Both science fiction and fantasy.

Science fiction was my favourite genre, and I dreamed of what it would be like to travel out among the stars... because that beat trying to imagine what it would be like to survive a nuclear strike. In the late nineteen-seventies, early eighties, kids in the Alice were very aware of the Cold War and what we called 'The Space Base' south of town.

And we all knew it made us a potential target... whether it really did or not.

Fiction was a refuge from being afraid, whether I was reading it, or writing it. The worlds in my head were much safer places than the one I lived in... regardless of who got eaten, or whose ship crashed into a swamp of stinging fish, or who was trying to shoot who, or blow who up. In my stories, things eventually went right for people, no matter how wrong they went to start with.

Like they did for Keill Randor, Douglas Hill's Last Legionary, or his Huntsman, or the Colsec survivors. Those stories, along with Anne McCaffrey's and Andre Norton's fiction were my constant companions, and form some of my fondest memories. Their character's stand alongside Tom Baker and Jon Pertwee as some of my fondest childhood memories, and their stories were a welcome escape from the hazards of everyday life, where it was hard to not get yelled at at home, or bullied at school, or to worry about what was happening in the world around me.

Their stories taught me to dream, and to work towards my dreams, to not give up, and to believe in the impossible. When I write, those are the stories at the back of my mind, the stories I hope to find every time I sit down at the keyboard.

Thank you for coming on this part of that quest with me.

MARCH 13, 2019

THANK YOU for not only reading this story but these *Author Notes* **as well.**

(I think I've been good with always opening with "thank you." If not, I need to edit the other *Author Notes*!)

RANDOM (*sometimes*) THOUGHTS?

So, my colleague (in crime...not really, just thought it sounded fun) just spoke to her memories of Dr. Who, and if that didn't give away her British background, certainly the other author names she mentioned did.

It so happens that I am in England at the moment, attending the London Book Fair, and Dr. Who was mentioned yesterday during a business meeting discussing the vast need for IP (Intellectual Property), which television and movie companies are supposedly in desperate need for.

Personally, I don't think they need 'more' IP, they need to discover the massive amount of IP that is already available. Barring that, perhaps there needs to be a better discovery tool which provides those who need to review the already-available IP in a form (usually graphical) which allows for an easier understanding of the premise.

For those paying attention, if you want your book to be reviewed more often for video, create a bite-sized chunk to show someone. The days where (most) will read the book are gone, and the chances someone will read it all the way through are dwindling.

On the positive side, you can be ahead of the game by planning ahead.

The London Book Fair (for me) is the bigger brother of Book Expo America (New York) for Indie Publishers. I will see this May if BEA has continued to relegate Indie publishers to the sidelines, or if they have figured out that Indie Publishers are just a new generation of publishers whose companies only know the new paradigm of publishing.

And refuse to do business like the old.

For myself, I've studied major parts of the old system (of which Barnes & Nobles is a major player) and I am working to completely bypass it. To accept returns (a remnant of a problem from the Great Depression in America) is not part of my DNA. I feel that a different type of distribution system can be created to help both parties, and I intend to implement to the best of my abilities a test of this system.

Will I fail?

Possibly.

But if I succeed, we will have changed an industry.

FAN PRICING

$0.99 Saturdays (new LMBPN stuff) and $0.99 Wednesday (both LMBPN books and friends of LMBPN books.) Get great stuff from us and others at tantalizing prices.

Go ahead. I bet you can't read just one.

Sign up here: http://lmbpn.com/email/.

HOW TO MARKET FOR BOOKS YOU LOVE

Review them so others have your thoughts, and tell friends and the dogs of your enemies (because who wants to talk with enemies?)... *Enough said ;-)*

Ad Aeternitatem,

Michael Anderle

CONNECT WITH THE AUTHORS

Colleen Simpson Social

Amazon author page:
https://www.amazon.com/C.M.-Simpson/e/B0086QFGFO
Blogspot:
http://cmsimpson.blogspot.com.au/
Facebook:
https://www.facebook.com/CMSimpsonWriter/
Pinterest:
https://www.pinterest.com.au/cmsimpsonauthor/
Twitter:
https://twitter.com/simpsoncolleen1
Mailing List:
https://mailchi.mp/718baa508302/cmsimpson_newsletter_signup

Michael Anderle Social
Website:
http://www.lmbpn.com

Email List:
http://lmbpn.com/email/

Facebook Here:

https://www.facebook.com/OriceranUniverse/
https://www.facebook.com/TheKurtherianGambitBooks/

www.ingramcontent.com/pod-product-compliance
Lightning Source LLC
Chambersburg PA
CBHW031620100726
47898CB00006B/1878